BLACK LIGHT

🎧 Hear the music

at

www.dekaydence.com

BLACK LIGHT

Susie
Cornfield

Black Light
Published by Garret Books in 2008
ISBN 978 0 9552279 2 9

Copyright © Susie Cornfield

The right of Susie Cornfield to be identified as the author of this work has been
asserted in accordance with the Copyright, Designs and Patents Act 1988

The publisher is grateful for permission to reproduce the following extracts:
'Stormy Weather', words by Ted Koehler and music by Harold Arlen, © 1933,
Mills Music Inc., USA. Reproduced by permission of EMI Music Publishing Ltd
London WC2H 0QY and lyric reproduced by kind permission of Redwood Music Ltd (Carlin),
London NW1 8BD, for the Commonwealth of Nations, Germany, Austria, Switzerland,
South Africa and Spain
'Bad Moon Rising', words and music by John Cameron Fogarty. © 1964 Jondora Music.
Administered by Warner/Chappell Music Ltd, London W6 8BS. Reproduced by permission

Garret Books Ltd Reg. No.: 5647052
Registered address: Suite 210, Maddison House, 226 High Street, Croydon, CR9 1DF,
Surrey, England, UK
www.garretbooks.com

A CIP catalogue record for this book is available from the British Library

Designed and typeset by Caroline and Roger Hillier, The Old Chapel Graphic Design
www.theoldchapelivinghoe.com
Copy editors: Anne Askwith; Ros Lavine. The author takes responsibility for any mistakes

Printed and bound in Great Britain by Bookmarque Ltd, Croydon, Surrey

FOR FAITH

Ruth Alltimes, Donna Ambler, Jessica Bashford,
Jane Bowling, Barrie and Jane Cooper, David Crombie,
Bob Crothers, Callum Dolby, Hilary Foakes,
Odette Gilbert, Tom Heron, Dominic Kelly, Chris and
Jago Kerr, Alison, Victoria and Charlotte Middleditch,
Maggi Ovink, SMOBAIGH Rapoport,
Pat Shalhoub, Keith and Rosemary Turner,
Anne Westnedge, Patience Wheatcroft and
Young Miss Burgess

FOR HOPE

Ted Martin

FOR LOVE

Ian Edwards

WITH THANKS TO THE MIDWIVES

Florence B. Cooper, IDE, and Alma Jaques

And in memory of Janet Yeates, the Godbookmother,
who journeyed through much of the long pregnancy of
this book, never once complaining

Susie Cornfield trained as a journalist on a local newspaper before
joining the staff of *The Sunday Times* where she was the paper's
radio critic. She went on to become a columnist on the *Sunday
Telegraph Magazine*, a writer for BBC TV and a presenter/producer
for United Artists TV.

Reviews of *Black Light*:

A racy, pacy, crazy book. Like Philip Pullman on speed!

Piers Plowright

A rollicking read that a modern Jonathan Swift would have been proud to produce. Beneath the entertainment is a disturbing allegorical tale, packed with characters unnervingly reminiscent of those who have been making the news seem stranger than fiction.

Patience Wheatcroft

A fast-paced, well-plotted thriller filled with futuristic details and good, old-fashioned drama. A definite "must-read", the book's sense of place and sympathetic characters will linger in the reader's mind. Highly recommended. Looking forward to reading the sequel; thank you, Susie.

Fran Crumpton, The Book Partnership

Mad, bad and dangerous to read. I want more. Now!

John Kippen

Fascinating characters and relationships, complex layers of ideas and plot all come together with deceptive ease. The 'heroes' are inspiring but very real people; the 'baddies' and their world insidiously credible – terrifying! Extremely readable for all ages. Can't wait for next instalment.

Kate Tyson

CONTENTS

DRAMATIS PERSONAE

Angelica Nera *Ruby Q's mother*

Arnold Mulch *original lead singer, the Dipstick Five*

Bianco *habitué of the Grey Zone, GeeZer territory*

Bodkin *Dekaydence laboratory assistant*

Butt *drummer, the Dipstick Five*

Cage Martin *an eighteen-year-old, the Martins' eldest son*

Edwina Gardening-Fork (pronounced Spade) *Editor*, Shed Monthly

Elsa D. Cooper *Ruby Q's grandmother*

The Face *leader, the GeeZers*

Geach *serious fraud investigator*

Grout *Dekaydence laboratory assistant*

Innit *a teenage thug*

Jack Martin *a sixteen-year-old, the Martins' third son*

Kane Martin *a seventeen-year-old, the Martins' second son*

Killivy *Dekaydence gardening contractor*

Lars Sparks *internationally renowned photographer*

Lizard *guitarist, the Dipstick Five*

Lorenzo di'Abalo *head of the Company of Dekaydence*

MacCavity *head of Dekaydence Security*

McCarbon *deputy head of Dekaydence Security*

Mr and Mrs Treasure *Elsa Cooper's housekeeper and gardener*

Mr and Mrs Martin *parents of Taylor, Jack, Kane, Cage and Meryl*

Nevis *guitarist, the Dipstick Five*

Petty Masters *avant-garde fashion designer*

Phlegm *Signor di'Abalo's butler*

Piccolo *a sixteen-year-old runaway musician*

MacMinor *Red Tartan Guard*

MacNoodle *Red Tartan Guard*

The Professor *head of Dekaydence Research & Development*

Rallan *a drummer*

Randall Candelskin *Signor di'Abalo's right-hand man*

Ron *a guide, the Palace of Dekaydence*

Ruby Q Cooper *a fifteen-year-old*

Schneek *rollerblading assistant to Petty Masters*

Sinus *the King's butler*

Sir Harrison Catgut *composer of avant-garde music*

Spiky Hair *a broadsheet journalist*

Taylor Martin *a twelve-year-old, the youngest in the Martin family*

The Crown Prince *heir to the Crown and Bowler Hat of Great Britain*

The King *constitutional monarch of Great Britain*

The Prime Minister *elected head of the British Government*

The Suit *a tabloid journalist*

Will *a sixteen-year-old, the King's great-nephew*

Young Miss Burgess *right- and left-hand woman at* Shed Monthly

1 GONE TO POT

'I blame the teabag for the collapse of civilisation,' said the King, watching the butler drop a sachet into a teapot. Above his head, the Day Crown, a coronet set on a bowler hat, swayed gently on a golden pole held by a bewigged footman, while outside, in the intense summer heat engulfing London and all the Union, dark-suited armed men sweltered unattributably on His Majesty's behalf.

'Ah,' said the Prime Minister, distracted by a song on the gramophone: '*Don't know why, There's no sun up in the sky, Stormy weather ...*'

A few hundred yards away, in his suite within the Royal Palace, Will adjusted the controls on the monitor hidden in his wardrobe to focus on his great-uncle, the King, and saw the Prime Minister glance discreetly at an indiscreetly expensive adservarum on his wrist. He knew the PM was supposedly appearing 'live' on TV at that very moment, fuelling speculation of a major GeeZer attack. So what was he doing here, in the King's Armageddon Conservatory?

'A teabag is designed for one cup, one person,' the King continued. 'Such a self-centred solitary little package – it mirrors much in modern life.'

The Prime Minister's eyes glazed over and Will guessed

he thought the King was following family tradition and going mad. Running his hand through his mane of dark hair, Will thought of his elder brother, dead three months, and wondered how long it would be before his own sixteen-year-old mind cracked. If only— From over his headset came a congratulatory curse of positive feedback, enabling him to relax: it hadn't been easy, hiding the webcams in the new conservatory, with the rare Verdeccio world map set into the floor, as the King himself had overseen its construction.

'Have a care, Sinus, there's a good fellow!' the King snapped at the butler, who was struggling to control a tremor as he served refreshments. 'We don't want tea stains on the Baltic!'

The King turned to the Prime Minister.

'But then the future of the Baltic, if not the entire planet, is in doubt, if one believed the Grey Zoners, or GeeZers as I've heard them called. Is that not so, Prime Minister?'

Will leant forward, his dark eyes intent on the screen.

But the King didn't give the Prime Minister a chance to respond.

'It's natural for the young to have ideals. What concerns me is that today's teenagers appear incapable of outgrowing them. Every day I learn of GeeZers attacking government or commercial buildings and now I hear that cells of these young eco-terrorists are springing up all over the Union—'

'Sir,' the Prime Minister interrupted, shifting his large frame in his chair. 'The world is not coming to an end. The ISB, the government's independent scientific body, refutes the Grey Zoners' scaremongering and blames power cuts and shortages on the inadequacies of previous governments and, of course, this extraordinarily hot weather.'

'Prat!' a voice growled in Will's ear.

'I've no doubt the planet is safe,' said the King, testily. 'Neither have my Archbishop, the Royal Astrologer, nor my butler, from whom I take regular soundings. But this increasing civil disobedience among the young – Prime Minister, I want every GeeZer found and dealt with, especially their damned elusive leader, the Face.'

The voice in Will's ear gave a dark laugh.

Will glared angrily at his great-uncle. The old man was so intent on safeguarding his throne that he was blind to anything else, whereas it was obvious to most young people, himself included, that if radical measures weren't taken and quickly, there'd be no future, because the planet was heading for environmental meltdown. World leaders, including the Prime Minister, might make promises but they never actually did anything – except lie, outlaw eco-pressure groups and arrest, or eliminate, their leading members.

Was it arrogance or ignorance? Will wondered. Whatever, politicians and business had to be won over somehow. Meanwhile, the only reliable sources of information were the IWs, the illegal websites run by GeeZers, where blacklisted scientists posted dire warnings. There were secret cells of supportive adults, but mostly adults appeared ignorant of or apathetic to it all.

It seemed only GeeZers took action. Only GeeZers were prepared to fight to save the planet. Some, like his brother, were prepared to— He dug his fingernails into his palms. Death was something that happened to other people. Not to someone of eighteen. Not to someone bursting with fun and energy. Not to your brother.

The King sighed. He looked older than his long years. 'I dread a war and the destruction of magnificent old buildings.'

Will saw the Prime Minister try to hide a smirk by glancing down at his manicured nails, and recalled the recent picture on an IW showing the PM proudly resplendent in the uniform of Commander-in-Chief of the Army, Navy and Air Force.

'Not to worry,' said the Prime Minister. 'We have a plan.'

'Excellent!' said the King.

'It's called the Sticky Rock Café,' said the Prime Minister.

Will frowned: the PM was not known for his humour.

'The Sticky Rock Café?' repeated the King. 'You think a café can prevent a civil war?'

'Oh, yes,' said the Prime Minister, a knowing smile slithering over the folds of his glistening face. 'This café is utterly different, and utterly irresistible. With its own music and fashion, young teenagers will become glued to Sticky Rocks. They'll have no time for Grey Zoner eco-garbage.'

Will stared at the Prime Minister in disbelief.

So did the King.

'Prime Minister, GeeZers are demanding we change our entire way of life. Some have died for their cause. Do you honestly think they'll stand back and watch you buy off their younger siblings and friends with a pair of designer knickers or whatever? No, they'll damn well fight you!'

'He's not wrong there!' snarled the voice in Will's ear.

The Prime Minister smiled as though he were dealing with a child, or an MP, and adopted the patronising tone he used often when abroad.

'Sir, Sticky Rocks are designed specifically to – how shall I say? – persuade youngsters to our way of thinking. They'll play with environmental projects but play is all that it will be as they quickly become immune to any Grey Zoner eco-garbage. As for Grey Zoners, or GeeZers as you and the general public prefer to call them, they'll find out soon enough that, from today, anyone aged eighteen and under caught on the streets between eight pm and eight am, without a pass, will be arrested and dealt with.'

'How dealt with?' the King inquired.

The Prime Minister tapped a forefinger against his nose.

The King nodded slowly.

Will shuddered. A spittle of abuse shot down the headset.

'The first Sticky Rock Café opens next month here in London,' the Prime Minister continued. 'Then they go nationwide.'

'You have proof that Sticky Rock Cafés work?' said the King.

'Indeed, sir. I followed the prototype as it was tested on teenage boys in a remand centre. Real no-hopers. I recall the ringleader, Bodkin, an especially nasty piece of work. He now works happily as a lab assistant.'

'A happy ending – how rare. And these Sticky Rock Cafés are your idea?'

'I can not deny an input.' The Prime Minister smiled, smugly. 'But the research and development was funded by Signor Lorenzo di'Abalo.'

'The head of the Company of Dekaydence!' the King exclaimed.

Will sat up with a jolt: Dekaydence! The name was scrawled on a scrap of paper in his brother's room but neither he nor his brother's friends had any idea why his brother had been interested in the conglomerate with its global interests in media and confectionery.

'Why on earth should di'Abalo fund this project?' said the King. 'I'd have thought he was too busy with his new hi-tech edu-playground for children.'

'Sir, the Palace of Dekaydence is, like the Sticky Rock Cafés, part of a thank-you for what this country has done for him.'

'Really?' said the King, musing. 'And you feel quite comfortable doing business with a man who wears an earring?'

'Actually, the rainbow stud is a security device, sir,' said the Prime Minister. 'All staff and any visitors to Dekaydence premises are obliged ...'

Will listened while the Prime Minister praised the company whose boss, Lorenzo di'Abalo, had recently hired the PM's friend and former MP, Randall Candelskin, to be his right-hand man.

'Besides,' the Prime Minister continued. 'The Signor is a generous man. If he has a fault it is his understated humility.'

'Really?' repeated the King.

'You see, sir, if my – if your – if our government buys into the Sticky Rock Cafés, with its ability to *nurture* the young tender roots of the GeeZer tree, our country's reputation in the Union will be much improved.'

The King snorted. 'Yours might, Prime Minister! I doubt it'll do a pig's ear for my ...'

The roar of a powerful engine drowned his words as a Harley-Davidson motorbike shot past the window. Careering across manicured lawns, between ancient oaks, the leather-clad rider clutched a handlebar with one hand while swigging from a champagne bottle held in the other.

'My boy. Or so I'm told,' said the King, as His Mediumness,

the Crown Prince, crashed through a hedge and landed in the lake built many years before by his grandfather.

Will snapped shut the link to the Armageddon Conservatory; from the other open line, a voice snarled into his ear.

'So they're going to brainwash kids!' said the Face. 'Pull the plug on their minds, as they pull the plug on the planet.'

'Aye, and with my uncle's consent,' said Will, bitterly.

'Don't take it personally.'

Why shouldn't I? thought Will, tying back his hair. It was the goddam reason he'd left the Highlands and come to London. To find out exactly what had happened to his brother.

'I wonder how they'll do it?' said the Face.

'I don't know, but now we know di'Abalo's behind it—'

'We'll deal with it. You take that break, and that's an order! After what you've been through, you must need it.'

Will said nothing. He'd already made up his mind. He'd told everyone he was going sailing off the northern isles with a cousin. So no one could track him down. Not his family, the royal officials, not even the Face. But sailing was the last thing on his mind. He'd been useful as a spy in the camp but—

He couldn't sit around any more. He was no longer a child, no longer a kid brother, and, given what he'd learnt today ...

He knew the King wasn't a bad man, just deluded. If Will could get evidence and show it to him, he knew his great-uncle would see the ignorance and evil surrounding him, and recognise that action needed to be taken before it was too late.

He pressed a button on his adservarum and Creedence Clearwater Revival began singing: *'I see the bad moon arising. I see trouble on the way. I see earthquakes and lightnin'. I see bad times today ...'* 'Bad Moon Rising': it had been one of his brother's favourites. Now it was one of his.

2 MIRROR, MIRROR

I'm looking in the mirror. I'm there, but only in part. If you were standing next to me, you'd see what I see: a fifteen-year-old girl, average height, average weight, green eyes, tortoiseshell glasses, black jeans, pink check shirt bought from a charity shop, and— What? It's dark red— Of course it's my own hair. Yes, it is on the wild side of curly. So?

Who are you talking to, Ruby Q Cooper? And what's the music?

It's Tebbit and the Toe-Rags. And go away, I'm not talking to you, or rather to myself, any more. I'm preparing for a job interview.

With a mirror?

No, with the editor of a newspaper.

Brilliant! So you've had a response to one of your zillion job applications?

No, but it doesn't matter.

Why?

I've quit school.

What? Does your dad know?

No, he's on tour again, isn't he? That's why I'm back here in this box room at Grandmother Elsa's house. And I've had enough of it. I'm not a child any more. If I've got to live out of a suitcase, it's going to be because I choose to.

But—

No buts. I can't hang about any more. There's no point learning about French verbs or paddy fields when, at any moment, the entire world could go down the pan. I've got to do something. And I've got to do it now!

You've been at those IWs again, haven't you?

Yes, because now the Union's new laws have put a stranglehold on newspapers, radio and TV, the illegal websites are the only way of discovering the truth.

So what have you found out?

You wouldn't be interested.

Try me.

OK. Every summer, thousands die in the UK alone because of the high temperatures caused by global warming. In fact, the number of deaths is rising so steeply that the government has stopped issuing figures.

Gosh.

More people are wearing protective filtration masks when they go outside because of pollutants in the air. But what's the point when millions of us are suffering and dying from cancers and brain diseases caused by chemicals sprayed on food, water and clothes, and in schools, homes, offices and factories? Do you know, they've found traces of carpet cleaner in women's breast milk, which is so contaminated that you couldn't legally sell it?

Yuck!

Oh, and there's a high risk of getting Alzheimer's or dementia from drinking water containing aluminium at half the level that's permitted in UK tap water. I mean, if I know this stuff, doesn't the Prime Minister? And if he does, what kind of man is he for ignoring it?

You're on your soapbox again.

Yes, I am. Because every 24 hours more than 200,000 babies are born worldwide. In a year, there'll be 80 million more mouths on the planet to feed. We'll need an extra 26 million tonnes of grain, an extra 50 million tonnes of oil for their heat, light, transport and manufactured goods. Where's it to come from when it takes 10 tonnes of the earth's resources to produce one tonne of products? If we don't do something to clean up the planet, feed people and save species from extinction, it'll soon be over for us all. We won't have a future!

Right, then we must become GeeZers and fight the oil-slickin' bastards on the beaches etc!

I can't.

Why not? It's easier for you than most. You haven't got any family to worry about, apart from your dad, Elsa and me. You got no friends, either.

Thanks. Can I remind you that you don't make friends when you're forever trailing after a dad who travels about to find work. Anyway, look at me: I'm too weedy to do what most GeeZers do – drive lorries, scale bridges, climb high buildings. And I don't want to live in the shadows, as they do, constantly on the run, on the alert. Besides, no editor will employ me if they think I'm sympathetic to the Grey Zoner movement.

I thought you supported the GeeZers? You went on one of their underground workshops. Remember, you met that dishy chap who—

'Course I support them. And it's as that chap said: everyone can help the movement in different ways, cleaning rivers and streets, planting trees, and spreading the word. So, when I'm a journalist, I'll work for them under cover, passing on any information I can— Oh, there's also this.

A photograph?

Spot on, Sherlock.

Let's see: a family outing to the seaside. There's a girl, maybe five years old, with the same wild hair as— Ah, moving on: there's a chap in specs. Looks nice but his swimming trunks look dodgy. He has his arm around an attractive dark-eyed woman. My, her hair is so shiny and beautiful. It's the colour of autumn leaves. It's your mother, isn't it?

I'm looking in the mirror. I'm there, but only in part.

I don't know what you mean.

Yes, you do. It was that night my mother left. The night I started getting nightmares.

Don't remind me. I hate clowns. Why do they keep haunting us?

I don't know. But I don't care any more. Life's too

short. And if I sit around doing nothing, there's a good chance it'll be shorter still. I've got to join the fight now! And when I'm a journalist perhaps I'll also have a better chance of finding my mother ... I'm looking in the mirror. I'm there, but only in part. Maybe one day I'll be complete.

Are we still friends?

Of course. To the bitter end.

Don't say things like that, Ruby Q Cooper. It spooks me.

3 BEATING A RETREAT

Piccolo had learnt to keep his head down from an early age. His mother could drink and swear, as much and as hard as the Big Bloke who'd moved in with them. They'd hit him regularly, stubbed out cigarettes on his body, locked him in the bathroom with no food, light, heat, nothing. For comfort, he'd clutch a bar of soap, smelling the soothing scent of lavender.

Maybe a neighbour heard something through the flat's thin walls, because the social services sent round a woman. His mum cried and sobbed, and said he'd done it all to himself. Her performance was so good that Piccolo knew the woman believed her. He would have done.

So he'd run away. When he was a kid. The police had found him and brought him back. To more beatings. There was no one he could tell. Nowhere he could go. He had no friends, no family. When they realised he was useful to them, they kept him off school, claiming he was sick. He learnt that the more useful he made himself, the less they lashed out.

He grew bigger and stronger. Brighter and angrier. And he never forgot things: like the night years before when he'd seen the Big Bloke beat his father to death, while his mum watched.

The moment he realised that he too could kill was the moment he knew he had to get away.

One night, when his mum and the Big Bloke were drunkenly asleep in front of the telly, he'd taken his mum's savings from the biscuit barrel, together with the Big Bloke's social, and slipped out of the flat. He had only the clothes he stood up in and, in his pocket, the only thing he prized, something his dad had given him: a wooden piccolo.

The landing was dark. The communal lights and security cameras hadn't been repaired in months. A druggie staggered past him on the stairs, mumbling into a telephone receiver ripped from a call box. In a corner, two drunks were rolling about on the floor in their own blood, swearing as they lashed out in a fight over a broken bottle of meths. He passed by them all, unnoticed.

When he got to the edge of the estate, he ran to the nearest petrol station. He waited in the shadows until a pick-up truck pulled in and slipped unseen under its flapping tarpaulins. He listened out and watched the road signs, changing between trucks and lorries in the motorway garages, where he pilfered food, until he reached London.

He kept away from the other youngsters hiding out, living rough, and slept alone where he thought he'd be safe – under bushes and, one night, inside a broken settee thrown into a skip. He scavenged for food and for places where he could compose and play the piccolo, unseen and unheard. For the first time in a long while, he felt at peace. There was no one to cause him grief or pain.

Then he met Will.

4 STREET FRIGHT

Despite the blistering heat, the rationing and the new curfew, there were scores of youngsters on the streets, or rather hiding in the derelict sites littering the capital, all keen to join the GeeZers, whose scouts were forever on the lookout for suitable recruits.

Will weaved in and out of them, listening but keeping his own counsel. He discovered sources of food and water and a safe place to build a hideout not far from London Bridge and therefore close to Dekaydence headquarters. If only he could get inside, maybe he'd discover what had intrigued his brother, and what had ultimately killed him ... But how to get in? The entrance barrier was guarded day and night.

One day, he noticed pots of paint, ladders and dustsheets piled up beyond the barrier. Decorators! And judging by the amount of stuff, they were there for the long haul. He hung about for longer than was safe but no one vaguely resembling a decorator ever showed. He decided to return early the next day to see which pub or café they went to. He'd blag his way into persuading them he was useful.

That night, he forced down his excitement to get some sleep.

He awoke suddenly and instinct told him that beyond the oppressive heat and the electricity of an impending storm something was wrong. He slipped from the shelter and shinned up the old yew tree by the wall. Most street lamps no longer operated and the only light was from a thin nail clipping of a moon. But at the end of the road, he saw it: an open-top bus, moving at a snail's pace, its lights out and its engine purring softly like a cat. Then it turned the corner and was gone.

Will was up and over the wall, and round the corner in time to see a handful of figures jump from the bus and sprint off into the night.

He dropped to his feet and slid under a burnt-out car. Footsteps approached and, seconds later, he caught a glimpse of a tartan kilt as a figure passed by.

He felt his heart beat wildly. He'd seen that uniform before: on the Red Tartans, the security guards at the Company of Dekaydence. That meant the bus must be one of the special Tartan Buses which, every day, carried parties of youngsters to and from the Palace of Dekaydence, the newly opened children's edu-pleasure park, reckoned to be one of the wonders of the man-made world. But what was it doing out at this time of night? He waited, still and silent, as he'd learnt to do when out hunting with his brother. At last, he heard footsteps.

Cautiously, he peered round the car: five Tartan Guards were carrying several large sacks on to the bus, which then drove off.

Guessing their destination, Will sped along back alleys, along the riverside, and up the steps and into the shadows close to Dekaydence HQ, as the bus arrived at the entrance. The barrier rose and, as the gates beyond were wedged open by the decorators' paraphernalia, the bus drove straight inside.

He watched as the Tartan Guards got off the bus and emptied the contents of the sacks on to the floor. Despite the heat, he felt his skin go cold: lying there, by the guards' feet, were the bodies of three teenagers.

5 A TREEMENDOUS ENCOUNTER

Why are we sitting in the garden in the middle of the night, Ruby Q, listening to Erik Satie's first Gnossienne? You must be well gloomed.

I can't sleep.

Which means I can't. Poxy heat! Poxy nightmares! Poxy clowns!

It's nothing to do with that. And just for the record, Erik Satie is ace.

Is it because you've had no replies to your job applications?

No.

What then? Are you scared of dying if the planet does go down?

'Course! But I'm joining the fight to stop that happening. It's just ...

What?

Well, if it *is* too late – before whatever happens happens, I want to find my mother. I want to know why she left me, and my dad, without a word of explanation, without a note. I want to know more about her, about her family. I want to know where I come from, who I am. I want to talk to her about things that matter and things that don't.

Nine years is a long time, isn't it?

Yes. No word then. No word since. And my memories are fading.

But you've got a clue, n'est-ce pas? Another photograph.

Yes. It was in a box in a cupboard in my room. I reckon it was taken at my parents' wedding. Everyone's dressed up, with flowers and smiles. There's a woman in the picture I don't recognise and a couple who I think are friends of Dad. I found their phone number in an old diary in the box and I've left a message on their machine.

You think this pair can help you?

I don't know. But as Dad and Elsa refuse to even speak about my mother, they're the only hope I've got.

Understa— Hellfire, Elsa's mangy poodle has gone mad!

No, she's after that cat.

Shhhugar, a sausage has fallen out of the sky!

No, it fell out of the tree. So did that cake. And the biscuits. They've distracted the dog but what—?

There's something else up there!

'I'm bored with these twigs sticking in my bum,' said a girl's voice.

'It's your own fault,' said a boy's voice.

Watch out, Ruby Q! That something up there, it's coming this way!

A boy jumped out of the tree, landing beside Ruby Q. He was tall and slim, with a long pale face, cropped brown hair and chestnut eyes.

'Hi,' said the youth, with a dimpled grin. 'Hope I didn't

startle you.'

What's wrong with your stomach, Ruby Q? It gave a funny lurch.

'My sister won a bet and demanded a midnight feast up a tree, and as our garden is concreted over ...' said the youth. 'Oh, by the way, I'm Jack Martin. We're your new neighbours.'

He held out his hand.

There goes your stomach again. What have you been eating?

The branches above them swayed wildly and they both ducked.

'Looks like I'll to have to introduce myself,' said the girl, crossly, appearing upside down amidst the branches. 'I'm Taylor. I'm twelve years and three hundred and fifty-nine days old and I'm named after Elizabeth Taylor, the most beautiful film star ever, until I get on the screen. If you're nice to me, you can come on my birthday treat. Mum bought me tickets to the Palace of Dekaydence. My best friend was coming but she's got measles. Do you want to come?'

Yuck, you won't like that. All that kiddiewinky wizardry stuff.

'Actually—' said Ruby Q.

'Jack's coming,' said Taylor, with a wide-eyed innocent smile.

'I'd love to come, thanks,' said Ruby Q, quickly.

What ...? Oh, I see. You're going because the chap who

dreamt up the Palace of Dekaydence is rumoured to be behind the new eco-friendly Sticky Rock Cafés. And he's your new green hero.

'It's not compulsory,' said Jack, sitting down beside Ruby Q. 'And don't mind my sister – she's harmless. Most of the time.'

'I'd love to come,' Ruby Q laughed, and felt herself blushing.

Oh, I get it: it's this boy you like.

'Now, about the rest of us ...' said Taylor, swinging herself upright.

Wow, what a beauty! Heart-shaped face. Huge sapphire eyes. Thick dark lashes. And long dark tresses, so neat and tidy and— Ouch!

'... Mum and Dad aren't divorced, unlike other people's parents. You've met Baghilde, our cat, and Jack. He's sixteen. Meryl's ancient ...'

'Yeh, like she's twenty,' said Jack.

'... she's away at college. There's Kane. He's seventeen. He sleeps for England and don't talk much, unless you're fluent in grunting. Are you fluent in grunting?'

Ruby Q laughed and shook her head. She thought Kane must be the extremely handsome lad she'd seen sunbathing in the Martins' garden.

'And there's Cage. He's eighteen. He don't live with us any more but he rings in to stop Mum worrying.' Taylor lowered her voice. 'Don't tell anyone, but he's a top GeeZer.'

'Taylor,' said Jack, warningly.

Ruby Q, did you hear that?

'Of course, it's Mum's fault. Ever since I can remember, she's been in one of those groups which secretly support the GeeZers and—'

'Taylor, for God's sake!' snapped Jack.

'What?' said Taylor.

'Your brother, Cage, do you think he could help me?' Ruby Q interrupted. 'You see, I want to be a journalist. I want to help the GeeZers, by working for them under cover. But I can't get a job. I know their leader, the Face, doesn't give interviews, but if I did get one – I know you don't know me but—'

'Oh, we know all about you, Ruby Q Cooper,' said Taylor. 'Except what the Q stands for.'

'Oh?' said Ruby Q.

'Your grandmother's cleaning lady told us about you,' said Jack.

'And so did her gardener,' said Taylor. 'Sorry and all that.'

'For what?' said Ruby Q.

'Well, everything,' said Taylor, surprised.

Don't get upset. Elsa's housekeepers aren't called the Treasures for nothing and they wouldn't say a word against you. So what's this jealousy? 'Cos they've got two parents, brothers, a sister, a home and a cat? I bet you think their mum bakes cakes and their dad does Sunday lunch, and they both help the kids with their homework.

Yep, and it sounds pretty good to me.

'A teenager interviewing the teenage leader of a teenage movement,' said Jack. 'It's a great idea, Ruby Q, and I'll tell Cage so when he rings.'

'I will, too,' said Taylor. 'So, Ruby Q, what does the Q stand for?'

You're blushing.

'Pestilence, is that the time?' said Ruby Q, standing up.

You're not wearing your watch, so how—?

'I'd better go back in before my grandmother wakes up and finds me and the dog gone. I'll tell you some other time.'

Bet you don't.

6 OUT OF THE FRYING PAN ...

Will stood rooted to the spot until music alerted his senses. Rising, as light as a bird, the sound flew past him towards the Tartan Guards. He ran down the steps to the river and there, under an archway, was a tall, scrawny mixed-race boy, about his own age, playing a piccolo.

'Shut it!' Will called, as loud as he dared.

The boy paused in his playing and stared at him.

Will heard footsteps overhead. The boy heard them, too.

'If you want to live, follow me!' cried Will.

The boy didn't hesitate. He raced after Will, along the embankment, down deserted side streets and alleys, the footsteps never far behind.

Will doubled and trebled back, before stopping in a street of half-demolished buildings.

'Up there!' he ordered the boy, nodding at an ivy-covered wall.

The boy gawped. The wall was twice his height.

'Man, you gotta be jokin'!'

'No!' Will snarled. He grabbed the boy's feet, thrust them into the ivy, and shoved at his butt. The boy yelped, as he clung to the vegetation like a baby to its mother.

A staircase is about his limit, thought Will, as he shinned up the wall, snatched hold of the boy's collar and hauled him to the top.

He ordered the boy to jump. The boy stared back at him and at the drop, and then, hearing footsteps approach, he hugged his arms to his chest and stepped into the darkness. Will followed. The boy was crawling out of a nettle patch, moaning and rubbing his stinging flesh.

Will glowered at him to keep quiet, as the bus pulled up on the other side of the wall. There were guards everywhere, and dogs. Apart from the sound of boots and the animals' panting breath, all was silent.

Will and the boy stayed crouched down, listening, until they heard doors slam, and the men, dogs and bus move off. When Will was sure it was safe, he indicated to the boy that he should follow him in silence. They walked past long-abandoned graves. Suddenly, Will ducked down, disappearing into a mound of dry leaves. Cautiously, the boy went after him.

Will struck a match and lit a candle in a bottle, illuminating three branches holding up a thatch of leaves and a floor area where soft springy boughs supported a layer of moss, a few blankets and old plastic sacks.

'Impressive shelter,' said the boy, shyly. 'Fit for a king.'

Will scrutinised him. 'You eaten?' he asked.

The boy shook his head.

Will divided some bread and cheese he took from a bag hanging on a branch.

'My name's Will,' said Will, handing the boy a bottle of beer.

'Mine's Piccolo, after ...' said the boy, tapping his hand on his T-shirt pocket, from which the piccolo peeped out.

For the first time in months, Will smiled.

Piccolo woke at about three o'clock in the morning to find himself alone in the shelter. He struggled out of the blanket-and-sack sleeping bag and went to look outside. It was already light, silvery and fragile.

Will was crouched by a large tin with holes in the side. He glanced up as he threw something resembling bright yellow pitta bread into a pan resting on the tin. It sizzled satisfactorily.

'What's that?' said Piccolo, his stomach gurgling its enthusiasm.

'Chicken of the woods,' said Will. 'It grows on that old yew tree. It's not bad but it'd be better with some bread or in a stew.'

'You sure it's not poisonous?'

'I'm still here, aren't I?'

'You a GeeZer or something?' said Piccolo.

'Is it a problem?' said Will, tossing his ponytail over his shoulder.

'Nope,' said Piccolo, hastily. 'Course, he knew of the GeeZers – who didn't? They were terrorists, weren't they? Always causing trouble, always in the news. He'd never met one. But then, the way he'd lived with his mum and the Big Bloke, he'd scarcely met anyone.

'When we're done eating, I'll be off,' said Will, handing him a metal plate of the fried fungus. 'If you want out, leave within the hour. Use the gate in that other wall. It leads into allotments. It's never opened, so climb over it. Whatever you do, keep your head down and keep the piccolo quiet. And for God's sake, remember the curfew.'

Piccolo had nowhere else to go so he stayed on.

Over the next few days Will took off at different times of the day or night, never saying where he was going, always returning with food. Left to his own devices, Piccolo taught himself how to climb the old yew tree and, when no one was around, he'd play. Softly, but he'd play. Because he had to.

Will taught Piccolo basic survival skills: to make fire without smoke by splitting open cramp ball fungus and using it as tinder inside the old tin-can brazier. And to place wood in a pebble-based pit, pouring water into holes in the ground before and after the fire.

'Think about it, Piccolo. You light a fire, a root smoulders and there's your forest fire.'

Piccolo was tucking into a fish Will had caught, stuffed with wild sorrel and steamed in the pan. He'd never thought of it before but then at home he'd never thought about much, except his music. And his father. And how to survive. He felt that Will, with his rich deep voice sounding like a taut Highland drum, was kick-starting his brain.

'Did you know that every year 34 million hectares of

forest are destroyed or damaged, mostly for beef cattle farms?' Will asked him. 'That every hour four species of life are lost ... Half of the world's grain and one third of all fish caught are fed to farm animals ...'

Every day, Will went on, passionately, relentlessly, reeling off facts and figures, until one day Piccolo walked away and went to lean against the yew tree.

'What is it? What's wrong?' demanded Will.

'All this stuff you keep telling me, it's doing my head in! Anyway, there ain't nothing I can do about it,' said Piccolo.

'You're wrong,' said Will, vehemently. 'Every one of us can do something! You, me, governments – We can reuse, recycle or compost. We can protect forests, and eat less meat and endangered fish. We can tax manufacturers for the rubbish they produce and, if we banned the processes which use poisonous chemicals to produce plastics, cleaning products, anti-freeze, pesticides, herbicides, fungicides and batteries—'

'Shut it!' said Piccolo, covering his ears. 'Just shut it!'

Words dried on Will's lips.

Piccolo glared at him. 'D'you know, I ain't never seen a forest, 'cept in a book.'

Will said nothing.

'The grub at home was either past its sell-by date, or nicked. Like my clothes. It ain't the likes of me destroying the planet 'cos us'll never afford half the stuff you're talking about. It's you lot, with the money.'

Will said nothing.

'But you've made me think, Will man! I'm like them fishes. I reckon I'm an endangered species! So, why aren't GeeZers fighting for me?'

'We are,' Will said, quietly, and he walked back to the shelter.

It was some time before Piccolo joined him, and they lay on their makeshift sleeping bags, together but alone, in the silence and darkness.

Eventually, Will got up and turned on a tiny portable solar dabcam. GeeZers were the lead story in the late-night news: they'd brought the City to a standstill by abandoning hijacked dustcarts loaded with rotting, stinking rubbish on the main arterial roads into London. There was an angry statement from the Prime Minister, whose voice Piccolo thought sounded like a congested tuba.

'But what if it's all too late, Will man?' said Piccolo, softly.

'Then it's too late,' said Will, with a shrug. 'But you can't give up without a struggle, can you?'

Piccolo shook his head. 'I dunno,' he said. 'But tell your GeeZer friends to get rid of the Prime Minister. I reckon he's got enough bullshit in one fart to wipe out a continent.'

Will laughed. So did Piccolo.

'And when they're done,' said Piccolo, happy to have broken the tension between them, 'tell them to bin the Royal Family. They're one load of screwball space-wasters.'

Piccolo laughed, not noticing Will's sudden silence.

When Piccolo woke the next morning, Will had gone. And he hadn't returned by the eight pm siren. Piccolo waited up all night, watching from the yew tree.

'Where are you, Will man?' Piccolo whispered to himself when the eight am siren sounded and still there was no sign of Will.

7 PETTY THOUGHTS

Randall Candelskin grew hot under the collar of his Savile Row suit as the tiny, plump young woman sitting opposite him in his office at Dekaydence HQ parked her heavy metal-studded boots on his expensive, uncluttered desk and began noisily picking at her teeth with a paperclip, spitting the debris on to the floor.

But with the launch of the Sticky Rock Café looming, Candelskin knew he had to tread carefully with this woman, as he did when the celebrated fashion designer refused to wear a Dekaydence security stud, claiming an allergy to its bright colours. Secretly, he wished he'd done exactly what she'd done: the damn thing so irritated his skin.

''Xpect it was 'im indoors, ol' di'Abalo, who got Claud Canapé to do your office refurb,' Petty Masters said, looking around admiringly. 'Only the likes of him can afford Canapé's maximus bill for his minimalist style.'

What did this woman know of style, thought Candelskin, with her voice pitched somewhere between loose elastic and south-east London? Why, you only had to look at her: silver studs down one pale cheek, eyes black-ringed like a lemur, her hair an electrocuted mass of tiny black plaits. Worse, she was wearing what appeared to be a T-shirt made out of stained dishcloths and combat trousers cut from sacking and egg boxes, with a gun belt at her waist.

Only the seriously rich, the seriously trendy or the criminally insane, he decided, would buy such ghastly designs, let alone wear them.

He ran a hand through the boyish haircut he knew took years off him and flashed one of his famously enigmatic smiles.

'Do you know,' he said, leaning forward conspiratorially, 'before he'd even consider the job, Canapé sent his astrologer to explore the building's birth chart to determine its "harmonious forces"?'

'Yeah, well, he's bonkers, inn'ee? That's why you and the seriously rich and trendy love 'im. Like you do me.' Petty winked. 'Anyways up, Candy-Pandy, after working me rubber gloves off for months, it's been fab having a break here. You serve the best caviar and champagne in the Union, and as for that chocolate nut sundae mud bath last night ...'

She undid the top button of her trousers. Candelskin looked away.

'And that great greasy breakfast this morning – the fried eggs, sausages, bacon, mushrooms, fried bread, black pudding and baked beans—' She belched. 'Better out than in.'

'Quite,' said Candelskin, adjusting his shirt cuffs.

'But it's no good, Randy-Pandypants, I won't do it. I got me posh clientele and gutter cred to think of. If it got out that I was designing free stuff for a load of manky kids and some 'orrible spotty new boy band wot don't exist as yet and will've split up by Christmas ...'

She took a match from the gun belt, struck it across the desk and lit a small cigar, inhaling long and deep.

Under the table, Candelskin clenched his fists.

'It wouldn't matter but your final offer ain't quite good enough for me pension, you see,' she said, exhaling a cloud of foul-smelling smoke.

'Such a shame.' Candelskin gave a delicate cough. 'Signor di'Abalo is so keen to flex his worldwide media muscles on your behalf.'

Petty gave a raucous laugh.

'And such gorgeous muscles, or so I'm told. But you'd know that more than most, Randy-Scandalskin, or so I'm told. Run to your rescue, didn't he, the Gobfather, after you were – well, you know your story about being sacked better than me.'

She stamped her metal boots on the wooden floor, hard and fast.

Candelskin gave a thin smile. If he'd been that type of man, he'd have been tempted to hit her. As it was, he knew he had to be careful: he bruised so easily.

Petty stubbed out her cigar on the floor and stood up. 'OK, it's time to say ta-ever-so, bye-bye, etc. If one of your gormless guards with Scotch mist for brains could organise a taxi.'

'Of course. There is one thing—' Candelskin gawped

in horror: having used the paperclip to explore her ear, Petty was wiping a large globule of wax on to the back of the chair. He swallowed hard before continuing. 'It is Signor di'Abalo's custom to offer his guests a small gift on their departure. He has an uncanny ability to match a gift to a person.'

'You don't know me that well,' Petty said, brazenly.

'Oh, but we do. It's simply that Dekaydence editors have been told to spike the stories,' said Candelskin. 'For the time being.' He smiled sweetly.

Petty stood transfixed.

'Come with me,' said Candelskin. 'Oh, you'll need this.'

'It's not the new Dekaydence 321 perfume, is it? The one you wear — the one available only to royalty and celebs,' she said, in a voice half sneer, half excitement, as she took the parcel Candelskin offered her.

'Wait and see.' Candelskin winked and led her from the room, as an inner voice screeched at him that, in reality, there was no time to wait.

8 THE PALACE OF DEKAYDENCE

Phew, Ruby Q, you know I don't do running, so why—?

'Sorry for the rush, Ruby Q,' said Jack, after he, Taylor and Ruby Q had raced along the High Street to catch the mid-morning Tartan Bus bound for the Palace of Dekaydence. 'Dad's in a state: he's starting a new job today.'

'Lucky man,' said Ruby Q, thinking of her pile of rejection letters.

'Lucky all of us,' said Taylor, slumping into a seat on the top deck.

Ruby Q looked questioningly.

'He's been out of work two years,' said Jack. 'The accountants at his old firm said his job could be done more cheaply by a youngster. That's why we rent next door to you. We lost our home. Well, we lost everything.'

'It's why Mum does so much supply teaching,' said Taylor.

So much for happy families, Ruby Q Cooper.

'I'd no idea,' said Ruby Q.

'That's the way it is today,' said Jack. 'I just hope the job lasts.'

'So you won't feel guilty when you walk out on us,' said Taylor.

'Why, where are you going?' said Ruby Q.

Can't you guess?

'As soon as I've finished the Grey Zoner induction courses, I'm off, to become a full-time GeeZer, like Cage,' said Jack.

Ooo, was that your stomach sinking to the floor?

Ruby Q looked out of the window. Shoppers laden with carrier bags went in and out of the stores, while beggars slept in the doorways of boarded-up shops. Paper, cans and dog shit littered the street, while inside the shops, on the shelves that weren't empty, everything, including the assistants, looked perfectly packaged. How could this happen? thought Ruby Q. Yet it did. And somehow life went on. For the time being. She knew Jack had to go but ...

'Wow-erooney!' exclaimed Taylor, as they stepped off the Tartan Bus outside the Globe containing the Palace of Dekaydence, which shone like a huge golden ball, its myriad windows sparkling like diamonds.

'"Sited by the river, on London's south side, the Globe covers an area the size of 36 football pitches,"' Jack read from a brochure. '"It has 27 glass supporting plinths, 100 metres high and 25 metres in diameter, all with lifts or stairs ... The laser boundary wall protects it against attacks—"'

'Who would attack such a beautiful building?' said Taylor.

'You stupid or what?' sneered a hooded youth behind them. 'Given half a chance, GeeZers spoil everything, dunnai?'

Steady, Ruby Q!

'No, actually, they don't,' said Ruby Q, turning round. 'It's politicians who are the professional polluters, spoilers and—'

'Leave it,' said Jack. 'His type are only interested in trouble.'

Yes, Ruby Q. This is Taylor's birthday treat and not the time or the place to get into a row.

Ruby Q was about to say something but Tartan Guards began ordering them to an entrance booth, where a girl stood waiting, a colourful Dekaydence stud in her ear and a smile as bright as her yellow suit.

'Please take the motorised pathway,' said the girl, with an American accent, as she collected their tickets. 'And remember, now that you're Adventurers, Have a Nice Dekaydence Day!'

'Have a Nice Dekaydence Day!' some Adventurers chorused.

The pathway took them through a park, in which colourful fountains, flowers and a shrubbery advertised Dekaydence products. It seemed that almost everything was for sale within the Palace of Dekaydence, through points awarded in competitions or by paying—

Over the odds, to be sure, to be sure.

They took a lift into the Globe and arrived at the Palace of Dekaydence, its crystal towers and turrets fanning out like sunrays on a dawn sky, and stood, gazing at the great Fanged Doors at the entrance, when a large red glass bubble flew out, hovering to a standstill close by. A yellow-suited youth, with a broad grin, appeared at the cockpit window.

'Hi, Adventurers! Welcome to the Palace of Dekaydence! I'm Ron, your Guide for today!' Ron proclaimed, in a transatlantic drawl. 'Please, step aboard your Orbobubble and I'll take you to your first game, dodgems on hot ice, where big winners achieve big points!'

'Why is everyone here American?' said Jack.

Ruby Q shook her head.

'Because Americans are better than us at smiling,' said Taylor, knowingly, as they found places on the rotating seats. 'They have better teeth. You see it in all their movies. That's why I'll get my teeth fixed.'

'But you don't need to,' said Ruby Q.

'That's not the point,' said Taylor, patiently.

They flew into a vast rainbow-coloured entrance hall, reverberating with the sound of music, laughter and chatter. Red, blue, green and yellow Orbobubbles glided through a laser light show happening above the crowds of Adventurers buying Dekaydence clothes, sweets and trinkets in the shops and cafés. As though there were no tomorrow, which one day there might not be, thought Ruby Q as she turned and saw something at the centre of the hall: a massive living sculpture, writhing with fire, earth, wind and water.

'Wow, these things must work on anti-gravitational tracks,' said Jack, as the red Orbobubble travelled through first one floor then another and another.

They passed a hologram in which Adventurers in racing cars were encouraged by the Guides to knock down pedestrians in a busy high street. In another, Guides cheered on Adventurers to speed eat their way through mountains of cakes, colas, burgers and sweets; while in a third, Guides rooted for the Adventurers who could endure the loudest sounds.

People will do almost anything in order to win, especially these days.

Would you?

I hope not. But I can't be sure.

The red Orbobubble entered a hologram and came to rest by the side of a lake veiled in a fine mist. A smiling yellow-suited Guide, with a cheery American voice, allocated everyone to one of twelve strange-shaped vessels. By the time Ruby Q, Jack and Taylor boarded Vessel Twelve, the cabin was packed with other Adventurers already strapped into seats, while at the wheel stood the hooded youth from the bus.

'Move your butts!' he snarled. 'And watch out for the dragons!'

Dragons?

'What dragons?' said Jack. 'This is a dodgems, isn't it?'

'Shut your mouth and peel open your eyes!' snapped the youth.

'It ain't worth arguin' with Innit,' a girl said with a sigh. 'I should know – he's me bruvver. This is water dodgems, on 'ot ice, between Steam Dragons.'

Steam Dragons?

Ruby Q peered through a porthole and the thickening mist. A vessel rose up, its hull unfurling like wings, its prow uncoiling like a swan's neck. All at once, scalding steam shot from its nostrils straight towards them, throwing Adventurers into the backs of their seats.

'Game's begun!' Innit shouted, above the shrieks of fear and delight. 'Remember, we gotta win!'

Steam Dragons careered in and out of the clouds, roaring and snorting steam, while Adventurers called out the positions of other vessels.

'Fantastic machinery,' said Jack. 'But what are we doing exactly?'

'A watched Steam Dragon never boils,' said Innit's sister. 'So while we're on the lookout for the others, we have to keep out of their sight. The winning Steam Dragon is the one that boils and whistles first.'

'Dragon at starboard!' an Adventurer cried.

Innit yanked hard on the wheel. A piteous yelp came from below.

'Two dragons to port!' someone shouted.

Innit spun the wheel. There was another dreadful cry.

Machinery or not, that noise is unbearable!

'Stop!' Ruby Q called out.

He's ignoring you.

'Innit! Stop it!' Ruby Q called, louder, above Adventurers' warnings.

'Shut it, carrot head!' Innit shouted, jerking the wheel hard in the opposite direction. A yowl rose from the vessel's bowels.

'Whatever this thing is, you're hurting it!' cried Ruby Q, struggling in vain to release herself from the safety harness.

'Yeah – so what? Big hits get big points, tomato top!' sneered Innit.

Steady, Ruby Q.

'If that's true, then stuff this game and you!' Ruby Q shouted, folding her arms and staring up pointedly at the ceiling.

Cursing, Innit made a move towards her.

'I'm with her!' Taylor cried out suddenly, crossing her arms.

'Me too!' said a young boy, putting his feet on the porthole.

'You'll be for it when I tell my mum about you, you big bully!' piped up a little girl.

Looking as though he might self-combust on the spot, Innit went to speak.

Other Adventurers folded their arms.

'OK!' snarled Innit, glaring at them all in turn. 'I'll be gentle.' And he turned the wheel with exaggerated care. The cries from below ceased.

Ruby Q uncrossed her arms. The others did likewise.

Not long afterwards, their vessel made a sound like a whistling kettle. More whistles followed until a horn blew, the mists cleared, the Steam Dragons drifted back to the jetty and the Adventurers disembarked.

'Twelve points to each Adventurer in Vessel Nine,' proclaimed a Dekaydence Guide, and gave ten other scores. 'And finally, a point to each Adventurer in Vessel Twelve! Well done, y'all! Have a Nice Dekaydence Day!'

'Have a Nice Dekaydence Day!' the Adventurers chorused.

Don't say anything to Taylor – this is her birthday treat – but there's something nasty about the games in here. It's as if they're encouraging us to behave badly. And as for those grinning Guides— Look out! It's—!

'You're trouble, you are,' Innit muttered under his breath as he sidled up to Ruby Q. 'But then I remembered sommat: so am I.' He sneered as he crunched his knuckles.

'You don't scare me, you bully,' said Ruby Q.

He scares the proverbial out of me!

9 ... INTO THE FIRE

It was deep into the night and Will had been following the Tartan Bus when someone grabbed him from behind. He'd put up a furious struggle, realising that although his assailant was a Tartan Guard he was different: he was solid muscle, his kilt was not red but black and his eyes were screened by red tartan sunglasses.

The Black Tartan had bundled him into a sack and, before he lost consciousness, he'd thought that was it. The end. For a split second, he felt anger: at his stupidity for getting caught, and because there was so much more he had to do. Had his brother felt the same at the moment when he too had ...?

The next he knew he was lying on flagstones, alongside two other youths. Then they were marched off, and as they left he saw a barrier descend. As well as relief that he was alive, he felt a surge of excitement: he was inside Dekaydence HQ – the very place he wanted to be!

They were led into a compound, secured by lasers and cameras. The Black Tartans took away his adservarum and eyed him suspiciously. Few people his age had such luxuries. He gave a false surname, and said he'd worked on a farm but had run away to London. It was true, up to a point. Each youth had a rainbow-coloured security stud punched into one ear before being ordered to strip, wash and dress in black trousers and T-shirt; then the youths were taken off in different directions. Will was taken to the kennels.

A small boy, several years younger than him, was preparing food for the caged dogs. He nodded at Will, indicating the cameras.

'New boy?' said the boy, out loud, as they filled up the bowls.

'Aye,' said Will, noticing scars on the boy's arms.

'When the stud flashes,' said the boy, lowering his voice and fingering the stud in his own ear, 'that's when they come for you.'

'And then?'

The boy brushed a finger across his throat.

'What does that mean?' said Will.

The boy looked around nervously.

'The Black Tartans take you underground,' he whispered, 'to the White Room. You don't come back.'

'Why? What happens?' Was this what his brother had discovered?

'No one knows,' said the boy, shrugging.

'I have to find out what's going on there,' Will whispered, urgently.

'Then you're crazier than the Tartans!' the boy snorted.

'Maybe.'

'Listen, they tell you this is a rehab centre for street

youngsters but ...' muttered the boy. Then he raised his voice. 'Here, shove the bowls under the bars of the dogs' cages. I'll deal with the haggoids.'

'Haggoids, what are—?'

But the boy was off, dragging a large bulging plastic sack to the far corner. Will set about his task, sensing unease among the dogs. He kept glancing at the boy, who was taking all manner of rubbish from the sack and stuffing it through the bars of a heavily strengthened metal cage.

Suddenly, the boy shrieked. The dogs broke into a frenzy of barking and howling.

Will dropped the bowl and ran across.

The boy was crumpled up against the bars of the cage. When he saw why, Will felt his insides curdle. Two dog-like creatures were staring back at him with wild, blood-red eyes. They looked like terriers, but their teeth, jaws and bodies were made entirely of steel. One had its jaws clamped on the boy's wrist.

'Give it more rubbish!' cried the boy, his face contorted with pain.

Will didn't stop to ask questions. He pulled a handful of rubbish from the sack and thrust it through the bars, just out of the haggoid's reach.

'Drop!' he said firmly.

The haggoid regarded him with its mad eyes.

'*Drop!*' he commanded, holding the creature's gaze.

The second haggoid leapt up at the bars.

Will snatched his hand away as its jaws snapped on to the rubbish.

The first haggoid yowled, letting go of the boy's arm and hurling itself at the other haggoid. Rubbish flew everywhere as the yattering haggoids fought, metal against metal.

'You OK?' said Will, turning to the boy, who was slumped on the floor, nursing and licking his wound.

'I'll live,' the boy muttered, grimly. He looked up and the wan smile froze on his face. He stared at Will in horror. He tried to say something. He went to touch the side of his head. That's when it began to dawn on Will.

The haggoids had stopped fighting and were staring at him, and he realised that their infra-red eyes and thin vibrating tails were probably transmitting information about him. Information that would tell someone, somewhere, that the stud in his ear was flashing.

10 PICCOLO'S SONG

Piccolo felt fear gnawing at his gut. Had Will been captured on one of his missions? Or hurt? He wondered what to do and decided to wait in the cemetery, in case Will showed. There was enough water but only a small chunk of cheese, which he quickly devoured.

It was an oven-hot day, the air sticky-thick like porridge. No one was about. He sat up in the yew tree, playing softly and thinking over the things Will had told him. The song came easily, the words forming in his head as he composed the melody.

> *Deep inside*
> *Like it's alive*
> *I'm plagued*
> *With volcanic rage.*
>
> *I turn the page*
> *Of another day*
> *And still they say*
> *I'm of the age*
> *To suffer*
> *With volcanic rage.*
> *What do they expect*

When they neglect
To see the world they've wrecked?
I look for truth
And can only deduce
It's a golden goose
Laying rotten lies
In a world they've crucified.

I'm a young man now
And I won't kow-tow
To the ways and means
Of their rotten machine
Which rides o'er the world
In blind unconcern
For my tomorrow.

Volcanic rage
With which I'm plagued
Helps me to fight
To get what's right
To lift the crippled world from off its knees
To see it live, at peace, at one
For my son, and for his.

He took the piccolo from his lips. 'Volcanic Rage', he'd call it. It was a song for Will and his GeeZers. He wondered when, or if, he'd ever play it for him.

He heard rustling in the grass and looked down. At the

far end of the cemetery, leaning against a gravestone, his back to him, was Will.

He jumped down and ran towards him, calling out his friend's name but, as the figure turned, he saw it wasn't Will. Nothing like. Piccolo pulled up. This youth was older, maybe nineteen or twenty, taller and more powerfully built, his skin dark and shiny as though it had been polished.

'Man, yous can play!' said the youth, his rich, deep voice reminding Piccolo of an oboe, his smile revealing teeth like polished pearls.

He breathed in the youth's apple-blossom freshness, so at odds with everyone and everything else on the streets, which smelt anything but, and decided the youth was the most beautiful being he'd ever seen.

'Yous hungry, music man?' said the youth.

Piccolo realised that delicious smells were coming from a bag at the youth's feet. Hot dogs and coffee? The youth took out a bun, oozing with ketchup and fried onions.

'Who are you?' said Piccolo. Not that his stomach cared.

'Name's Bianco,' said the youth, grinning as he held out the bun. 'I was passin' when I heard your little wooden bird. Man, you make it fly!'

Piccolo took the bun and plunged his teeth into it, savouring the glorious combination of meat, ketchup, fried onions and bread. It was gone too quickly. Bianco handed him a coffee and leant back against the ancient gravestone, watching as Piccolo swallowed the sweet, frothy drink.

'You know there's trouble brewing, music man,' said Bianco, casually. 'Theys out to get GeeZers, d'you know that? And they ain't about to stop and ask if yous a musician, if yous get my drift.'

Piccolo nodded, staring into the empty cup.

'So howzabout comin' to the Promised Land?' said Bianco.

Piccolo looked up, frowning. 'You mean like in the Bible?'

Bianco laughed. The sound made Piccolo smile.

'Yeh, something like that. It's safer than here.'

Piccolo nodded slowly.

'I'll come for you tonight. I got me some things to do. Keep your head down. I'll find you – you can't escape me.' Bianco winked.

Piccolo hesitated. Bianco was beautiful. Mesmerising. Tempting. But who was he? Was he another GeeZer? A friend of Will? Something stopped Piccolo asking. He supposed that, although he'd never had one before, Will was his friend. He savoured the thought, as he'd savoured the burger. Yes, Will was a friend and he had to find him. He said nothing.

When Bianco left, he quit the cemetery. He asked on the streets about Will but no one could help. He was close by the place where they'd met when he heard the sirens. He leapt into a burnt-out car.

It was hot and humid. Thunder rolled round the sky.

Piccolo watched from inside the car, trying to ignore his empty stomach's cries for more burgers and coffee and instead imagine a promised land. What might be there for him, and for Will? He yawned. The sirens moved away. He closed his eyes. He was at a party, his party. Will was there. So was Bianco. Tables were laden with food and flowers. People were smiling and making a fuss of him, and then his dad came in, arms outstretched and—

He awoke with a start. He was being dragged from the car and shoved into a sack. He punched and kicked out. But it was no good. The silent assailant tying the sacking around his head was immensely strong.

For a moment, Piccolo panicked, thinking it might be his mum's Big Bloke. And then he breathed in the most tantalising aromas and stopped struggling. Treacle pudding and custard. Ice cream and hot chocolate sauce. Roast chicken, roast potatoes and gravy. He was salivating, clutching the sacking as if his life depended on it. He no longer felt hungry, or afraid. Thoughts of the Big Bloke, his mum, Bianco, even his dad and Will drifted from his mind.

Through a rent in the sacking he was vaguely aware of a swirl of tartan and the growl of a diesel engine. But he was soon lost in the actual taste of the most meltingly fluffy light lemon meringue pie in the world.

If this was his time to die, he thought dreamily, so be it.

11 CREAM CRACKERED

Having ushered Petty Masters into an elegant drawing room, Candelskin went up into the gallery to join the Professor, Dekaydence's Head of Research and Development.

The Professor was fiddling with the controls of monitors that focused on Petty Masters and the room below. Candelskin sat down in the next seat, without acknowledging him. They had neither music nor clothes for the new cafés. Why? Because the Professor had insisted on choosing the designer and musicians. Where had it got them? Nowhere. And with nothing. Only closer to the Sticky Rock Café launch. Quite what this wretched experiment would achieve where a chocolate mudbath had failed, Candelskin couldn't imagine.

The Professor flicked a switch and ordered up some Bach. Candelskin groaned inwardly: he longed for Wagner, the ninth great wonder in the world.

Collapsing on to a *chaise longue*, Petty Masters ripped open the package to discover a pistol, which she stuffed dismissively into her gun belt, and an envelope, which she opened with great care. She feasted her eyes on the white powdery contents before breathing it in. A fire coursed through her body. Closing her eyes, she slumped back into the seat and sighed contentedly. A few seconds later, she was frowning.

'This ain't right,' she muttered, wiping sweat from her face. She opened her eyes and looked around in disbelief.

The room had vanished. She was still sitting on the *chaise longue* but—

'I'm in the middle of a bloody jungle!' she exclaimed, staring at trees, stretching high into the sky, and dense undergrowth of leaves, roots, fallen branches, ferns and red-flowering heliconia. She looked back at the door, now the buttress root of a tree, some eight metres in diameter.

And there was the heat: the studs in her face were burning her skin.

A green flying snake skimmed her body before landing some ten metres away.

She screamed and a chorus of deafening shrieks splintered the air. The jungle throbbed with hidden life and everywhere water dripped from leaves and branches, as well as from her body, hair and clothes. Her heart was racing.

'Wow! This stuff is ex!' she said. 'And after only a few grams!'

She stood up, took a few steps and slipped. A lizard skittered over a puddle. This time, she didn't scream. She tore back the thick vegetation and strode deeper into the jungle. The light was poor but she plunged on.

It was then she heard laughter. Laughter without a trace

of humour. It was coming closer. A startled bird flew up into the sky. The laughter stopped and started again. Hand shaking, Petty reached into her gun belt, cocked the pistol and held it high.

Crashing at full pelt though the undergrowth came a tall, spindly creature, followed closely by another. The two creatures saw her, and the gun, and stopped dead in their tracks.

Petty blinked. Each creature had the head, arms and legs of a man but the body of a huge, square, brown biscuit, flecked with creamy yellow spots.

'Don't shoot!' screamed the first creature, holding up its long trembling arms.

'Don't shoot!' cried the second, holding up its long trembling arms.

'I wasn't intending to!' she snapped.

'That's a relief,' said the first, hand on biscuit hip.

'It surely is,' said the second, and both hooted with laughter, triggering an explosion of noises from unseen creatures.

'Who are you?' Petty demanded. 'And what are you doing here?'

'More to the point, *what* are you?' said the first, haughtily.

'My name is Petty Masters.'

'Possibly, but that doesn't explain *what* you are,' said the second.

'What on earth are *you*?' retorted Petty.

'It's obvious, we're crackers!' screamed the first cracker, while the second burst into such hysterical laughter that it fell over.

'Oh, crumbs!' cried the first cracker, wringing its hands and hopping from one leg to the other. 'Give us a hand, you Petty Masters creature.'

Pocketing her gun, Petty stepped forward and reached out a hand. The second cracker sank its teeth into her skin. She yelped, the creature let go, and she felt warm blood flowing out through a wound.

'Never bite the hand that feeds you!' the first cracker tutted.

'That's OK,' said the second cracker, jumping to its feet, 'because to the best of my knowledge, that hand has never fed me.'

'You're right!' cried the first, and they both screeched with laughter.

'Look here!' said Petty indignantly, wondering vaguely if she could get blood poisoning from a cracker.

'Where?' whispered the first cracker, looking around, fearfully.

'What are you on?' Petty demanded. 'Why do you keep laughing?'

'I told you!' snapped the first cracker. 'Are you stupid or deaf or something? We are crackers! Completely and utterly crackers!'

'Worse!' said the second, pointing to the blotches on its body. 'We've been genetically modified into ice-cream crackers.'

'God, I've no idea what's going on,' said Petty, clutching her head.

'That explains one thing,' said the first cracker. 'You've either just arrived or been here even longer than us.'

Petty stared at the crackers. They were standing on their heads. So was the jungle. She collapsed into a clump of ferns. There was a clap of thunder, and another, and she realised it wasn't thunder: it was gunfire.

'Do some good in the world, you Petty Masters creature,' cried the first cracker, hastily covering her with ferns and leaves.

'Yes, you can't help us, but you can help others through the Sticky Rock Café,' cried the second.

The two crackers scuttled off into the undergrowth. There were more shots, and first one and then the other cracker fell to the ground. Petty choked back a sob. If only she could've helped them, she thought, before she lost consciousness.

'Miss Masters will give us no trouble now,' said the Professor, as the drawing room quickly replaced the jungle. 'I really must congratulate young Bodkin on his excellent hologram. If only the boy could spell.'

Candelskin said nothing.

'I find it fascinating,' the Professor continued, 'how those who powder their nose so easily lose the ability to see beyond it. D'you know, Herr Candelskin, that

that powder Miss Masters thought she so desperately needed young Bodkin and I concocted from icing sugar, ground syringa and dandruff from the Signor's cats? And it worked.'

The Professor chuckled. 'Yes, it will go down excellently well in the cafés, in tea, cappuccinos, colas and those strange smoothies you like so much.'

Candelskin didn't answer. He was watching a woozy Petty Masters stare at her bleeding hand while distractedly stuffing cream crackers into her mouth with the other. He glanced at the calendar. Less than two weeks to go before the Sticky Rock Café launch. He swallowed first two and then a handful of indigestion tablets.

Sometimes he yearned to know why di'Abalo so often let this lunatic have his head; mostly, he sensed it was best not to ask.

12 OVER AND OUT

'You're for it now!' said the boy, staring at Will's flashing stud.

'At least I'll get to see the White Room,' Will muttered, grimly.

'Then you're dead meat.'

Will thought of his brother. 'I have to know what's going on,' he said. 'I think my brother was in here. Maybe, you knew him. Tall, thick set—'

'Same weird accent?' said the boy.

'Aye,' said Will, alerted.

The boy shook his head.

For a moment, Will was silent.

'I've got to find out about this White Room,' he said at last.

'You a GeeZer?' said the boy.

'Aye. Problem?'

'No,' said the boy.

The haggoids started to yatter.

'Shite!' said the boy, wincing as he tried to move his arm.

'What's with them?' said Will.

'Greed. If they don't get more junk, they'll flip. And we'll be for it.'

'Where's the junk kept?'

'In bins at the edge of the compound, but—'

'I'll go,' said Will firmly, taking an empty can from the rubbish.

'But ...' The look of horror on the boy's face increased as he watched Will use the can's sharp edge to score at the surface of the stud.

'Well?' said Will.

'It's not quite as bright but—' said the boy, doubtfully.

'It'll do,' said Will, releasing his long hair from its band and heading for the door. 'I'll see you in five.'

'Then I'll show you how to change the bag inside the haggoids.'

Will turned round. 'You are joking?'

'No. But don't worry. You only do it when the bags are full. The haggoids crash, you throw a switch on their back, open 'em up and do the business. You get a minute before alarms go off at central control.'

'Aye, well, I'll take cover while I watch you, if you don't mind,' said Will.

The boy grinned.

As the boy had guessed, the Black Tartan on duty in the corridor was so absorbed in a soap opera on Dekaydence TV that he waved Will through, without looking up. A door opened and Will stepped into a yard six metres square, with twelve bins labelled 'Haggoids' and lasers enclosing the yard blocking any view beyond.

He was pulling paper, bottles, board and tins from a bin when he smelt something decidedly rancid and heard a man's voice he recognised, coming from the other side of the barrier.

'We're getting the clothes but the music ...'

Will sensed anxiety in the man's voice. But who was he?

'Signor, we must delay the opening.'

Of course! It was Randall Candelskin, the PM's former friend. And he must be talking to his new boss, the head of the mighty Dekaydence empire, Signor Lorenzo di'Abalo.

'Signor,' said Candelskin. 'This eleventh-hour way of conducting affairs – In business, it serves you excellently well but in politics, which is what the Sticky Rock Café comes down to, it will cause your reputation to suffer.'

'My dear Randall, I trust you implicitly, as I hope you trust me,' a man replied, quietly yet firmly, in an accent threaded with Italy and Eire.

Will strained to hear more.

'But how—?' said Candelskin.

'Randall, I think Sir Harrison Catgut is in need of a special treat.'

'Like the farewell treat we have in store for the Prime Minister?'

'No,' said di'Abalo, with a dry chuckle. 'Something less dramatic. For the time being.'

The voices moved off and Will realised his hands were shaking. Had he heard right? A farewell treat for the PM?

Was this the start of the coup the media were always hinting at? Was this what his brother had discovered? Was that the reason he'd been killed?

And was this the real reason Candelskin had quit parliament — so that he could join forces with a man whose fortune could easily fund such a project? But if so, why? Questions collided in his mind. Will knew one thing only for sure: that if the PM were killed, the King would be next. And the rest of the Royal Family, his family, would follow.

He had no liking for the PM but he realised if the man was killed, the GeeZers would take the blame. They'd be hounded by the media, sought out and exterminated. There'd be no one left to fight for the planet.

He had to get out of this place. He had to get a message to the Face. At all costs, the assassination attempt had to be stopped. Another part of his brain fired up. What of the teenagers who went missing inside Dekaydence? What of the White Room? What of the boy in the kennels? What of his brother's death? And his body?

An alarm bell startled him, bringing him back to his current plight. Had they discovered he'd gone missing? Had the haggoids' software informed someone somewhere that the stud in his ear was flashing?

A door opened and he slipped behind the bins as a dozen laughing, chattering teenagers in bright yellow suits hurried towards the laser wall opposite, which parted sufficiently to reveal a Tartan Bus.

A newspaper article flashed into his head. These teenagers must be Dekaydence Guides, the all-American cheerleaders and jocks imported, it was said, to inject some enthusiasm into their more morose British counterparts. His mind raced on. They must be on their way to the Palace of Dekaydence, which meant the bus would be stopping regularly to pick up – Adventurers. That was what the young visitors were called.

The last Guide had boarded the bus and the laser wall was starting to close.

Will raced across the compound, sprinted through the opening and leapt on to the bus. The laser wall closed and the bus doors locked fast behind him. He glanced around. No one seemed to have noticed him. There were no hidden cameras, or Tartan Guards, Black or Red. The only adult on board was the driver, in his cubicle, who was intent on manoeuvring the bus out of Dekaydence HQ into the narrow street beyond.

Will felt his heart pounding. He'd escaped!

He ducked down under a seat, and remembered the last time he'd been on a Tartan Bus. But this was broad daylight, he reasoned, drawing comfort from the presence of the lively young Dekaydence Guides. As soon as the bus stopped to pick up passengers, he'd mingle with the crowd getting on, slip off the bus and run. No one would be any the wiser.

He waited and watched, knowing he must get to the Face before it was too late.

'Stop,' he urged the bus as it travelled alongside the River Thames.

Under a stormy overcast sky, the river looked like thick, grey gravy. The bloated body of a dog drifted by and he wondered how long it'd be before desperate humans took to drinking from the filthy, polluted waters.

The bus continued its slow progress. Petrol rationing had reduced traffic, but power cuts meant traffic lights were frequently out of action, and here and there wreckage was strewn across the streets.

Will spotted a Dekaydence bus stop, surrounded by a crowd of young teenagers. The bus slowed down. He tensed himself, ready to make his escape, but, all of a sudden, the bus picked up speed. He caught sight of the disappointment and anger on the youngsters' faces as the bus sailed past them. He ducked down under the seat.

What was going on?

'This is a game, right?' hissed an American voice, close to his ear.

Startled, he looked up. A pretty girl was standing over him, grinning.

'You're an Adventurer, right?' she said, excitedly. There was something reverential in her tone of voice.

Will swallowed. What should he say? He smiled.

'Gee!' The girl's eyes widened. She turned to the others. 'Hey, everyone. Come meet our first Adventurer.'

He slid into a seat as the group surrounded him.

'Are you the only Adventurer here?'

'Is it your birthday?'

'How many points d'you get for riding with us?'

'Do you need the bathroom?'

They were friendly enough, he thought as he answered their questions, but something about them put him on edge. What was it?

'Which game is this?' a cheerful boy asked.

'It's a new game,' Will replied, more confident than he felt, as an idea occurred to him, should the driver see him. 'So, I need your jacket.'

The boy happily took off his jacket and handed it to Will, who slipped the yellow garment over his black T-shirt and smiled.

The boy smiled back. 'Hey, you're one of us now,' he cried.

'Aye,' said Will. 'But listen, for this game, you have to tell me everything you know about the White Room. And quickly.'

The teenagers looked blank.

'Come on, somebody must know something,' Will cajoled.

The boy was about to answer when the bus stopped. Will cursed under his breath but, smiling and nodding, edged his way to the door.

'Wow,' said the boy, peering out of the window.

'Wow,' said the other youngsters.

Will's heart sank.

Instead of a bus stop, a large, circular yellow craft

hovered close by the door while, in the near distance, a giant golden orb glittered in the sunshine.

He hadn't escaped. He'd simply walked into another of the spider's webs: the Palace of Dekaydence.

13 CLOSE ENCOUNTERS

The red Orbobubble containing Ruby Q, Jack, Taylor and the other Adventurers sailed through the DekAquarium, where everyone was encouraged to zap marine life using their personal mini-coms. They flew through the DekUniversarium, where they were egged on to destroy planets and stars. In the Movie House, points were deducted for a lack of knowledge of Dekaydence films and TV soap operas, while in the Music Room, all were chivvied to sing along, as loudly as they could, with the unmanned instruments playing the Palace's anthem:

> *Have a Nice Dekaydence Day!*
> *Come to the Palace and play!*
> *There's much to do and much to eat,*
> *So come to the Palace, get your points and treats*
> *And ... Have a Nice Dekaydence Day!*

I wonder who invented all this techno-spectacular stuff?

I don't know, but why does everything here encourage cheating and lying, if not downright ignorance and violence?

Ruby Q, get real: this is life today.

Not everywhere. I doubt the GeeZers—

If they were all saints, Ruby Q, they wouldn't survive.

It was time for the finale. The red Orbobubble flew them to the basement, where scores of Adventurers stood waiting on a station platform, with a group of new over-excited Guides.

Ruby Q heard the sound of crunching knuckles behind her.

'Final journey, GeeZer girl,' sneered the familiar voice of Innit.

'Look here.' She spun round, furious, and came face to face with a tall dark-eyed youth, with long dark curls, who certainly wasn't Innit. Was he a Dekaydence Guide? He was wearing a bright yellow jacket but his security stud was flashing and, far from smiling at her, he stared at her with an unsettling, penetrating gaze.

''Ere, what's your—?' snarled Innit, but a glance from the dark-eyed young man stoppered his mouth and temper.

'You're a GeeZer?' The youth spoke quickly and Ruby Q was surprised to hear not an American but a Highland accent.

'Not exactly,' she said, and she saw an anxious look cross his face.

'Actually, my friend Ruby Q Cooper is a journalist and she's going to interview the Face,' Taylor boasted in a low voice.

The youth started. 'I have an urgent message for the Face,' he hurried on. 'It's ...'

His words were drowned by the Adventurers' cheers as an open-topped train, the WeatherCoaster, chugged out of a tunnel towards them. Scores of Adventurers disembarked and scores more surged forward to get on the train; and, in the ensuing chaos of struggles, scuffles and raised voices, Ruby Q and the youth were separated. When she found herself shoved into an auto-locking seat, she looked around. Taylor was next to her, Jack a few seats away; Innit was in a scrum in the next compartment but of the youth she saw nothing.

She shrugged. They'd meet up later, she was sure, when she'd put him right about Taylor's boasts before he told her his message.

You can be a prig, Ruby Q.

At least I sleep easy at night.

No, you don't.

You're right. The clowns.

The klaxon sounded and the train chugged back into the tunnel. A display of red and green light-works exploded in the darkness overhead. The Adventurers gasped, cheered and applauded.

'In the polar regions,' Jack mused, 'charged particles from the sun get trapped in the earth's magnetic field ...'

Adventurers tapped his words into their mini-coms in answer to the questions. If it meant more points, and more prizes, so what if it was cheating?

Innit yawned loudly. 'Yeah, it's the Aurora Boring,' he said, switching on his inaudirum and deafening Adventurers sitting even a distance away.

There was a clap of thunder; then came the rain. Cussing, two Red Tartan Guards ran for shelter under the Globe.

'What's up with the wee beastie, MacNoodle?' said one, shivering, as his colleague struggled to control a yattering haggoid that was straining at its leash to climb a supporting plinth.

'Ach, MacMinor, it's not the haggoid, it's the software in these wretched studs,' said MacNoodle, tapping his ear. 'And I'll tell them so on my training day next week. It interferes wi' 'em, and sends 'em half crazy, so they go for anything that doesn't move. And anything that half resembles a lamppost, like this yon plinth – They're that powerful, these wee beasties, you're safer letting them go.'

'Is that right?' said MacMinor. 'Poor wee sods.'

'Aye,' sighed MacNoodle, patting the creature's head. 'I know they're only bits of metal but I find I'm getting rather fond of this wee thing. Don't say anything, but I've called it Cromarty.'

'Och, that's nice,' said MacMinor.

'My other one's Ross,' said MacNoodle, proudly. 'Aye, but they're getting terrible trouble in the kennels. Real green-eyed stuff from the dogs. They don't mix. Like us and those cursed Black Tartans.'

MacMinor sniffed. 'You don't like them 'cos they keep themselves to themselves.'

'Aye, and doesn't it make you wonder why?' MacNoodle snorted. 'We have some unpleasant duties, but what is it those Black Tartans do in the compound which has to be kept so damned secret?'

MacMinor stepped out from under the Globe and sneezed. 'It's eased off, MacNoodle,' he said. 'Best press on.'

MacNoodle grunted. 'Och man, this is a waste of time. If there is a young 'un escaped here off the rehabilitation programme, Cromarty would've sensed it. No, my bet is this is another software malfunction at HQ. Either that, or it's one of those scheming Black Tartans sending us off on a wild goose chase.'

In a glorious dawn, the WeatherCoaster slowly descended a snow-covered mountain. Skiers and snowboarders shushed past as Adventurers answered questions on their mini-coms about the three countries remaining in the world that boasted snow-covered mountains.

'It's marshmallow!' Taylor squealed, tasting the snowball on her T-shirt thrown by one of the bobble-hatted youngsters hiding in the bushes.

All at once, there was a splintering sound and a deep shudder, and the Adventurers saw a mass of snow hurtling towards them. They shrieked and struggled in vain to free themselves from their seat belts, as trees, skiers, snowboarders and bobble hats vanished inside the avalanche which shot by, a metre from the train. Seemingly oblivious, the Guides chatted among themselves, as the avalanche disappeared from sight.

'We must help!' cried Ruby Q, tugging at the seat belt.

Innit yawned loudly.

'It's fakin' make-believe, dolthead,' he said, kicking out at his weeping sister. 'To spook you. And it's done its fakin' job, annit? I knew it first time round, and that's what gets me points and makes me the winner. Yeah, death, destruction, 'avoc – that's right up me fifth avenue.'

He leered at Ruby Q, as he honked with laughter.

Ruby Q watched pulleys drag trees, skiers, snowboarders and the bobble hats out of the snow and back up the mountainside. She frowned. Everything had looked so real. But then so had the Steam Dragons.

She turned and saw the dark-eyed youth in the next compartment. He was watching her intently. She nodded and was relieved when the WeatherCoaster went into another dark tunnel, sparing her blushes.

The train re-emerged into warm spring countryside and Innit began ripping off branches from the overhanging shrubbery.

''Ere, try this marzipan,' he said, chewing noisily on a handful of leaves and thrusting some at a pretty dark-haired girl, who ignored him.

'All ri'. Try this,' he said, shoving a twig into the girl's face. ''S chocolate. All girls like chocolate, dunnai?' He kicked his sister's ankle.

The pretty dark-eyed girl took a tentative bite out of

the twig and smiled.

Innit smirked.

'How about the peppermint blossom?' he cried. 'Or daffodil toffees, jelly gladioli or a few rum truffle berries?'

The Adventurers discarded their mini-coms and followed Innit's lead, devouring any vegetation in reach. Soon the landscape was laid bare, the ground becoming a chocolate mud with a scattering of red marzipan petals. Whatever the point of the game, thought Ruby Q, Innit's smug expression told her he'd won it, as well as the girl.

The WeatherCoaster chugged into another tunnel before arriving at its final destination: the seaside.

A summer sun shone on a bright blue sea. Youngsters – or were they automatons? – played and picnicked on a sandy beach. There was a white pier, with stalls and a funfair, and a brass band of youngsters in pink-and-white-striped suits performing in an open-air pavilion. The band reminded Ruby Q of her dad, touring South America, and she wondered how, in this day and age, phones could be so unreliable: unusually, there'd been no word from him, and neither could she get through to him.

'Adventurers!' said a voice in the ether. 'It's Party on the Pier time! Your Guide will take your mini-com and give you your personal Bank of Dekaydence credit card, on which your points have been placed and which you can use here in the Dekaydence stores. All you have to do is—'

'Have a Nice Dekaydence Day!' sang the Guides and

Adventurers, as they clambered on to the pier.

'These Guides are something else,' Ruby Q muttered.

'Yes. Who in their right mind would wear yellow?' said Taylor.

'Yes,' said Jack. 'They're about my brother's age but Kane and his friends don't do smiling, like this lot. They don't do much except sleep.'

'And why are they so indestructibly happy?' said Ruby Q, catching sight of the dark-eyed youth, making his way through the crowd towards her.

Taylor saw him, too.

'Come on, Jack,' said Taylor, dragging off her protesting brother, who'd seen nothing. She winked at Ruby Q, who blushed.

The youth stood before her. 'There's no time for pleasantries, Ruby Q Cooper,' he said, brusquely. 'I must know. Are you committed to the GeeZers' cause?'

'Yes, of course, but I have to tell you—' said Ruby Q.

'Listen!' the youth commanded, fiercely. 'Tell the Face that I – that Will told you there's a plot to assassinate the Prime Minister and—' He stood immobilised, encased in a fine net of light.

Ruby Q stared, uncomprehending, as two Red Tartans marched past her and led him away, on a thin chain of light.

'Wait!' she cried.

She went to follow but Jack was there, holding her back.

'No, Ruby Q,' he said, quietly.

'Why on earth not?' Ruby Q said angrily, struggling to free her arm from Jack's grip and watching the Red Tartans escort Will off the pier and head for the exit.

'Because—' Jack began.

'Heavy stuff for not having a ticket,' said Taylor. 'Shame, 'cos he was cute and he obviously fancied you, Ruby Q. Oh, well, come on.'

Reluctantly, Ruby Q let herself be led away to fight computer battles at ScreenAgers, ride the helter skelter, and have her fortune told by a Bearded Lady with huge biceps and a deep voice. At Whelkcome! they bought gobstopper onions pickled in fizzy Blooza Jooza – Just For Yousa, and sent postcards to the Treasures and the Martins' parents. And at Dek-U, Taylor bought a red outfit sold only to first-time Adventurers.

But all the time Ruby Q thought about Will, and his message for the Face. And why, thinking her to be a GeeZer, he should imagine that she'd care a fig about the PM being murdered, when he was among those responsible for allowing millions round the world, as well as the planet itself, to die.

It was nearly time to go and they were leaning against the railings, eating ice creams and gazing out at the bright blue sea, when something hit Ruby Q hard and sharp in the back.

She fell forward, grabbing at the wooden railings, which gave way in her hands. Someone screamed. Was it her? The next she knew, she was crashing into the sea, swallowing not salt water but sweet, fizzy Blooza Jooza.

Ruby Q, do something! We're too young to die!

She tried to force herself up to the surface, but her limbs felt leaden. And her head hurt. Something grabbed hold of her ...

She opened her eyes.

She was lying on the pier, drenched, dizzy and nauseous. Beside her the Bearded Lady, soaking wet and looking even less ladylike, was offering her a drink. Jack and Taylor knelt by her side. A few Adventurers gawped at her, while Innit, his arm round the dark-haired girl, stood close by, expressionless.

The drink revived her considerably and she stood up. Everything looked so hazy.

'For the little lady who dived in to save her specs!' cried Ron, encouraging the Adventurers to applaud and cheer.

It was then Ruby Q realised that her spectacles were in her hand. She put them back on.

'What happened?' she mumbled to Jack and Taylor.

'Innit pushed you!' said Taylor.

'Taylor, you didn't actually see—' said Jack.

'I didn't need to,' Taylor retorted, sharply. 'He was standing right behind us. That nasty smirk on his face. Oh, it was him all right.'

'Wait!' cried Ruby Q, clutching her head. 'It doesn't matter. What's important is that I get Will's message to the Face!'

'What was the message?' said Jack.

'There's a plot to kill the Prime Minister!' said Ruby Q.

'That's not news, Ruby Q. Even I know about that,' said Taylor.

'There was something else before the Red Tartans, I just can not ...' Ruby Q shook her head.

'Ruby Q, the websites are full of rumours about assassination threats,' said Jack. 'So are the papers, TV and radio. The Prime Minister thrives on it all, to rule harder and harsher. You know that as well as I do.'

'Yes, but—' Ruby Q began.

'Listen, Ruby Q,' Jack said. 'Even if you did have something new to tell the Face, you won't get the chance. I didn't know how to tell you this before but Cage rang last night. The Face still refuses to be interviewed – by you or anyone.'

'Did you get any of that?' snapped Bodkin, one of the Professor's assistants, who was sitting in Central Security at Dekaydence HQ.

'No, the computer crashed again when someone said the words Blooza Jooza,' said Grout, another assistant, as he fiddled with the controls.

'Who was on duty last? No, don't tell me,' said Bodkin, kicking the control panel. 'Boggin' Red Tartans! They couldn't operate a tea strainer without a manual.'

14 NOTATION

The butler cleared his throat, less discreetly than before, and a man swathed in a deep blue velvet hooded cloak lifted his sweating head from a bowl of steaming hot water and scowled.

With a grand theatrical gesture, Sir Harrison Catgut, the avant-garde composer recently knighted for his services to loud music, swept his long grey hair from his noble aquiline face.

'Yes?' he said, imperiously.

The butler gave a curt bow and pushed a trolley closer to the table.

'Roast hedge, sir,' he said, lifting the lid on a silver dish. 'Slightly underdone, as I believe you like it. With an Aconcagua, 1924.'

'My, a celebration, Phlegm?' said Catgut, watching greedily as the butler eased the cork from the bottle and poured the rare vintage water into a glass.

'We can but hope, sir,' said Phlegm. He bowed and left the room.

Catgut grabbed the bottle and took a deep swig. Then another.

There wasn't much time left. And what did he know about Young People, let alone the music they liked? Less than nothing. And if that wasn't enough, there were the constant demands from that damnable scientist to play the popular classics. God's teeth! He'd been promised a king's ransom. Was it worth it? Because if he failed ...

A little way off, in the elegantly furnished ivory room overlooking the River Thames, a tall handsome man in an expensive dark suit and cream silk shirt, his eyes the colour of a Caribbean sea, switched off the tiny custom-built adservarum he wore on his wrist. Sir Harrison Catgut, together with the 1924 Aconcagua, disappeared from the screen.

A noise distracted him and the man looked up. In the corner of the room, by the marble fountain gushing tall hot flames of fire, he saw two cats, their gaze intent on a fluttering moth. Suddenly, the white cat leapt into the air and, in a flash, clawed at the moth, brought it to the ground and then walked away, leaving the black cat to bite off the insect's head.

Lorenzo di'Abalo smiled indulgently. Really, it wasn't that different from the game he was playing.

15 CUPBOARD LOVE

By the time Piccolo arrived in the dormitory, word was out that a teenager had disappeared. And not to the White Room, which was the usual route, he was told. When the whispers said that the teenager was a tall brooding Scot with long, dark, wavy hair, Piccolo could have cheered. But when the whispers murmured of the haggoids' savagery, he refused to listen, instead imagining Will free and back fighting with the GeeZers.

As the security stud was punched into his ear, he was told he was lucky to be in one of the country's top rehabilitation centres for street youngsters. On one level, he didn't understand or care. Why should he? He was given a bed, clean linen and clothing. And unlike on the outside, there was water sufficient to have a daily shower. Best of all, there were three regular daily meals, with delicious puddings and sweets. It was better than living rough. It was much better than living at home.

To Piccolo, used to a life of chaos and disorder, the rules were, on that first day, a novelty. There was a time to get up, a time to go to bed, a time to eat. There were lessons in the morning, work in the afternoon in the kitchens, the laboratory or the kennels, and, in the evening, team-building sports. Music was everywhere. Some said it did their head in. Some didn't seem to hear it. For Piccolo it was sheer joy.

But by the end of the first day he knew he had to escape, because he yearned beyond desperation to play. He understood this feeling: it had been with him since he'd first held the piccolo. What he couldn't understand was how much he missed Will.

For most of his life, he'd survived without friendship, without trust. Next time – except there wouldn't be a next time, he told himself angrily – he wouldn't be so stupid. He wouldn't make himself vulnerable to anyone. He of all people should know that was the only way to survive.

But he couldn't survive without playing. It was worse than not talking because the piccolo was his voice. It spoke his feelings, his thoughts. He'd guessed the piccolo would be confiscated. That's why he'd hidden it in a cubicle in the lavatory when he was first brought in. That's why he and the piccolo kept silent, though his fingers moved restlessly, searching for the fingerholes. If he could only find a safe place, he knew he could get by. Until he escaped, like Will.

That first morning on the second day, he sat on the loo, composing a song in his head, and realised no one else was about. He looked at the watch they'd given him. He was late! He'd been warned about being late. He was pulling up his pants and trousers when he heard the outer door open. He tucked up his legs on to the lavatory seat.

Someone with a wheezy chest shuffled past his cubicle, opened a door, cussed and shuffled back out.

Piccolo peered round the cubicle door. A store cupboard, usually locked, stood open. He waited before moving swiftly across the room. He examined the cupboard. It reeked of bleach but—

He heard footsteps and dashed back into the cubicle, leaving the door ajar.

An old man shuffled into the room. He was pushing a trolley stacked with lavatory rolls, which he threw into the cupboard, before locking it and shuffling back out.

Piccolo looked at his watch. Seven minutes since he'd last checked. He raced to the classroom, where a short-sighted teacher was writing on the blackboard and continued to do so until the lesson ended.

The next day, Piccolo again missed the first few minutes of class, risking whatever punishment lay in store. This time, the Shuffler left the block for eight minutes.

The following day, it was nine.

Piccolo reckoned he had six safe minutes. Not long but better than nothing.

On the fourth day, he took the package from the lid of the cistern and, the moment the Shuffler left the room, he ran to the cupboard, took the piccolo out of its wrapping and lifted it to his mouth.

Softly, he trilled up and down the scales. Hearing the sound of the instrument felt like a waterfall in a desert. He played another song he'd composed in his head for Will.

After six minutes, he forced himself to stop, returned the piccolo to its hiding place and ran to his class. He ached with desire to play more.

The next day, he transcribed a piece he'd heard in the laboratory and went on to play another new composition. He caught sight of the time. Eight minutes! The Shuffler was overdue. So was he. He'd be for it! He was reaching for the handle when he heard a slow handclap and smelt something deeply unpleasant.

He pushed open the door.

A tall, fair-haired, expensively dressed man in his thirties stood before him, wearing a smile chiselled from ice. He gestured for Piccolo to walk on ahead into the corridor, where the Shuffler and another old man in a dark suit were hastily stubbing out their cigarettes.

'Phlegm,' said the fair-haired man, his voice, thought Piccolo, sounding like cold treacle trickling over cold suet pudding, 'I found this truant wasting time in the lavatory. It might suit MacCavity.'

'Yes, Mr Candelskin,' said the old man in the dark suit, clearing his throat. His voice sounded to Piccolo as ancient as the world.

Candelskin walked off, leaving the nasty aroma lingering in the air.

He could escape, Piccolo thought, wildly. What chance did two old men have against him? But which way was out? He scanned the corridor, this way and that, for cameras and heat sensors.

'Don't waste your time,' Phlegm said, offering him a cigarette.

'Why not?' Piccolo shouted, knocking the cigarette from Phlegm's hand and seizing him clumsily by the collar.

Now what? he thought. He'd never fought anyone in his life, let alone an old man. Living with the Big Bloke, he'd scarcely dared think about fighting until that day he realised he could kill. He heard music and his grip faltered. It was a song he'd written for Will. But how –?

His whole body went rigid, and a scream stuck in his throat. Only his startled eyes could move sufficiently to see that he was encased in a web of light, which must have come from the pen-like instrument Phlegm was pointing at him.

'You're like the rest of them,' the Shuffler spat at Piccolo, his voice of sand and ash. 'Think I'm too old to see what you're up to. But I ain't.'

Phlegm lifted a web-thread and Piccolo felt his legs working out of his control as he was trailed along the corridor, as a child might drag a toy.

'That was one of the boy's compositions,' said the Shuffler, abruptly, stroking a mini-recorder in his hand.

'A composer?' said Phlegm, stopping in his tracks. 'How interesting.'

16 HOME TRUTHS AND LIES

Imprisoned in a web of light, Will heard the two Red Tartan Guards arguing as they led him off the pier and across the beach. They were still arguing as they went behind the scenes of the WeatherCoaster and from nowhere, a yowling, red-eyed haggoid leapt up at him, its metal fangs bared. He screamed but the sound never left his body.

'Good boy, Ross,' said one of the guards, throwing the mechanoid an empty crisp packet as he unleashed it from the wall.

The haggoid jumped at the plastic bag, devouring it in one go.

'Och, MacNoodle, there'll be all hell to pay, if anyone finds out,' said the second guard, nervously, as he unlocked a door disguised within the brickwork and the four descended a steep underground staircase.

'So who's going to tell them, MacMinor? You?' said MacNoodle.

'Och, man, of course not, but—'

'Do you know, on reflection I don't think it was the Black Tartans who put us on yon boy's trail.'

'You don't?' said MacMinor, aghast. 'What's come over you?'

'I reckon it was an automatic alarm that went off. It

was our luck we picked it up, wasn't it, Ross?'

MacNoodle patted the metal head of the haggoid, which yattered appreciatively.

'So you're not blaming the Black Tartans, for once? I'm amazed.'

'I'll find another occasion, MacMinor, don't you worry, but I was counting up how many of them are off sick because of the stench of fresh paint everywhere. Great wee wimps that they are.'

'Aye, that's true. MacGluten in the kitchen told me—'

'So, all this sickness must mean there's times when security cameras are unmanned. And as there's nay cameras down here anyway, who'll see us? Och, it's only a wee joke, man. For a few days. It's time those snotty Black Tartans got their comeuppance. And think how good we'll look when we come up with the lost goods.' MacNoodle nodded in Will's direction.

MacMinor looked cheered as he nudged Will into an open cell and locked the door on him.

'The web-lock'll wear off in a wee while, sonny,' said MacNoodle, through a grille on the door. 'You won't remember a thing.'

'When we "find" him, so to speak, d'you think we'll get a bonus or a pay rise?' MacMinor asked, eagerly.

'Och, what planet are you from, MacMinor? Aberdeen?'

MacMinor looked offended.

'This is bigger than money, man,' said MacNoodle. 'This

is payback time. This is "Up the Reds!"'

'Gosh!' said Grout, sitting back from the control panel.

'You could say that,' said Bodkin.

'Lucky the Professor put us on voluntary security watch.'

'Yes,' said Bodkin. 'And lucky that I saw the wisdom of installing a few extra webcams in that hell hole. Lucky for the Prof, considering how partial he is to strays for his figgin' animaloid experiments. And lucky for us, 'cos that lad'll earn us quite a bit of extra dosh.'

Will soon discovered that the Red Tartans were wrong: when the web-lock wore off, he remembered everything – from the moment he'd told the girl reporter about the assassination plot to the moment, seconds before, when through the grille, he heard the guards talk about him as though he were a pawn in some squabble with the Black Tartans, to be handed back in a few days.

A few days!

Time enough for Candelskin's plot to go ahead, for the Prime Minister to be assassinated. He clenched his fists and, in desperation, prayed to a god whose existence he doubted – his brother's god, who'd failed him in his hour of need – that the girl reporter would pass on his message to the Face. If she didn't ...

17 SURPRISE, SURPRISE

In the box room of Elsa's house, Ruby Q sat on the bed, thinking. Why couldn't Will deliver his message to the Face, even if only by the internet? Why did he look like a Guide, with his jacket and stud, but act nothing like one? As for the rumour that he'd got in without paying, Ruby Q didn't believe it: he didn't look like a cheat. She wondered what had happened to him after he was marched off. And whether he had told her something else. And if so, what?

She was distracted by the telephone. She rushed to answer it, hoping it might be her dad. Instead, the call was from a guest in the wedding photograph who'd returned from holiday and picked up Ruby Q's message that she was searching for her mother. Would Ruby Q like to come over? Yes, Ruby Q would.

Are you OK, Ruby Q?

Yes.

Only we've been standing on the doorstep for three point thirty-nine minutes. And Mrs Wedding Guest is kindly fitting you in between pupils.

Yes, I know but—

Are you a bit wobbly after that dip in the Blooza

Jooza?

No, but – I'm bit nervous.

Understand. Take a deep breath. Now ring the doorbell. At-a-girl. Grief, we've come to a zoo!

A discordant symphony of barking, squawking and shouting grew louder and more discordant as the front door opened. A harassed-looking, youngish woman stared blankly at her.

'Hello, I'm Ruby Q Cooper,' said Ruby Q.

''Course you are! Come in!' cried Mrs Wedding Guest above the noise, her face relaxing into a smile as she flung open the door.

She led Ruby Q through a hallway filled with shoes, rucksacks, bats and brollies, to the kitchen.

'Sorry, my brain's not working today,' said Mrs Wedding Guest. 'I thought you were a pupil arriving early. Excuse the noise. The triplets have got friends here and the parrots are jealous. The dogs are always loud.'

Mrs Wedding Guest shut the kitchen door. The noise level diminished.

'What does your father think of what you're doing?' she said, as she set about making a tea substitute, using water from a storage tank.

'I don't know,' said Ruby Q. 'He's on a contract in South America. I've only got his mobile number and it's always out of range.'

Mrs Wedding Guest nodded. 'As I said on the phone, Ruby Q, I'm not sure I can help you. Since your mother left, your father has never spoken about her to us. And living on opposite sides of London, with jobs, children and everything, we've rather lost touch.' Mrs Wedding Guest served tea and sat down.

'I haven't seen my mother since I was six, nine years ago,' Ruby Q said, flatly. 'I've never heard from her. I've got only a sketchy picture of her in my head and fuzzy memories. Dad won't talk about her; neither will my grandmother. I've no idea about her family. I've never met them. I feel a bit of me is missing and that doesn't feel right. Does that make sense?'

Mrs Wedding Guest looked sympathetic. 'You must remember, Ruby Q, I didn't really know your mother. Your father was our friend. The first time we met her was at their engagement party. The next time was at the wedding. We met up a couple of times a year after that before—'

'What was she like?' Ruby Q asked.

'Very beautiful,' said Mrs Wedding Guest, with a wistful smile. 'Very fair, clear skin. Eyes so dark you couldn't see the pupils. And the most fabulous hair. Like a bright shiny copper coin. When the sun was on it—'

'But what was she *like*? Inside?'

Mrs Wedding Guest frowned. 'Very serious. Maybe she was shy, but I don't think she approved of us musicians, our black humour or our lifestyle. Certainly, her parents didn't.'

'Did you meet them?'

'No, but when your mother told them she was getting married, apparently her father cut her out of his will and wouldn't have anything more to do with her. He had his own business, a hotel in Switzerland.'

Switzerland?

'Switzerland?' Ruby Q stumbled. 'How come?'

'That's where your mother came from, Ruby Q. The Italian part. Hence her name, Anjelica Nera. Didn't you know?'

No!

'No,' said Ruby Q, struggling to steady her teacup as well as herself. 'Dad always called her his Angel so I thought that was her name.'

'Did you know that she was very clever? That she was a student when she met your father, and then she landed a top job in the City?'

'Yes, but I never knew where.'

'It was a well-known firm. What was it called? An odd name. Well, three odd names. Sounded like an optician's. But I can't quite ... My husband will remember. I'll ask him when he gets home and let you know.'

Ruby Q fell silent, trying to take it all in.

'You don't look like your mother,' Mrs Wedding Guest reflected.

'I know,' said Ruby Q, gloomily.

'You look like her sister, Lily.'

What sister?

'Sorry?'

'You've got the same hair as her,' Mrs Wedding Guest continued, blithely. 'She was tall and slim like you. Different-coloured eyes but attractive, like you. She was a nice woman. And such fun. I liked her a lot.'

'Er, I thought you hadn't met the family?' said Ruby Q, fazed.

'I didn't meet your grandparents but I met Lily. Didn't you know about her, Ruby Q? Oh dear, obviously not.'

'Is Lily the other person in this picture?' said Ruby Q, showing Mrs Wedding Guest the wedding photograph.

'Yes, she defied your grandfather and came to the wedding.' Mrs Wedding Guest chuckled. 'She had a disaster at the hairdresser's and went next door to a charity shop and got that dreadful hat. Only just made the ceremony.'

'What do you know about her?'

'Not much,' said Mrs Wedding Guest. 'She was older than your mother. An artist. She came to the wedding with a family friend, who took the photographs. He was charming. He and Lily were "stepping out", as they used to say. Lily was certainly smitten with him, though ...'

'Yes?'

'Well, my husband told me I was imagining it but I thought this chap had rather a soft spot for your mother,' said Mrs Wedding Guest.

The doorbell rang. It was the next pupil. Mrs Wedding Guest said a hurried goodbye after making Ruby Q promise to keep in touch.

Ruby Q stood outside on the pavement, which felt as unstable as Elsa's temper. She was trying to take it all in. Her mother was Swiss or Italian. Or both. Her mother had worked for a City firm with an optical name. She had grandparents who owned a hotel. And she had an Auntie Lily who was cursed with the same radical, free-thinking hair.

You need a cup of tea, Ruby Q. Or something stronger.

18 PICCOLO PLUCKED

'Piccolo! A pleasure to meet you, formally, as it were. My name is Randall Candelskin,' said the man with the smelly aftershave. 'I hear you're doing excellently well on our rehabilitation programme for young street people.'

Yeah, and so what else goes on in this place? thought Piccolo. And what's with the Mr Nice Guy act when a few minutes ago you were ready to bin me? But he said nothing.

'I hear you're performing to an audience of lavatories and bleach bottles which, to the best of my knowledge, aren't known for their musical appreciation,' Candelskin continued, with a little laugh, which Piccolo thought sounded as genuine as a fairy light. 'You should've spoken to the Professor. You know how he loves his music.'

Candelskin wiped an imaginary speck from his desk.

Piccolo stood on the other side of the bare desktop and shifted his feet. Candelskin made him feel edgy. Like his mum's Big Bloke had done. You never knew which way they'd jump. The only thing you knew for sure was that they held your life in their hands.

'While you made your way here, the janitor played me his recordings of your music. You have great talent, Piccolo.'

Piccolo remained silent.

'So much so that I wondered if you'd like to join us in an important little musical project we're working on.'

'After that, do I get sent to MacCavity?' Piccolo couldn't stop himself. 'Or to the White Room?'

Candelskin looked pained. 'Dear boy, you'll not be sent to MacCavity. Or to the White Room, whatever you mistakenly take that to mean. No. I'm keen for you to meet a fellow musician.'

Piccolo said nothing but his eyes betrayed a flicker of interest.

'Sir Harrison Catgut has a devoted following and a name synonymous with – what would you say, Phlegm?'

Phlegm cleared his throat. 'Car exhausts, sir?'

Candelskin tittered. 'Yes, he's not exactly Wagner, but Sir Harrison Catgut is an acclaimed composer, Piccolo. He's composing a new sound for young people, for the new Sticky Rock Cafés. I expect you've heard of them. Somehow, I feel sure he'd welcome your assistance. What do you say?'

Piccolo chewed the inside of his mouth. Maybe it was a trap, but what option did he have? At least he'd be able to play and compose. In fact, he'd be fulfilling a dream. And he'd be working with a proper musician, albeit a celebrity he'd never heard of. On an important project, Candelskin had said. Perhaps life in this place wasn't so bad after all. Perhaps his escape route was inside, not out of, this place. If only he could share his good news with Will.

'All right,' said Piccolo, trying to sound casual.

'Excellent!' said Candelskin, and he nodded at Phlegm, who ushered Piccolo towards the door.

'Oh, I nearly forgot: a mutual friend sends his regards,' Candelskin called out. 'Said he hoped you hadn't forgotten him. I told him no one could forget the beautiful Bianco.'

Piccolo was on the verge of rushing back into the room and demanding Candelskin tell him more when a thought occurred to him: what had Bianco to do with Dekaydence?

19 SHADOWBOXING

It was another blisteringly hot and bright summer's day but behind the boarded-up windows of the derelict house there was a chill in the dark air. The house was deserted but for the bare upstairs room in which a sturdily built figure, dressed in a fleece and baggy trousers and sitting by a brazier, was sending and reading coded text messages on an adservarum.

A board on the stairs creaked. The figure jumped up and moved swiftly and silently to the door, taking a steel knife from a pocket. If it had been one of the others, they'd have used the signal, but there was nothing, no sound; and in any case they weren't due home for hours.

All at once, the room was filled with the scent of apple blossom as the figure felt its wrist held in a vice-like grip and its mouth clamped shut by a hand held hard over its mouth. The knife fell to the floor.

'Gotcha!' whispered a voice. 'Yous getting careless, Face.'

Abruptly released, the Face spun round and stared furiously at a row of perfect white teeth set in a teasing smile.

'Blast you, Bianco! You always arrive out of the back of nowhere!'

The young man grinned. 'Only way to travel. Ass class. Yous should know that.' He winked.

'One day, you'll get yourself killed.'

'Moment ago, seemed yous the one gonna get youself killed.'

The Face cursed, and walked back to the brazier. 'D'you want some soup?'

Bianco grimaced. 'Not unless it got additives and colourings and everything ba-ad.'

'I've no idea what it is,' said the Face, frowning into a pot of simmering broth. 'Looks like vegetables.'

Bianco rolled his eyes dramatically. 'I don't eat vegetables, unless it looks like they gonna eat me first.'

The Face ignored him, dunked two mugs into the steaming broth, handing one to Bianco, and sat down by the brazier. 'So what brings you here?'

Bianco squatted down, mesmerised by the molten coals. 'I was wondering about your plans.'

'Is that before or after a sex, drugs and rock'n'roll orgy? Or is tonight another black-tie film première?' said the Face, dryly.

Bianco chuckled, and then asked, 'Any plans for movin' on?'

'Save your skin, will it, if I tell?' said the Face.

'Face!' said Bianco, affronted. 'Might save yours, though.'

'How's that?' said the Face.

'Dekaydence is setting you up.'

'So what's new?'

'This time I got a feelin' they is planning to take yous off the map.'

The Face snorted. 'They'll never do it. We're great scapegoats for their abominations.'

'True, but mebbe you should take a back seat for a bit.' Bianco saw fire reflected in the Face's eyes.

'Bianco,' said the Face, in a diamond-hard voice, 'we're facing disasters and deaths on an unimaginable scale. If people don't change their way of life, if politicians and business don't put their tin-pot ambitions on hold and look to the bigger picture, we can kiss goodbye to this planet. If we carry on doing nothing, there'll come a time of no tomorrows. GeeZers must get this message across, through civil unrest or bombarding the web with information. We must fight—'

'But yous don't fight, Face.'

The Face gave him a withering look. 'You don't have to spill blood to save it.'

'Tommo thought different. And wasn't his blood royal?'

'Tommo was an insubordinate fool,' said the Face, icily dismissive.

Bianco said nothing.

'Tell your bosses, Bianco, I'm not about to give up, now or ever.'

Bianco stood up. 'OK, OK. But don't forget, I don't often get to visit pads like this and I'd be well peev-éd if they went missin' from my life.'

Something akin to a smile flickered about the Face's mouth. 'You've got to realise, Bianco, we're in this for real. You're the one playing a dangerous game. And I still don't know why.'

The Face turned to look at Bianco but he was gone.

20 WILL'S TESTAMENT

If the Prime Minister were killed ... Will tried and failed to shut his mind to the consequences not only for his family but also for the GeeZers. And the planet.

He had to get out of this place.

He searched for a door, a window, any way out of the sparsely furnished cell in which they'd dumped him, with its bed and thin blanket, lone light bulb, bucket and tap. He explored every crack and crevice in the floor, walls and ceiling, and climbed a rusty metal ladder attached to the wall, only just saving himself from crashing to the floor when a loose screw fell out, but the ladder led only to an air vent.

He slumped on to the bed, turning to stare at the far wall, and watched a steady trickle of water running the length of the room. Did it lead to the sewers? To the river and freedom? Even if it did, he thought desperately, how could it help him get out of the cell?

'Come on, Will. You're the one with all the grey matter.'

He heard his brother's teasing voice in his head, remembering the great big idiotic grin. And he felt the now familiar pain, a dull ache within a void. Losing someone you loved – it was like the flu, he thought. It knocked you for six, or more, and when you kidded yourself you were getting better – not over it, just a bit better – then, wham! It knocked you down again.

He stood up and began pacing the floor – anything to distract himself. Sooner or later, he supposed, a Red Tartan would bring him food and ...

That was it! It had been some time since the last meal. He stood by the door, listening, waiting. He thought of the childhood fights with his brother. However hard he'd tried, he'd never beaten him but ...

He grew thirsty and went to take a drink from the tap when he heard footsteps echoing in the corridor outside. He hurried back to the door, flexing his fists.

The door opened slowly. He was ready but, before he had time to think, a haggoid flew at him, knocking him to the ground and sinking its metal jaws into his leg. He cried out, as he struggled to wrench it off, while all around shouting voices crashed into one another.

'Get that tin can under control!'

'Cromarty!'

'The Professor will be furkin' furious if the goods are damaged.'

'Heel!'

When the two Red Tartans had the haggoid under control, two young men in white coats stepped forward.

'Get up!' shouted the one with a thin, mean face, kicking him in the stomach.

Will groaned, but he attempted to stand.

'Steady, Mr Bodkin,' said one of the guards.

'And stand up straight!' Bodkin snapped at Will, nodding to his colleague, who bustled forward with a small automatic centi-rod, which took readings of Will's height and weight.

'And what would this be for?' Will gasped.

'Och,' Bodkin mimicked, with a smirk. 'Another jock strapped for a brain! All you need know, kiltboy, is that you're helping to advance science.'

He turned on his heel and left the room, followed by his assistant and the two Red Tartans, with the haggoid.

'You OK, laddie?' muttered MacMinor over his shoulder.

Will nodded.

'Stinking Sassenachs,' hissed MacNoodle, as he locked the door.

Will collapsed on the bed, cradling his stomach and his leg. It seemed that worse was to come. If he'd needed proof, which he didn't, Bodkin's manner only confirmed that whatever fate, or scientific research, had in store for him, it would not be pleasant.

He must find a way out. There was so much he had to do. His brother must not have died in vain.

It was then he heard music.

21 BREAKING NEWS

Why are you looking in the mirror? What's up?

I've got news to tell, so I thought I'd practise being a newsreader. And before you ask, no, I haven't got a job interview.

Ah, sorry. But carry on. I'll do the terrible background drum music that they use on Channel Dekaydence news.

If you must ... Well, go on then.

Ratatatat!

'Hello, my name is Ruby Q Cooper and here is today's news.'

You sound very professional! Sorry ... Ratatatat!

'Swiss detectives track down Ruby Q Cooper's family!'

What? Sorry ... Ratatatat!

'GeeZers say no again to Ruby Q's plea for an interview!'

There's a surprise. Ratatatat!

'Ruby Q's dad's mobile phone remains out of range!'

Oh, no! Ratatatat!

'Here is today's top story: in response to her email inquiry, the Swiss Chamber of Commerce tracked down Ruby Q Cooper's grandparents but regret to inform her that their search ended in a cemetery, as they're both dead. Killed in a plane crash a few years back.'

Oh, no!

'Yes. A stunned Miss Cooper told us: "One moment, there's no one. The next, I discover I have a family. Then I learn they're dead. It's difficult to take it in." Later, she confided: "I wish I could've met them. Known them. But they never wanted to meet me, so who am I kidding?"

'The Chamber confirmed also that Miss Cooper's Auntie Lily was not a passenger on the plane but moved from Lugarno after the family hotel was sold to a multinational conglomerate. No one knows where Miss Nera is. And Miss Cooper asks anyone with information concerning her aunt's whereabouts to contact her at rubyq@rubyq. info.'

Ruby Q, I'm so— Sorry. Ratatatat!

'Also, today ... After Cage Martin informed his brother, Jack, that the Face will not be interviewed, the GeeZers' website complains of constant misrepresentation by the media.

'Said Miss Cooper: "I'm not sure whether to feel annoyed or flattered. After a fortnight's work experience on a local newspaper, am I a media person?

'"But I won't give up. Until they change their minds, I'll keep posting my request on their website. And I'll keep sending them stories I find on the illegals – such as the increased underground volcanic activity in the world; the number of cancers in people living around airports; and the Union fishermen fishing off the African coast, driving local fishermen inland, where they're forced to seek work cutting down forests essential for a healthy global climate.'"

At-a-girl, Ruby Q. Ratatatat!

'Ruby Q Cooper is unable to contact her dad on his mobile; nor has he sent her any of his usual text messages, using the title of a song— Excuse me, the telephone is ringing.'

OK, I'll keep the audience amused. Have you heard the one about the whale who went up to the loan shark, plonking something down on the table, saying: 'Here's the sick squid I owe you!'?

'Breaking news just in: in her relentless pursuit of her mother, our investigative reporter Ruby Q Cooper trawled the web, looking for an accountancy firm with a name like an optician's, and discovered a name fitting the bill. Mrs Wedding Guest's husband later confirmed that the name was indeed Cataract, Cyclops and Mote. But under the Data Protection Act, CCM cannot give out personal information on personnel.

'However, within the past few minutes, Miss Cooper has talked to a student doing work experience in their human resources division, who is sympathetic to her cause and promises to ask around. We'll bring you more stories after the break.'

Ratatatat! Great! Can we expect a story with a happy ending?

I hope so.

22 DUET

'Remember, sonny, that for security reasons you'll find there are certain restrictions,' said Phlegm.

Before Piccolo had a chance to ask what he meant, Phlegm had departed, leaving him with two huge, silent Black Tartans, their eyes screened by red tartan sunglasses.

They took him deep underground until they reached a vast, arched brick area, softly lit and furnished, with eating, sleeping and games areas set around a raised concert platform filled with chairs and music stands. Overhead, Eye-Spies, small multi-lensed globes, moved slowly round the room, scanning everything, including the entrances to a number of different-sized tunnels.

Piccolo saw at once that the twenty-odd men were musicians. Huddled together on seats or leaning against the walls, many clasped their instruments tightly, as a child might clutch a teddy bear. As he passed them, they stared or turned away.

He was taken on to the platform, where a long-haired, haughty-looking man of indeterminate age, dressed in baggy cream trousers and shirt and a blue velvet cloak, stood on a podium.

'I am Sir Harrison Catgut,' said the man, in the timbre of

a French horn, addressing him as if he were an audience of thousands. 'I've been informed you are to be my assistant, and that you have some talent. Play!'

Piccolo stifled a nervous giggle and, taking the piccolo from his pocket, gave life to the little bird.

'Enough! Time to work!' Catgut shouted out after Piccolo had played no more than a dozen bars. 'Please note, Young Person, there will be no idle chitchat. We discuss the project and nothing else.'

Piccolo's spirits soared. He was working with a real musician, composing music for young people, which would be on a CD, for sale in shops and on the internet. OK, so Catgut was a self-centred bullying tyrant obsessed with his health, and the underground set-up with the Eye-Spies was weird, but did any of that matter when you were fulfilling your dream?

He felt inspired. Partly by love, he realised, and friendship. So thoughts of his father and of Will and his commitment to the GeeZers wove their way into his work, alongside thoughts of the mysterious Bianco. By the end of the first day, he'd written nine songs – words and music.

He was ecstatic. He knew Catgut was too, although he tried to hide it. But one musician, a cheery bespectacled bear of a man with a cosy armchair voice, slapped him on the back and congratulated him.

It was later that night, long after the dirty dishes had

been sent back to the kitchens via the delivery hatch and while the musicians were chatting quietly or playing table games, that the Black Tartans returned, accompanied by two of the Professor's white-coated assistants. He recognised them instantly: Bodkin and Grout. They worked in the laboratory. One was a thug, the other his dim assistant. No one said a word, but each musician went to lie down on his bed.

Piccolo watched as Bodkin attached a small pad to a musician's head. The man yelped and passed out. Bodkin moved on to the man in the next bunk. Grout worked from the opposite end.

Piccolo sat, frozen in horror, until he felt a hand on his back.

'No!' he cried, and he lashed out, but the Black Tartan's grip tightened. He was tossed over a shoulder and carried back to his bunk bed.

'What are you doing?' he shouted as the Black Tartan flung him down on the bed and Bodkin's face appeared by his side.

He felt a sharp stab in his head, heard himself scream and saw Bodkin's satisfied smirk, before — he saw his father and Will, and Bianco.

When he woke the next morning, it took Piccolo a moment to recall where he was. He touched his scalp, but the pad had gone. He got up, his head throbbing, and crossed unsteadily to the dining area, where he poured himself a strong coffee.

'Over here,' said the cheery bespectacled man, who was sitting with a group of musicians at a trestle table.

Piccolo hesitated. The others at the table eyed him suspiciously.

'Come on, we don't bite. Well, not often,' the cheery man chuckled.

Piccolo sat down.

'Name's Rallan,' said the cheery man, holding out his hand.

'Mine's Piccolo, after the ...' said Piccolo, tapping his pocket.

Rallan nodded and smiled. 'Don't let this place get to you,' he said. 'Sooner we're done, quicker we're out of here.'

A couple of the other musicians snorted.

'You're all the same, you drummers,' said a man with a high-pitched voice. 'Dreamers and madmen. When will you get it into your head that we're never going to get out of this place?'

The others muttered in agreement.

'What do you mean?' Piccolo demanded.

'Don't listen to him,' said Rallan, soothingly. 'What does he know? He plays the viola.'

'I don't and I agree with him,' said another, in a clipped voice, his fingers tapping nervously on a violin case.

Everyone fell silent.

'Listen to me, boy,' the violinist continued, watching

the Eye-Spies. 'We're here, wherever we are, to play for a weird scientist. And Catgut is supposed to be composing stuff for him for some new secret venture. But our agent never said anything about any head-pad stuff. So when we realised Grout sometimes fails in his task, we said the next time the head-pad fell off, that person would make a break for it and raise the alarm—'

'It was our drummer,' said the viola player. 'He went through one of the tunnels. Nothing was said for two days. We thought he'd escaped and would be raising the alarm. Then a Black Tartan showed us his body.'

'His body?' Piccolo repeated, and shuddered.

'For all the world, he looked as though he were asleep but – It's hard to describe,' said the violinist, shrugging.

'No, it's not,' said a trumpeter. 'It's simple. He'd been miniaturised.'

'What?' said Piccolo, feeling ice crawl through his blood.

'He was less than a foot in length,' said the trumpet player. 'He looked like a doll. A dead doll.'

Piccolo saw that the room was spinning. And somewhere inside it was Will. He put his head in his hands, trying to stop his mind disintegrating, as his dream splintered into a thousand nightmares.

That second day, Catgut drove him on relentlessly. Piccolo didn't care. It gave him less time to think. All he knew was that he wanted out. He'd had enough. He felt ashamed of his own stupidity. And scared that when his work was done, he'd end up with MacCavity, as Candelskin had threatened, or in the White Room, or, like the drummer ...

There were tunnels in almost every wall and not all, he reasoned, could be guarded. Not all would lead to death or— He spotted a grille in the wall behind his bedside cabinet. Maybe ...

By the end of the day, they'd completed four more songs. Catgut informed him they must do two more and Piccolo reckoned he'd be safe for a third day. But beyond that ...

The second night was the same as the first: the fear and dread, the struggle, and then the glorious escape into a fantasy dream.

He woke late on the third morning, groggy as before, but knowing it had to be that morning, while breakfast was being unloaded, while men congregated in the dining area. In fact, it had to be now. He bent down to tie his shoelaces, waiting until the Eye-Spies flew by, and then edged the cabinet away from the wall.

Something sharp prodded him in the back. He turned. Catgut was standing there, baton in hand. Piccolo saw another Eye-Spy approach and the moment for escape vanish.

'We have a vital duty to perform,' Catgut announced.

'What is it?' snapped Piccolo. There would be another moment in the day, he told himself. There must be.

'My music requires a name – like pop, garage or rock'n'roll.'

Piccolo slumped to his knees. A name for the music? He looked round wearily. The musicians were herded together in the dining area, like animals in a—

'Pen?'

Catgut grimaced.

'Prison?'

Catgut sneered.

'Abattoir?'

Catgut grimaced and sneered.

Piccolo thought some more.

'OK, what about – what about – shed?'

'Shed?' Catgut frowned and scratched his forehead with his baton. 'Shed? Shed Music! Yes, that's it! It's so completely lacking in meaning! It's perfect!' He hurried off, making a call on his adservarum.

Piccolo saw a break between the Eye-Spies. This was it, another chance. He tore away the grille cover and clambered into the tunnel.

He was flat on his stomach, unable to turn round, stand or sit up. He held his breath and listened. Nothing. No sound, in front or behind. He'd escaped! He blinked, trying to adjust his eyes to the half-light.

He heard a whirring noise in front of him. Something soft and wet touched his face. He brushed it away. It felt like a cold, throbbing jelly, yet it had stung his hand.

Then he saw it. A long thin white luminous limb. There

was another and another, coiling through the air towards him, like a lasso. As the tentacles reached for his face, he recoiled, stifling a scream. It was some kind of mechanical octopus.

Something clamped hold of his ankles in a vice-like grip and yanked him backwards with such force he thought his bones were being crushed.

His scream was smothered in a mouthful of brick dust, as he fell out of the tunnel on to the floor by his bed.

'For God's sake, Young Person!' yelled Catgut, letting go of Piccolo to brush dust from his hands and clothes. 'This is no time to be fooling around in tunnels!'

Piccolo sat quite still, unable to speak.

Catgut stared at him, his anger turned to a horror mingled with fear.

'We've got an emergency on our hands, Young Person. We have to write another twelve songs by Thursday week! They want a second CD.'

Piccolo looked up at Catgut: he didn't know whether to laugh or cry.

23 MORE BREAKING NEWS

'Welcome back for news just in!'

Ratatatat!

'A group calling themselves the Real GeeZers are tonight claiming responsibility for the deaths of nine people working in a chemical factory in Cumbria. Many more have been seriously injured. In a statement issued within the last half-hour, the Real GeeZers say the time for peaceful protests is over and warn that anyone, whatever their age or gender, who is wilfully harming the environment will meet the same fate.

'A spokesman for the GeeZers denies any association with the Real GeeZers, saying they strongly condemn violence. Meanwhile, a government spokesman is urging for calm and vigilance and has said that all terrorists will be hunted down and dealt with in the appropriate manner.'

This could turn nasty.

Yes, 'cos however much the GeeZers protest they're not connected with the Real GeeZers, if people get injured, no one will stop to think and they'll want the whole lot of them punished. Any kind of split plays right into the Prime Minister's hands.

And any in-fighting takes time and energy away from

the real fight – for the planet.

Exactly. Especially when—

Sorry ... Ratatatat!

'Hundreds of thousands of people are missing in Canada and Russia as earthquakes hit major cities in both nations. And after the spring typhoons and tsunamis that devastated Japan and Australia come TB, encephalitis and killer viruses. The death toll rises.'

Oh, no! But what can the likes of you and me do, apart from send money and aid?

Lots. Even now. Switch off, 'cos it takes two power stations to cope with things like TVs and computers left on standby. Do something simple: don't use plastic bags because they take five hundred years to degrade in a landfill and we're currently using 150 million in the UK every week ... We must persuade the greatest pollutants, the politicians, that they have to clean up their act, fast, and globally.

I almost can't cope, but I'll get on the case. Thank goodness for music, and this stuff on the radio is distractingly good. What is it?

It's fantastic, isn't it? It's called Shed Music. It's a kind of green rock. The group's the Dipstick Five, and they're appearing live for the first time next week at the launch of the Sticky Rock Café.

24 OVERSIGHT

A storm was brewing and lightning flashed across the mirrored walls in the ballroom of the crystal Icosahedron, which rotated on an invisible axis round the Globe and cast a shimmering light on the country park. The mirrors reflected the smiling faces of the young musicians and several dozen young couples on the ballroom floor, the girls in gowns of rainbow shades through red, orange, yellow, green, blue, indigo to violet matching the bowties of their beaux attired in ivory or black dress suits. All wore a rainbow stud in one ear.

Amidst but apart, two men in expensive suits sat at a table.

Randall Candelskin refilled the Prime Minister's champagne glass and looked up at the Professor in the gallery above them.

'Ah!' gasped the Prime Minister, as, all at once, every musician and every one of the dancers was silenced and stilled, completely and utterly.

The Prime Minister looked questioningly at Candelskin, who smiled enigmatically and glanced up at the gallery. A moment on, music filled the air once more and the dancers again laughed and chattered.

The Prime Minister's look of admiration turned to one

of awe.

'A remarkable ... refinement, Randall. But is it – do you know ...? How shall I put it ...?'

'We are assured it is perfectly safe,' said Candelskin, adjusting his shirtsleeve, aware that his left eyelid was twitching involuntarily.

The Prime Minister downed his drink in one. Candelskin reached into the ice bucket. Clasping the bottle's neck with one hand, he slowly twisted the cork with the other until it popped out gently and softly, releasing a thin spiral of champagne mist. He refilled the PM's glass.

Mopping his brow with a tissue, the Prime Minister leant forward and whispered something to Candelskin.

'There's no reason to fret,' Candelskin replied, as he refilled the Prime Minister's glass. 'The Independent Scientific Body I set up works entirely to your instructions, which means Grey Zoners, Real or otherwise, condemn themselves by their own actions. And it appears our source is gaining the confidence of the Face.'

The Prime Minister nodded.

Candelskin leant back in his seat, relishing the highly toned muscles in his lithe body as much as the ridiculously expensive Maccaroni suit he'd recently acquired, courtesy of a Dekaydence bonus.

'In any event, PM, you'll cut a dash in military uniform.'

'Randall!' A look of sublime contentment settled like a pigeon on the Prime Minister's face.

'I'm going to enjoy working with you again,' said the PM. 'It's good that business with the loan was – well, you know, sorted. I'm only sorry there was nothing I could—'

'But you introduced me to Signor di'Abalo.'

The Prime Minister waved his hand in a dismissive gesture.

'Least I could do, Randall. And it appears you've landed on your feet. Obviously earning a few bob more than you were as an MP. Vintage champagne, Maccaroni suit, a life of Dekaydence – Perhaps we should swap places!' The Prime Minister chortled.

Candelskin's smile didn't quite reach his eyes.

'And now we're both going to take on the Union,' said the Prime Minister, his eyes glinting. 'It'll be fun, Randall, having you close by. Quite like old times.' He stared thoughtfully at the youngsters gliding by. 'Life is about control, isn't it, Randall? Music, dance, science and politics – one must have control.'

Candelskin glanced up at the gallery and realised that his other eyelid was twitching.

25 TRIPPING THE SHED FANTASTIC

Jack hoped the phone call was from his brother, Cage, so that he could tell him how idiotic the GeeZers were for not letting Ruby Q interview the Face, especially since the bloody arrival of the Real GeeZers. But the call wasn't from Cage. It was from his father. Mr Martin was phoning from his office at the gardening magazine *Shed Monthly*, asking if Jack knew anything about Shed Music.

'Dad, you've been listening to it for the past week.'

'Have I?' said Mr Martin.

'Yes, Dad. It's on the radio all the time.'

'So, Shed Music is quite popular with you youngsters?'

'I'd say "quite popular" is a bit of an understatement.' Jack had to laugh. 'Shed Music is *the* latest thing. You must've read about it, Dad.'

Mr Martin hadn't but he thought Mrs Martin probably had.

'Jack,' said Mr Martin, 'will you write an article about Shed Music?'

'What?' said Jack.

'I want you to write an article telling me all about Shed Music.'

'What?' repeated Jack.

'Jack, it's taken all my powers of persuasion to get the

Editor to agree to run a stop-press article on Shed Music in this month's issue but the copy deadline is tomorrow morning and I'm desperate. I don't know who else to ask.'

'I can't do it, Dad, but—' said Jack.

'Jack, I'll be honest with you. My job is on the line,' Mr Martin pleaded. 'This old gardening magazine will close down unless it takes a giant leap into the twenty-first century. I think we can save it with an article on Shed Music. We're being inundated with phone calls from Shed Music fans, big advertisers and agencies. They all think we're the official underground fanzine magazine. But when they find out we're nothing to do with—'

'Dad!' said Jack. 'I can't write your article but Ruby Q Cooper could. She wants to be a journalist and if you give her the job, she will be.'

'Does she know anything about Shed Music?' Mr Martin asked, nervously.

'Does she! She's the one who told Taylor and me all about it. So, how many words, Dad? When's the deadline? And what are you paying?'

'Three thousand words. The article must be in my hands by eight am tomorrow. I'll come back to you about payment. Jack, are you sure she can do it?'

'Dad,' said Jack. 'Trust me, OK?'

26 WRITING WRONGS

Ruby Q was in the kitchen, about to make a mug of tea while listening to the new Shed Music CD on her inaudirum, when Jack, followed closely by Taylor, burst in.

'Guess what, Ruby Q,' cried Jack. 'You've got a job as a journalist. The Editor of Dad's gardening magazine has commissioned you to write three thousand words on Shed Music, by first thing tomorrow.'

Has the boy gone mad?

'Sorry?' said Ruby Q.

Taylor repeated what Jack had said.

Grief, they've both gone mad. Simultaneously.

'I can't possibly do it,' Ruby Q spluttered.

'Why not?' Taylor demanded.

'It's obvious, isn't it?'

'No,' said Jack. 'You said you wanted to be a journalist and along comes this great opportunity and you turn your nose up at it.'

'It's not that,' said Ruby Q. 'I want to be a campaigning journalist, telling people what's going on in this corrupt, eco-unfriendly world before it's too late. I don't want to write about music.'

'Have you had a better offer?' Jack sneered.

'No. I'd have told you if I had,' Ruby Q snapped.

'What about a pot of Elsa's proper tea?' said Taylor, taking charge of the tea making. 'And we can sit down and discuss this calmly.'

Grudgingly, Jack sat down at the table.

'Are you scared, Ruby Q?' said Taylor, warming a teapot. 'I know I won't be on my first film, but you're different.'

Ruby Q sat at the table, as far away from Jack as was possible.

'The deadline's scary but no, I'm not scared as such,' she said.

'If it's about money—' Jack growled.

'It's not about money,' said Ruby Q. 'It's— I can't write about something I don't know about.'

Some people can.

'Doesn't stop most journalists today,' Jack muttered.

'That's a cheap remark, Jack,' said Ruby Q. 'There are journalists like that but I'm not going to be one of them. I'm not going to write fiction, like Elsa. I want to write the truth and to do that I need facts.'

'Here's a truth, Ruby Q,' said Jack. 'You know how long it's taken my dad to get a job. Now he's worried sick it mightn't last. And he's got it into his head that an article on Shed Music will keep the magazine and his job afloat. I'd write it myself but I can't write – not like you can, Ruby Q.'

He glared at Ruby Q, who glared back.

'So, until you're made the patron saint of journalists,' said Jack, 'how about writing this article to help us out?'

Ruby Q looked Jack in the eye. 'The answer's no, Jack. I'm truly sorry, but I can't do it.' She saw anger in Jack's face and something close to disgust.

'Ruby Q,' said Taylor, putting three teaspoons of tea into the pot and pouring in freshly boiled water. 'You say you need facts before you write about something. I was thinking, you know lots about Shed Music because you told me and Jack all about it.'

Ruby Q said nothing. She was wondering why she didn't feel better about sticking to her principles.

'So why can't you write down the things you told us?' Taylor persisted, setting Elsa's best bone china tea service on the table. 'About major and minor key changes, the rhythm and blues influence, the guitar riffs, the lead singer's voice, the words – Why can't you write that, Ruby Q?'

Ruby Q frowned. Did she know more than she thought?

'If you like, we could help you, Ruby Q,' said Taylor. 'Couldn't we, Jack? – Jack!'

Jack shrugged.

'OK, it's a crummy old gardening magazine but it is an incredible opportunity,' said Taylor, sipping her tea.

She's got a point. After all, how many job offers have you had?

'And if you can't actually save the world at this moment,' Taylor continued, 'the next best thing is to help people enjoy themselves.'

Remember Mrs Treasure talking about the last war? How

people had fun despite the bombs and the never-ending uncertainty of daily life?

'Besides,' said Taylor, pouring the tea, 'how do you know you can't do something until you try, Ruby Q Cooper?'

You've got to hand it to this girl: she is good. And she's right. Fear can hold you back, Ruby Q. And what a waste that would be. Fear shouldn't smother your life. Do you want to die, having never lived?

Ruby Q stared at Taylor. She so wanted to be a campaigning journalist. Not a music reviewer, even if the stuff was good. But maybe this was what life was about: you didn't always get to your destination by the route you planned or dreamt about.

She took a deep breath. And another.

'OK,' she said. 'I'll give it a try.'

'Ex!' said Taylor, clinking her cup with Ruby Q's. 'Ex! Ex! Ex!'

Jack, catching a look from Taylor, managed a brief smile.

'I wonder,' said Ruby Q. 'Wouldn't it be great to interview Dekaydence's top man, Lorenzo di'Abalo, and find out why he funded Shed Music, and what makes him so different from all the other adults who don't care a flying fig for this planet?'

Her mobile phone bleeped. She took it from her pocket.

'You OK, Ruby Q?' said Taylor. 'Only your face has gone pink.'

'It's a message from my dad!' said Ruby Q.

'Ex!' said Taylor.

'Great, how's he doing?' said Jack.

Ruby Q could've cheered: she'd got a message from her dad and Jack was talking to her again.

'He must be doing fine,' she said. 'He's texted me the title of one his favourite songs.'

'What is it?' said Taylor.

Ruby Q grinned.

'It's an old Beatles' number. It's called "Help!"'

27 RUMBLES UNDERGROUND

After supper, at the end of the first day's work on the second Shed Music CD, the musicians dispersed to chat, play table tennis or snooker, or watch the Dekaydence satellite channels. Catgut was working on his Symphony for Suburban Traffic, which involved recordings of diesel engines, white van doors slamming, car horns and raised voices.

Piccolo wandered round the compound, practising the piccolo while scanning the tunnels and grilles. He reckoned the second CD bought him time of a little over a week. He tried not to think of what lay beyond.

That night, Grout fitted the pad to his head. Or rather didn't, so Piccolo found himself wide awake in the early hours. In the quiet darkness, he was reviewing possible escape routes in the walls when he heard a scraping sound coming from underneath the bed. Then something hit him hard in the small of the back.

Winded but alert to a sudden gap in the Eye-Spies, he leapt out of bed, stuffed the pillow under the sheets and slipped under the bedstead in time to see a thin metal rod disappearing into a grille in the floor. He made a grab for it.

'Who's there?' he whispered.

He felt an increased tension on the rod and tightened his grip. He put his mouth closer to the grille.

'Who's there and what do you want?'

'Piccolo?'

Piccolo couldn't, didn't dare, believe his ears.

'Will?'

'Aye,' said Will. 'I might've guessed it was you making that racket.'

'What happened to you, Will man? And where are you?'

'It's a long story but I'm in a cell, below you. I think I'm lined up for some kind of experiment. Anyway, listen—'

'Holy shit!' Piccolo thought of the miniaturised musician. 'Will—'

'Listen to me, Piccolo. You've got to help me.'

''Course, man, that's what I'm telling you, this experiment, it's—'

'Piccolo, can you get out?'

'Will man, I'm trying but it ain't easy. We're in some kind of cellar. Me and this orchestra and—'

'Orchestra?'

'Yeah, I'm composing stuff for some new youf café but—'

'The Sticky Rocks!'

'Yeah, I thought my dream had come true but—'

'Piccolo, Sticky Rocks are a scam! They're planning to brainwash any teenager who walks into one!'

Piccolo fell silent. His splintered dream was turning

now to dust.

'Listen, Piccolo, I've got to get a message to the GeeZers. It's vital but in case I can't, you must do it. Do you understand?'

'I ain't goin' nowhere without you,' said Piccolo, stubbornly.

'This isn't a time for friendship, or loyalty, or sentiment,' said Will, brusquely. 'We must operate independently. If you get to a phone, this is the contact number, and use my code, which is xyx. That way, they'll know you're genuine.'

Piccolo took the scrap of paper Will shoved through the grille. 'Will, man, I been lookin' for you and I ain't about—'

'Piccolo, this is not about one life, yours or mine. This is about billions of lives. This is about the survival of the planet.'

There was a pause.

'Some choice you give me,' said Piccolo.

Will said nothing.

'OK,' said Piccolo, quietly. 'What's the message?'

'You must tell the Face there's a plot to assassinate the Prime Minister. That it's different from all the others, 'cos this one's likely to work. They must get to the PM, see him in person, to warn him.'

'Why?' said Piccolo.

'What?'

'After what you told me, he deserves everything coming

to him.'

'Piccolo, listen to me. This isn't a story. We don't flick a switch and, with that one action, save the world,' said Will, vehemently. 'This is real life, Piccolo, and it's not that easy. Killing the bad guys doesn't solve anything. In fact, it can make things a damn sight worse for the good guys. Do you understand?'

'No,' said Piccolo. 'But if for some reason yous rootin' for the bastard PM—'

'It's not like that,' said Will, urgently. 'Look, just tell them that they have to warn the PM that the plot is coming from his side, his people. I don't know why or how it's going to happen but I overheard them talking – the Dekaydence boss, Lorenzo di'Abalo, and that creep Randall Candelskin.'

'Oh my word, the graveyard shift has come to life,' said Bodkin, as he watched the monitor linked to the camera hidden under Piccolo's bed.

'I thought the Signor and Mr Candlestick were friends of the Prime Minister,' said Grout, frowning.

'They are,' said Bodkin, musing. 'So I wonder what they're up to? No matter, Grout, we'll make something out of it, whichever way the poisoned cookie crumbles.'

28. HOLD THE FRONT PAGE!

What you thinking about, Ruby Q? As if I didn't know. Come on, it wasn't your fault your mum left home.

You don't know.

You were six. What did you do that was so awful she had to go? Rob a bank? Kill the cat? Refuse to drink tea?

Don't be silly.

Hey, I'm not the one beating myself up over Will's message, when it all happened so fast. As for you getting hold of your dad, I couldn't track down someone in the world's fourth biggest continent without them giving me a contact phone number or address.

You're right.

I am mostly. So, let's get to work on this article.

OK, OK. Here goes. I'll think of my first reactions to Shed Music – the fierce power, the joy, the anger, the tenderness in the music and the lyrics ... The lead singer is a bit nasal – and the use of traffic noise is an acquired taste ... But the other Dipsticks – the range of instruments ... It's odd: there's no note on the CD sleeve about a composer, but I reckon they're young, genuinely influenced by the GeeZers, and loners.

Like you, Ruby Q.

No.

★ ★ ★

Look at the time!

Three thousand words. I've finished. I'm ready for bed ...

Crikey! It's the alarm already. It feels like I've hardly slept.

I must re-read the article, make a few minor alterations, before I print off a final copy – OK, I'll let myself out of the house without Elsa hearing and pop next door to drop the envelope through the letterbox—

Agh! There's man in a dressing gown, pacing up and down the Martins' garden, with a steaming mug in his hand.

'Good morning, Mr Martin. Hope this is OK,' said Ruby Q, trying to sound casual, as she handed him the envelope.

'I'm sure it is, Ruby Q,' said Mr Martin, sounding anything but sure.

'My mobile number is in there, if there's a query,' said Ruby Q.

'Fine,' said Mr Martin, distractedly.

'I hope it helps. I mean, I hope it's all right.'

'You know, Jack's got such faith in you,' said Mr Martin, handing Ruby Q his mug and heading back to the house.

Unusually, there was a bird in the tree. It was singing and Ruby Q's heart sang with it. She put the mug on the Martins' doorstep and went back to her room, blushing inside and out.

She was still in a dream at breakfast when she took a phone call from the assistant to the Editor of *Shed Monthly*. Young Miss Burgess, who sounded not that young, was accepting her 'most agreeable' article, with an apology for the small payment, standard for all contributors. The magazine would be on sale the next day, with a 'Stop Press!' on the front cover announcing her article.

Taylor arrived, demanding Ruby Q's autograph. Mr Martin had rung home, asking her to pass on his thanks.

'And this is for you from Jack,' said Taylor, handing her a small parcel. 'He did them before he went off on another of his courses.'

Inside the parcel, Ruby Q found scores of business cards, printed with her name, phone number and the word 'journalist'.

Ruby felt she'd flown past the bird in the tree: she was closer to heaven.

Taylor went off to visit her formerly measly friend and Ruby Q tried to settle back into a web-search for her Auntie Lily, all the while hoping for a phone call from the girl at Cataract, Cyclops and Mote.

'Course, Auntie Lily may have got married and changed her name, or maybe she isn't listed, or has moved to another country.

Thank you, I can do without your cheery input.

But the phone didn't ring and the searches produced nothing. Ruby Q went to bed and slept fitfully, waking only to realise she'd missed breakfast. She returned to the computer and her hopes for a phone call.

Later that morning, after she'd found a tray of cheese sandwiches and a coffee outside her door, deposited she knew by the Treasures, the phone rang. It was Young Miss Burgess. She sounded flustered.

'Miss Cooper. The switchboard, which is me, is being flooded with calls from teenagers praising your article and demanding more.'

'Gosh,' said Ruby Q, who'd quite forgotten that the magazine was now on sale.

'And having listened to the music, Miss Cooper, I think you've captured its voice perfectly. Congratulations.'

'Gosh,' said Ruby Q.

You've done it! Your first piece of professional journalism! The Pulitzer Prize here we come! And you're going to get paid!

Wow! As in wow! This'll help me get a proper job on a proper newspaper. If only I could tell someone, but who?

Get back to work and give yourself permission to be proud of yourself.

Ruby Q posted another interview request on the GeeZers' website, and tried to concentrate on the web-search for her aunt.

In the afternoon, after she'd found a Treasure tray of tea and fruitcake, the phone rang again. It was the girl from Cataract, Cyclops and Mote. She had no news and she must have sensed Ruby Q's disappointment.

'There is a list,' she said. 'Give me your address. But be quick: all calls are monitored.'

Ruby Q was giving her address when the line went dead. She realised she hadn't asked what was on this list when the phone rang again. It wasn't the girl ringing back, as she expected: it was Edwina Gardening-Fork (pronounced Spade), Editor of *Shed Monthly*.

'Miss Cooper!' said the Editor. 'Your fan club is expanding. Had hundreds of chaps and chapesses on the phone or in here at reception.'

'Gosh,' said Ruby Q.

'We're delighted. Sales are going through the roof, thanks to you.'

'Gosh,' said Ruby Q, hoping Mr Martin's income would soar, too.

'Got another bit of good news,' the Editor continued. 'It'll give you copy for next month's article ...'

Next month?

'... As our Shed Music correspondent.'

What?

'You and I have been invited to next week's Royal Gala opening of the Sticky Rock Café.'

'Gosh,' said Ruby Q.

Hang on – who said anything about more articles? And suddenly, you're a 'correspondent'? Ruby Q, she's desperate. Demand a pay rise.

'And, Miss Cooper,' said the Editor. 'I've saved the best 'til last. You're invited to be the first journalist to meet the Dipstick Five before their first public appearance at the launch.'

'Gosh,' Ruby Q repeated.

Come on, Ruby Q, you can do better than that.

'Er, who has invited me?'

'The man behind the entire venture, Signor Lorenzo di'Abalo.'

The top man! Ask for top pay, Ruby Q.

'G-goodness!'

'Signor di'Abalo's right-hand man, Mr Randall Candelskin, rang me a moment ago,' said the Editor. 'Word is out about your article, our magazine and our huge, new teenage audience. So, can you be at Dekaydence HQ at eleven am tomorrow morning?'

Demand treble payment!

'Yes,' said Ruby Q, quickly. 'No problem.'

Ruby Q!

'Jolly good,' said the Editor. 'Mr Candelskin gave me his telephone number for you to call him direct to confirm details. Got a pencil?'

Ruby Q wrote down the details, in a daze. She had an invitation to the Royal Gala launch of the Sticky Rock Café! An exclusive with the Dipsticks! Maybe she'd get to interview Signor di'Abalo himself.

Great! You bottled out of asking for more money and all you're worried about is what you're going to wear!

It's allowed. I'm a girl.

29 MACCAVITY'S PARLOUR

Working on the second CD was a hard slog. Piccolo knew he had to get on with it to stay alive but now, as well as cursing himself for his naivety about Dekaydence and the Sticky Rocks, he worried about Will. He must free Will before anything happened to him. But how, when he couldn't free himself?

By the third morning, he'd finished only two songs and, however much Catgut wheedled or shouted, Piccolo remained distracted or sullen.

'That's it!' cried Catgut, flinging down his baton. 'Coffee break.'

Piccolo was wandering round, listlessly, when two Black Tartans appeared. Instinct told him they were on to him, and to Will, and that he should fling himself into the nearest tunnel, but before he could do anything, his body was gripped in a web-lock of light. Sheathing their pens, the Black Tartans began dragging him from the room.

The musicians watched, in horror.

Rallan ran forward but Catgut pushed him aside.

'What on earth are you doing?' demanded Catgut, furiously.

The Black Tartans ignored him.

'What are you doing? You can't take him away. We

have important work—' Catgut threw himself in front of the Tartans, who tossed him aside as if he were a sweet wrapper. He lay motionless on the floor.

'I can't work without him, I simply can't,' Catgut wailed as the Black Tartans led Piccolo from the room. 'What's to become of me?'

The Black Tartans led Piccolo up flights of twisting stairs until he saw sunlight trickling through a window. He blinked. It was so bright. He squinted and saw a courtyard, a huge fountain cascading fire, a distant barrier ... before he was taken into a room on the first floor and released from the web-lock.

There was a window overlooking a river, but the room was dark and smelt of pine and fresh heather. A giant of a man, dressed in a red and black tartan cloak, with a head of closely cropped ginger hair, sat motionless at a desk, watching him with cool blue eyes. Piccolo knew from what he'd heard that this was MacCavity, Head of Dekaydence's Security, the man in charge of the Tartan Guards, Red and Black.

'So you're the laddie workin' wi' the pansy man?' said MacCavity, in a deep voice sounding like distant thunder.

Piccolo nodded cautiously.

'You play well,' growled MacCavity, 'for a Sassenach.'

Piccolo swallowed hard.

'You play, or play about with, some Scottish airs that mean a lot to me.' The thunder was drawing closer.

Piccolo shuddered.

'I don't like anything fancy, laddie. Remember that. You play them straight when you play for me – and for her.'

MacCavity nodded to a far corner of the room. Piccolo peered into the gloom and saw several curtains of the most delicate material he'd ever seen. He stared harder and his knees almost buckled. They weren't curtains. They were cobwebs. And at the centre of one was a jet-black spider, its body the size of a cat.

30 ONE OF OUR DIPSTICKS IS MISSING

Standing in a side street close to London Bridge, Ruby Q looked at the shabby Victorian warehouses that backed on to the river. She re-read the name on the archway above the entrance booth: the Company of Dekaydence.

The mighty Dekaydence HQ! Bit different from the Globe, isn't it?

'Can I help you, miss?' said a Red Tartan in the entrance booth.

'My name is Ruby Q Cooper and I have an appointment with—'

'Och, Miss Cooper,' said the guard. 'Mr Candelskin apologises. He had an urgent call to go on ahead but the car is waiting for you.'

A limousine purred into view and the driver, a guard in black tartan and red tartan sunglasses, emerged to open the door.

Ruby Q climbed in.

Taylor was born for this treatment. Yuck! What's that smell?

I don't know. And I can't work out how to open the window. Hell's teeth, what have I pressed?

'Miss Cooper,' said a recorded voice. 'Randall Candelskin here. I am so sorry to have missed you but we'll meet up very soon. In the meantime, do help yourself to some light refreshment. Should you have any questions, contact the driver via the gold intercom button at your side.'

Cabinets sprung open, revealing music CDs (mostly Wagner), the day's newspapers, and a stockpile of Dekaydence sweets and drinks.

Chocolates. Quick, fill your pockets, Ruby Q.

Stop it. I'll have a fresh orange juice.

She settled back to read *The Daily Unigraph*, glancing up occasionally to watch the driver negotiate the City streets and head south for the suburbs. After thirty minutes, the car turned into a side road, passed through a checkpoint in a perimeter fence and climbed a wooded hill where, at the summit, stood a magnificent Victorian church.

The Black Tartan led her to a descending flight of stone stairs and they followed a gardener, who'd carried out from his van one of many gloriously leafy or flowering potted plants.

As her eyes adjusted to the darkness in the church's crypt, Ruby Q sensed a tension in the air before she saw a dozen or so people anxiously adjusting cameras and lights focused on a burnt-out car, a handful of shrubs and a burnt-out garden shed covered in cobwebs.

A small, chubby, angry-looking woman in a bubble-wrap T-shirt, black pantaloons and combat boots rushed by, stuffing cream crackers into her mouth with a heavily bandaged hand. Ruby Q recognised her. It was Petty

Masters, the famous fashion designer dubbed PMT by the tabloids for her terrible mood swings.

Fridgefreezers! I see why no one but the rich, trendy or deranged buy her designs, let alone wear them. I bet that bandage is one of her new trendsetting gimmicks. Now, look over there: that's what I call style.

Ruby Q saw a youngish man, in a cool dude suit, appear at the bottom of the steps. He was deep in conversation with the gardener, who was holding a beautiful flowering shrub. She knew immediately from the smell in the limousine that the young man must be Randall Candelskin.

'I want them massacred, Killivy,' she heard Candelskin say.

She stopped dead in her tracks.

The gardener gently fingered the shrub's petals and said nothing.

'No leaves, no buds, no flowers, no sign of growth whatsoever. Try to understand: this is an artistic necessity,' said Candelskin.

The gardener shook his head and sighed.

Ruby Q was about to introduce herself when Petty Masters jabbed a finger in Candelskin's back. He spun round, a look of fury on his face, but, seeing Petty, and Ruby Q, he smiled.

'Ah, Miss Cooper, the new star writer with Shed-loads of readers. Welcome! And dear Miss Masters. Everything tickety-boo?'

'No, it sluggin' isn't,' snapped Petty, before Ruby Q could respond.

'Oh dear,' said Candelskin, giving Ruby Q a conspiratorial wink. 'Anything I can do to help?'

'Yeah, turn into a Dipstick,' said Petty, sarcastically, stuffing cream crackers into her mouth.

'Ah, if only I could,' Candelskin tittered.

'Well, you're going to have to do something drastic and fast, Randy-Candy baby.' Petty spat out the words through a mouthful of crumbs. 'A sluggin' Dipstick has vanished. So I've lost a model and you've lost one of your sluggin' band.'

Ruby Q saw Candelskin's smile freeze on his face.

'Good, innit?' snarled Petty. 'Any moment now, I've got a fashion shoot with one of the world's top fashion photographers. Any moment tomorrow, you've got the launch of the Sticky Rock Café with wall-to-wall VIPs, celebrities, the furkin' PM and sluggin' royalty.'

Ruby Q sensed Candelskin's mind go into overdrive.

'And I tell you this, Randy-Pandypants,' Petty continued. 'It'll get nuclear expensive if Lars Sparks has to hang around 'cos all the little Dipsticks aren't lined up and ready to rock'n'roll'n'Shed their stuff.'

She stormed off, stuffing more cream crackers into her mouth.

'Sluggin' things!' she shouted, spitting out the remnants of a half-digested cracker on to the floor. 'Why do I keep eating them? I hate them.'

Candelskin adjusted his cuffs and shot Ruby Q a quick smile.

'As you heard, Miss Cooper, we have a technical hitch, so I must once more crave your indulgence. Wait here, and I'll be back in a trice.'

'Mr Candelskin, can I—?' said Ruby Q, but Candelskin was already up the steps and out of the door, and the Black Tartan had moved to the bottom of the steps and was blocking the exit.

She watched the gardener hack away at the plant until it was bare of foliage and flowers. The man looked desolate.

And so, thought Ruby Q, did the entire situation. It seemed that the Dipstick Five had ended before they'd begun. Which meant the end of Shed Music, which meant the end of *Shed Monthly*, Mr Martin's job and an income for the Martin family.

And you can kiss goodbye to your first job in journalism.

31 NET GAIN

It was two days, or thereabouts, since he'd spoken to Piccolo. Will tried to calculate time by the meals he'd had. To date, it was five. He'd heard the music, but nothing more from Piccolo himself. Had he escaped or ...? Rather than brood on what he couldn't answer, Will determined on devising his own escape plan. It was a long shot but ...

Examining the flagstones, he felt a flicker of hope: the grouting was Victorian, made of lime. A soft touch, with any luck. With the screw from the ladder, he set to work, using tap water to wash away the dust. As he'd expected, the flagstones were dislodged easily. He could've cheered. If he couldn't go through the door, he'd damn well go under it.

He worked only when the music above his head had long ceased, when he reckoned it was deep into the night, the safest time to work. Any time a thought came into his head of the urgency, or futility, of the situation, he took it out on the grouting. And when he breathed in the stench of his own shit and urine from the bucket, he imagined the smell of heather on the moors and the brackish scent of the Highland streams.

He went through the daring episodes undertaken by

his brother and the local GeeZers, in their determined, courageous fight to save the planet. It was at these times that he came close to breaking. But he used his anger to drive him on. He had to escape, in order to carry on his brother's work.

There was another meal, another long period of silence above his head, before he began work again. He'd been working for an hour, maybe two, when he heard a tapping above his head. Three short, three long, three short taps. Piccolo!

He clambered up the ladder, excited and disappointed: Piccolo hadn't escaped, which meant he hadn't delivered the message.

'I thought you'd gone?' he whispered.

'Not yet,' said Piccolo. 'I've been playing for the Head of Security.'

'What?'

'I play for this guy only when he knows Candelskin isn't in the building. I've no objection, 'cos I can see a way out.'

'Great,' said Will.

'I don't like to leave you, you know that, but—' said Piccolo, shoving a knotted shirt down through to the grille.

'You must. You know why,' said Will, automatically taking hold of the shirt. 'What's this? Am I doing your dirty laundry while you're away?'

Piccolo gave a hollow laugh. 'It's things you might

find useful. But go carefully with the stuff inside the manuscript paper. It's from some kind of computerised spider and— Hell, I can hear something. I'd better go—'

'You leaving today?'

'Yeah,' said Piccolo, awkwardly. 'I'll see you around, Will.'

'Aye,' said Will. 'See you around.'

For a moment, in the dark silence, he felt a raw, echoing loneliness, as when he heard the news of his brother's death. He took himself back to the Highlands. The wind on his face. The deep, wide quietness. Even the irritating midges in the summer air. He descended the ladder.

He sat on the bed and untied the shirt. Inside were a pack of sandwiches, two packets of crisps, a tin of Blooza Jooza, an old torch and, oddly, a pair of rubber gloves. He carefully opened the manuscript paper and stared at the contents. What did he want with a sheet of netting? He went to pick it up, hesitated and studied it more closely. All of a sudden, he uttered a low, dark laugh.

He put on the rubber gloves and wet them under the tap, to make it easier to pick up the spideroid's web.

As the cell door opened, Will yanked on a thread. The spideroid's web fell from a pole fixed between the walls, enveloping MacMinor, whose struggles only tightened its hold.

Throwing the bolt on the cell door, Will took the path alongside what he hoped was the main sewer leading to the river.

He sped along the narrow slippery ledge, offering up thanks to Piccolo for his 'dirty washing'. He had no idea how long the journey would take or what he might encounter on the way. He had no idea when, or if, the Red or Black Tartans would come after him. But he'd escaped. And this time, he could taste freedom. He hoped Piccolo might taste it, too. And that one or other of them, or the girl reporter Ruby Q Cooper, would get the message to the Face before it was too late.

32 KANE AND UNABLE

Jack was in his room, busy with course work, when he heard a car pull into the drive and a key turn in the front door. He knew, without looking, that it was his dad.

At breakfast, Mr Martin, who was chauffeuring Ruby Q and the Editor to the Royal Gala launch of the Sticky Rock Café the following day, had said that he was using the office's precious petrol coupons and his own lunch break to check out the route, starting from home.

Jack reached for his headset. The Shed Music CD helped him work. So he didn't hear the thud in the next room. Or his father's heavy tread on the stairs as he rushed to see what was wrong. He didn't see Mr Martin's expression when he saw his second son, Kane, sprawled across the floor. And he had no idea that Mr Martin dragged his comatose pyjama-clad son into the car to keep an eye on him during the trial journey, thinking no one else was home and that Kane might be suffering from a head injury.

So Jack couldn't know that Mr Martin breathed a sigh of relief when, during the trip, Kane awoke sufficiently to sing along with the Shed Music songs on the radio and sang on after they reached their destination, when Mr Martin discovered he was out of petrol and had to run to the nearest garage to fill up a can, returning to find his son gone.

And, of course, there was no way Jack could know that a Red Tartan on duty told Mr Martin that Kane had gone to visit a friend near by, leaving a message that his dad was not to worry as he'd be staying over. Or that another Red Tartan told Mr Martin about his lost pet, which was like a son to him.

Pressed for time, Mr Martin returned to the office and the first Jack got to know what had happened was at supper that evening, when Mr Martin informed his family that Kane was staying with a friend for a few days.

'After that bit of business, we deserve promotion to the Black Tartans, and the salary and index-linked pension that goes with it,' said MacMinor, as they walked the perimeter of the Sticky Rock Café.

'After you lost my haggoid? Fat chance,' said MacNoodle, bitterly.

'Och, that's not fair. Something caught its eye and it took off. I bet you an hour's overtime that it'll come back to you wi' some bit of rubbish.'

MacNoodle snorted. 'How often have I told you, man: Dekaydence don't pay overtime.'

33 LARS MINUTE CHANGE

It feels like the day after Boxing Day. Like the day you get rotten exam results when you expected to come top or near enough. Like ...

... the days after my mother abandoned me. That's how I feel. For a brief moment, life tasted sweet. Now my job, and Mr Martin's, is going up in smoke, yet everyone carries on as if nothing has happened. As if a missing Dipstick doesn't matter. As if Shed Music isn't affected. It's like we know the planet is in danger yet adults carry on as if it isn't.

Ruby Q looked round the crypt. The Black Tartan guarded the stairs. Petty Masters paced up and down, maniacally devouring crackers. Killivy, the gardener, hacked away at his shrubs. And if anything, the mood of the photographer's assistants was even more tense, as the celebrated photographer himself had arrived.

With his long, chiselled face, pale blue eyes and trademark black clothes and loafers, Ruby Q recognised Lars Sparks from a self-portrait. He prowled round the set, climbed ladders, rolled across the floor or leapt on to chairs, framing imaginary shots with his long tapered fingers.

You can tell he's an artist.

'Remove that cobweb, pliz,' said Lars, in a chill, stern voice, as he emerged from behind the camera. 'This is not a vampire shoot.'

His assistants jumped to do his bidding.

A rollerbladed youth skated up to Petty Masters.

'They've got him,' cried Rollerblader. 'Well, one like him.'

'What do you mean, "one like him"?' Petty snapped.

Ruby Q followed Rollerblader's gaze. A massive Tartan Guard, in a red and black tartan cloak caught with a large spider brooch, was descending the crypt steps ahead of Candelskin. In between them were one, two, three, four, five youths. Ruby Q's heart soared. They'd found the Dipstick! Mr Martin's job was safe!

And so is yours!

'Miss Masters! Miss Cooper! Wonderful news!' said Candelskin. 'The Dipstick Five! And all yours!'

Ruby Q grinned and applauded.

Petty sniffed suspiciously, before surveying each of the five young men in turn. Four were dressed in rubberised wooden suits, with trellis braces and plaited ivy ties, gumboots and straw hats. But the fifth, a tall handsome youth with spiky fair hair, was dressed in blue-and-white-striped pyjamas, a combat-green dressing gown, black boots and a black baseball cap skewed sideways on. Ruby Q thought he looked familiar.

Everyone thinks that when they get close up to famous people.

Petty Masters spat out some cracker crumbs. 'They're not all originals,' she snarled.

Oops.

Ruby Q looked at Candelskin, who smiled on, relentlessly.

'And 'ow did this one get hold of the new look I'm doin' for the spring?' said Petty, ominously, pointing at the pyjama-ed youth.

Candelskin beamed at the youth, who seemed to be asleep on his feet. 'Well, now—'

'Excuse me, luvvies,' cried Rollerblader, blading towards them. 'Lars is extremely anxious to meet the group. Ooo, and can I see why.' He pirouetted, as he spotted the pyjama-ed youth.

'Charityshop.' The pyjama-ed youth yawned suddenly.

'*What?*' shrieked Petty.

Ruby Q thought Petty was about to throw one of her infamous PMTs when Lars Sparks distracted her.

'The Dipstick Five, I presume, Miss Masters?' he inquired.

Three Dipsticks nudged a fourth to speak.

'My name is Arnold Mulch and I'm the lead singer,' said a small, pale balding creature in a flat, nasal voice. 'We were a country and western group, spending three years touring local clubs and pubs when ...'

Ruby Q blinked. The Dipstick Five's lead singer sang OK but his speaking voice sounded like a lawnmower. And he looked worse.

'This is Nevis, Lizard and Butt,' Mulch droned on. 'They're trainee sales reps like me. So was Lincoln but he—'

Mulch fell silent as he met Lars's icy look.

'Had to move on. Unexpectedly,' said Candelskin, quickly.

'And you?' said Lars, turning to the pyjama-ed youth.

'Me?' said the youth, cheerily, in a New York accent. He scratched his hat. 'I only just got here. Someone said something about a cup of tea.'

He grinned and a dimple appeared in one cheek.

Hey, your knees buckled.

'What the boy means is—' Candelskin began.

'Miss Masters,' said Lars, lowering his voice but not enough to prevent everyone hearing. 'The world is full of Mulches. The star is the boy in pyjamas. His face carries the project's future. I must focus on him.'

Ruby Q wanted to cheer. Lars was right. Mulch might be nice but he was utterly devoid of wow factor. Shed Music was excellent, but it had to be fronted by the handsome, cheeky chap – in or out of his pyjamas.

Steady.

'It's no skin off my nose but tell 'im.' Petty nodded at Candelskin.

Lars turned to Candelskin. 'My photographs will be the first visual exposure of the Dipstick Five? And this will coincide with the launch of the Sticky Rock Cafés?'

'Yes, to both questions,' said Candelskin.

'Mr Candelskin, if you want the Dipstick Five to be a

success you must replace Mulch with the boy in pyjamas. The camera will adore him and, it follows, so will the fans,' said Lars, matter-of-factly.

''Ere, that's not the deal,' said a Dipstick, as Mulch's jaw dropped.

Ol' Lars doesn't mince his words, does he?

'Not possible. Sorry.' Candelskin sighed. 'Out of the question.'

'Mr Candelskin,' said Lars, 'wherever I go in the world, I see the GeeZers' anger. They point to a bleak future for us all. I tell you about this boy because I am a professional and because I want very much for your Sticky Rock Café project to succeed.'

'Your support is touching, Mr Sparks,' said Candelskin, 'but your suggestion is out of the question. We have spent a fortune on publicity.'

Ruby Q couldn't contain herself any longer.

'But he's right, Mr Candelskin. If you really want the Sticky Rock Café and Shed Music to succeed with young people, you must choose the boy in pyjamas. He is something else. Every boy will want to be like him and every girl will want to date him. The only thing is, can he—?'

'Why, Miss Cooper ...' said Candelskin, taken aback.

'Mr Candelskin,' said Lars. 'Here and now, with witnesses, I donate my fee to the Sticky Rock Café project. In fact, I double it, on one condition: that you take my advice.'

'Blimey! Bribery and emotional blackmail!' muttered

Petty, choking on the crackers in her mouth.

Candelskin smiled, and shook his head.

'Mr Sparks, Miss Cooper,' he said, at last. 'What can I say? Your persuasive arguments have persuaded me. I yield to your advice.'

Bits of saliva-ed crackers fell from Petty's open jaw.

'The only thing is,' said Ruby Q, 'can he sing?'

Candelskin laughed. 'It matters little, but if you think it's important, I'll make a call.'

He tapped a number on his adservarum. A few feet away, a ringing tone sounded and the massive Tartan Guard reached into his sporran.

'MacCavity, can the new Dipstick sing?' said Candelskin.

There was a pause. MacCavity made another call and rang back. Candelskin beamed happily.

'He can sing, Miss Cooper. And he knows all the Shed songs.'

'Fantastic!' said Ruby Q.

At-a-girl, Ruby Q. You've helped save the day for Shed Music, Shed Monthly *and Mr Martin's job, as well as your own. You've done your bit for Sticky Rock Cafés, which means you've also done something important in the fight to save the planet. And you didn't have to disguise yourself in a rubberised suit and outlandish mask!*

'By the way, Mr Candelskin,' said Ruby Q, 'what's his name?'

Candelskin looked blank.

'Stanley Halls, at your service, ma'am!' announced the pyjama-ed youth, with an exaggerated bow.

'That's right,' said Candelskin. 'He's just arrived from—'

'The US of A!' Stanley continued. 'When the call came, Stanley Halls was undressed and ready! Just waitin' to Shed his stuff!'

He winked and grinned, and the dimple dimpled further into his cheek. He burst into a song from the CD, and at the end, everyone applauded.

My word, can he sing! Even Mulch looks admiring. And it's funny, but, at this moment, Candelskin's odorous perfume doesn't smell half so bad.

34 FRIGHT PATH

It was close to midnight but as hot and humid as any day that summer and in the wooded grounds of the Victorian church, now the Sticky Rock Café, Tartan Guards, Red and Black, patrolled listlessly. A lone cloud drifted across the face of the full moon and two great birds – black kites with forked tails – plummeted from the sky and flew through a slit in the stone spire into the bell cage, disturbing a clutch of bats.

The birds flew round the seven bells and then down into the body of the church, past leafless shrubs potted in empty petrol cans, and burnt-out cars and garden sheds littering the aisles.

One bird flew along the nave, through a huge cobweb curtain sprayed black and silver. The other flew lower, jostling the clouds of black, red and silver balloons tied to tables on which stood black, red and silver candles in broken beer bottles.

The birds drew closer, flying together as one dark shadow, around the walls, past rows of blinking computer screens, and then, at speed, towards the chancel.

One bird landed on the rood. The other flew through the chancel, and on into the Sanctuary, landing on the carved stone that had served once as the sacred high altar and was now the Sticky Rock Café bar. The bird flapped its mighty wings and uttered a piercing screech, which travelled beyond the walls into the woods.

MacMinor shivered and crossed himself.

'There, there, laddie,' said MacNoodle, reining in the haggoid, which had begun to yowl horribly.

In the bushes, the Face tensed.

The ground was dry and every sound resonated.

The guards, and the haggoid, moved on.

There was a slight rustling in the trees. The Face readied the knife.

'Howdedoodee!' a voice whispered.

'You're late!' The Face snarled.

'Yeah, but I's worth waitin' for, ain't that the truth?' Bianco grinned.

'Shut your mouth! Your teeth are like bloody searchlights!'

Bianco's grin grew wider.

'What's so urgent that we had to meet here?' said the Face.

The grin disappeared. 'Your man, Will— Yow! For a peacenik, Face ...'

The Face released the grip on Bianco's throat.

'The Professor's got him. At Dekaydence HQ.'

'Stupid—' The Face spat on the ground.

'But he struck lucky. He's got a friend, Piccolo, the café composer, bunking above his head.'

The Face said nothing.

'Time's running out, Face. You keep telling me that. And those Real GeeZers are stealing your thunder. You've lost Tommo and now Will—'

'Shut it!' snarled the Face. 'Just find out what's going on in the White Room!'

'It ain't that easy, Face. No one's talking, mebbe 'cos no one knows. Not for sure.'

35 STICKY ROCK'N'ROLE PLAY

So, the list from Cataract, Cyclops and Mote doesn't have your mum's name on it. The Italian Tourist Office and the Embassy can't help in the search for your Auntie Lily. And the web-search has drawn a blank.

Yes, but I'm being positive. Today's the launch of the Sticky Rock Café. And I reckon it might encourage other businessmen to follow Signor di'Abalo's example, so we can all work together to save the planet.

It may encourage them only because they'll see that it's the 'in' thing to do. Odd, isn't it? Writing about Shed Music has turned out to be campaigning journalism.

In her black jeans, pink charity-shop jacket and the ruby-red earrings the Martins had given her as a present for helping them out, Ruby Q stood on the pavement with Mrs Martin, Jack and Taylor.

'You look fab, Ruby Q,' said Taylor. 'Even your hair!'

Jack groaned.

'Thanks,' said Ruby Q, and grinned.

Nothing was going to spoil her day, not even Elsa, who'd failed to appear to wave her off. Ruby Q climbed into Mr Martin's car, where a large woman sat, dressed in khaki and a tricorn hat decorated with geraniums.

'Edwina Gardening-Fork (pronounced Spade), Editor,

Shed Monthly,' the woman said, briskly, holding out her hand. 'Caught the bus over — saves Mr Martin fetching me and saves on petrol. Don't want to miss any fun, do we, Miss Cooper? Now, tell me about yourself and I'll tell you about the old mag.'

In no time at all, Mr Martin was dropping them off at the entrance gate. They walked up the hill, stopping at a gap in the trees to admire the views of London and the old church, now the first Sticky Rock Café.

'Sad to see the end of an old church,' sighed the Editor.

'But it's not an end, it's a beginning,' said Ruby Q. 'It's a birthplace, where for the first time teenagers and adults will work together to save the planet.'

The Editor nodded but said nothing, and they walked on to the front entrance, where Dekaydence Guides checked their invitations.

'Goodness me!' exclaimed the Editor, staring up at a sign above the door, which proclaimed in multicoloured flashing lights: 'Welcome to the Sticky Rock Café'.

Techno-yuck!

My thoughts exactly.

They entered the old church, exchanging the bright summer sunshine for a chill darkness lit by huge sconces of candles hanging from the walls. Mists swirled about their feet and an eerie glow emanated from rows of computer monitors lined up along the north and south aisles. Chatter, laughter and *Carmina Burana* echoed off the old walls.

Politicians, pop stars, actors, artists, journalists and film stars stood round pots of lifeless shrubs, queued at the font – which was flowing with Dekaydence champagne – or hung out in the Lady Chapel, where a vast monitor was showing trailers of the latest Dekaydence films.

Everyone who is anyone (and many, like us, who aren't) is here.

Ruby Q's eyes were drawn to the huge flames dancing wildly on the wall behind the high altar, now transformed into a coffee bar, where stood MacCavity, in his red and black tartan cloak.

He banged a caber on the floor. The music and chatter ceased, and Randall Candelskin emerged from the shadows. There was applause and cheers. Candelskin ran up the steps of an eagle-shaped lectern and held up his hand for silence. He was resoundingly ignored, and didn't appear to mind.

'Good to see Randy back to his old dandy self,' said a young woman with spiky green hair and wearing a purple suit, standing close to Ruby Q. 'He's a two-faced git, but at least he's fun.'

'He is that,' agreed a grey-suited man. 'Do you remember when he ...?'

The Suit whispered in Spiky Hair's ear.

She rolled her eyes. 'I'd forgotten that one,' Spiky Hair giggled, and then sighed. 'Poor old soul having to work on this green cappuccino nonsense with the PM.'

'Especially if he ever discovers that it was the PM who

set him up so that he had to resign as an MP,' said the Suit, smiling enigmatically.

What?

What?

'What?' said Spiky Hair.

'I'm surprised you didn't know,' said the Suit, casually.

Ruby Q edged closer but Spiky Hair and the Suit disappeared in the bustling crowd, which was shushing itself into quietness.

'Dearly beloved,' Randall Candelskin pronounced in a ringing tone, his arms outstretched as if to embrace the entire assembly.

'Candelskin for Pope!' a voice bawled and a cheer went up.

'Give me time.' Candelskin smiled coyly.

There were more cheers. Candelskin adopted a serious expression. The crowd fell silent.

'Welcome to the launch of the Sticky Rock Café, an extraordinary project funded by a extraordinary benefactor who wished to remain anonymous but, as some of you ladies and gentlemen ...' He surveyed the crowd. Several journalists shuffled uncomfortably. '... and ferrets of the Press ...' He pretended a stern look.

The crowd, relieved, laughed.

'... have revealed, the gentleman who aims to create a better world for us all is none other than Signor Lorenzo di'Abalo, head of the Company of Dekaydence.'

There was polite applause.

'And if you need proof that the Sticky Rock Café project works, look at the youngsters in your midst who are about to serve you.'

Oh no! Nine years in our nightmares and now they're let loose here in broad daylight!

Settle down. They're only teenagers dressed up as clowns.

But—

Hush.

The crowd beamed approvingly at the smiling young clown waiters offering them delicious canapés and drinks.

'Ladies and gentlemen,' Candelskin continued. 'I am proud to announce today that this unique project has the official backing of His Majesty the King, and of His Majesty's government. We welcome the Prime Minister and, at some point during proceedings, we hope sincerely that His Mediumness, the Crown Prince ...'

The crowd sniggered: despite his love of fast bikes (and faster women), the Crown Prince was well known for being incapable of arriving anywhere on time.

'The Sticky Rock Café is targeted at younger teenagers. It will open 24/7, and go nationwide this summer. Come autumn, it will go Unionwide. At Signor di'Abalo's insistence, all facilities at Sticky Rocks are free, including bed and breakfast, and clothes from that world-renowned designer who'd like to have us all in stitches – as long as they're hers: Miss Petty Masters!'

There was applause, cheers and a few wolf whistles.

'Miss Masters is somewhere about, attired in one of her own inimitable creations – a ballgown fashioned, she tells me, from roof tiles.'

Rowdy laughter and a cloud of crumbs erupted into the air, followed by a welter of swearing from a familiar voice.

'Ah, you've found her. Jolly good,' said Candelskin. 'But to continue. Our Sticky Rock clients will also have their very own music ...'

There was a roar from the crowd and many stamped their feet.

'... which, I am reliably informed, is proving popular with people a teensy bit beyond their teens,' said Candelskin, feigning innocence.

The cheers were deafening. Candelskin took a sip of mineral water.

'In fact, ladies and gentlemen, the new Shed Music CD is available here at reception at vastly inflated rates, which I know you won't mind paying because it's for a good cause and because, as we all know, it'll go on the old expense account and you won't be paying – your boss will be.'

There was laughter.

'So, ladies and gentlemen, as a reward for your presence, and in grateful anticipation of your generosity, and that of your boss, you are the first to see and experience, in public, for the first time – the Dipstick Five!'

Candelskin relished the crowd's wild enthusiasm before holding up his hand.

'Of course, we must remember that this project has come about because Signor di'Abalo believes it is time for adults to listen to what youngsters have to say, especially about their concerns for their future. In return, we ask only that youngsters give some time to work on environmental community projects, and enrol in the Sticky Rock job-search programme.'

Candelskin clasped his hands as if in prayer.

'Ladies and gentlemen, my dear friends, we, at Dekaydence, believe sincerely in the Sticky Rock Café project as the way to end the increasing conflict between young and old. We, at Dekaydence, believe sincerely that through Sticky Rock Cafés, youngsters and adults can work together, to rebuild society and, yes, even our world. The world our youngsters will one day inherit from us all here today. Thank you.'

There was a moment's silence before tumultuous cheering and applause. Candelskin bowed, skipped down the pulpit steps and disappeared from sight. The crowd called for his return. But he did not respond.

What a magnificent performance! He could be in films, with Taylor.

Maybe, but what's that about him and the PM?

Ruby Q looked around and saw the Suit and Spiky Hair. She was edging her way towards them when a voice called out over the speakers.

181

'Ladies and gentlemen, please welcome the Dipstick Five!'

Above the ecstatic cheers, Ruby Q heard Spiky Hair's voice.

'It's a fantastic story. Why haven't you published it?'

The Suit glanced around. Ruby Q stared fixedly elsewhere.

'Proof, dear heart,' said the Suit. 'A little matter of proof. Find it for me and we'll split a fortune when—'

Agh! What was that?

Something exploded! My God, look! The wall behind the high altar bar is collapsing!

People were screaming; some were fighting their way through the crowd, as Red Tartans directed those closest to the high altar into the nave or side aisles.

Agh! There's another one! We must get out!

No, it's OK! Look!

A black stage emerged slowly through the wall and the flames, and halted at the chancel. The screams stopped and those shoving to get out tried to push their way back as shock gave way to fascination. There was a lightning flash, a crack of thunder, and scores of red, white and silver lights burst into life. As the smoke cleared, the crowd saw on the stage a burnt-out shed, a burnt-out car, a load of twiggy lifeless shrubs and a lean, mean-looking motorbike.

The music started. A quiet introduction from a melancholic oboe, joined by a cello, then drums. Ruby Q and the many Shed Music fans in the audience cheered.

'Lost and Found'. It was one of Ruby Q's favourites. The song kicked into life and four young men, in mock wooden suits, gumboots and straw hats, leapt out of the car. Two picked up guitars, one went to a drum kit. Ruby Q saw Mulch sullenly pick up a triangle.

A few bars in and a fifth figure, lying prostrate on the bike, got up slowly. For a moment, Stanley Halls, clad only in his striped pyjamas, combat dressing gown and boots, his black baseball cap skewed sideways on, surveyed the crowd with a querulous pout. Then he winked and gave a broad grin, a dimple appearing deep in one cheek.

The crowd shrieked.

Ruby Q grinned from ear to ear. She knew it: Stanley Halls was a natural. The crowd was his to command. And then he began to sing.

> *'Bossed around,*
> *Crossed and*
> *Tossed around,*
> *Here I am lost and dumbfound*
> *In this crazy world ...'*

Oh look, here comes Lars the Lens.

'An excellent choice, Miss Cooper,' said Lars Sparks.

'Yes,' she said. 'And he'll be great on the second CD, won't he?'

The crowd moved and Ruby Q was pushed closer to the stage.

> *'Here I am blown about,*
> *Thrown about,*
> *Disowned and alone about*
> *In the Grey Zone ...'*

She stared at Stanley Hall's handsome face. But before she could think where she'd seen him before, the music had reclaimed her.

> *'And now I am found again*
> *Feet on the ground again*
> *Back from the drowned*
> *And crowned with a new sound.'*

After performing five songs, the Dipstick Five went to leave the stage but the crowd roared for more. Four Dipsticks looked at one another, unsure what to do, but not Stanley Halls. He said something to the Dipsticks, appeared to talk to a backing band hidden from sight, and then turned to the audience. He grinned and the audience grinned back.

'Hi, ladies and gentlemen,' Stanley called out in a New York kinda accent. 'How ya doin?'

'Fine!' the audience yelled.

'What a coincidence! 'Cos we're doin' fine, too!'

Stanley punched the air. The audience cheered its approval.

''And 'cos it's you, we're gonna do one more song!'

'Yes!' screamed the audience.

'And then we gotta go! We got a photo shoot – with the PM of GB!'

'Shame!' howled a voice, and the audience laughed.

'Just for you, we're gonna sing ... "Shed (Your Stuff)!"' cried Stanley.

The audience screeched with delight. Ruby Q grinned: the song's cheeky words and up-tempo beat would suit Stanley. And, at the end, the crowd cheered long after the band had left the stage.

Ruby Q spotted Spiky Hair and the Suit talking to Petty Masters.

Yuck, it's that scent.

'All this is thanks to your persuasive powers, Miss Cooper,' called a smiling Candelskin, as he passed by in a throng of admirers.

As the noise died down, Ruby Q realised her phone was bleeping.

It was a text message from her dad.

The title of another old song.

It's the one he sends when he wants you to know he's missing you.

Yes, I can even sing this one. It's by the Animals: 'We Gotta Get Out of This Place'.

Ruby Q tried to call back but again, there was no signal.

Never mind, at least you know he's OK.

36 TUNNEL VISIONS

It was the Black Tartans who came after him. Will heard the echo of their boots pounding along the tunnel or sloshing through the sewage. He took refuge in pipes in the sewer walls, which were far too narrow for the Black Tartans to enter or perhaps imagine that anyone else could.

But it wasn't long before he realised something else was after him.

He heard a humming sound echoing some way off. He ran back to the nearest narrow pipe and clambered in. He didn't have long to wait.

He recognised it from conversations between the Red Tartans, who saw it as another threat to their jobs – an Eye-Spy, with its myriad camera lenses scanning everything as it turned and twisted.

He pressed his body into the pipe's rounded wall and waited. After the first came another. They were quieter, swifter than the Black Tartans and, he reckoned, able to detect through darkness as well as body temperature.

He waited for them to move on, deciding that their presence meant he could no longer travel along the main sewer. It might take him a bit longer but he hadn't yet broken into his supplies. What worried him was the torch. Its flickering light told him the battery was running low.

But there was no way of telling how long it would last.

He listened, hearing only the sound of water, running or trickling through the pipes. He slithered forward and was about to climb out of the pipe when he heard a noise behind him. He froze. Was it an Eye-Spy that had found another way into the pipe? He remained absolutely still, trying to think what to do. There was another noise. A kind of whining. He turned slowly and felt his heart and ribs collide.

It wasn't an Eye-Spy.

It was worse.

He was staring at a pair of infra-red eyes and a metal jaw salivating thick oily gunge.

37 THE PM TEASE

Am I paranoid, or are these clowns following us?

Shhh! I want to hear what the Suit and Spiky Hair have to say.

'Drink, sir? Nibbles, madam?' A clown waiter held out a tray.

'What you got there?' said Spiky Hair suspiciously, squinting at the colourful array of liquids sparkling in the sunshine.

'Gutz beer. Bloat lager. Vintage pink Ziff ...' said the clown waiter.

'What's that?' said the Suit, pointing at a glass of colourless liquid.

'H20, sir.'

'Sounds familiar,' said the Suit, peering with interest at the glass.

'Yeah, but it went out of fashion years ago,' said Spiky Hair.

'Even more reason to try it,' said the Suit, decidedly, and took two glasses, handing one to Spiky Hair. They each took a cautious sip.

'Gah! It's different, that's for sure,' said Spiky Hair, pulling a face.

'It's exquisitely boring!' said the Suit. 'I must get a case of it.'

'You'll find it at the warehouse within Dekaydence HQ,' said the clown waiter, lowering his voice. 'Ask for it by name, sir.'

'Mum's the word,' said the Suit, tapping his nose.

'No, H20's the word, sir,' said the clown waiter, and walked off.

The Suit and Spiky Hair headed for the open-air arena where the Dipstick Five interview was to take place. Ruby Q followed along with rock, fashion, news and feature writers, each after their own scoop.

'To think, I once wrote an exclusive story about Candelskin becoming PM,' sighed Spiky Hair.

'So did I,' the Suit sighed.

Ruby Q was moving closer when she caught a familiar scent.

'Ah, Miss Cooper,' said Candelskin, brightly. 'Come with me, I've got a VIP seat for a VIP guest.'

Bother, that was getting interesting.

Ruby Q let Candelskin guide her through the crowd, losing count of the gracious nods he accorded his admirers on the way, and wondered what the PM had done to him, and why.

'Prime position, as 'twere,' Candelskin winked, ushering Ruby Q into a seat at the front. 'Apologies again, but you must excuse me.'

He is one high-energy dude. Ouch! Your hand's being crushed in two huge sweaty ones belonging to the fat man sitting next to you.

'Miss Ruby Q Cooper in person. What an honour.'

Ruby Q turned to look at her neighbour.

Grief, he looks much older than he does on TV. And he pongs worse than Candelskin's aftershave.

'I'll let you into a secret, young lady,' said the Prime Minister of Great Britain and Northern Ireland, leaning closer to Ruby Q. 'My children bullied me into taking out an annual subscription to your magazine. Cost me a fortune. I'll have to put up income tax.'

Lucky he supplies the laughter for his own jokes.

'My name will be mud if I don't get your autograph,' the Prime Minister confided, thrusting a Royal Gala programme into Ruby Q's hand.

'What are your children's names?' said Ruby Q.

'Jesus, Maria and Josef.' The PM dabbed his neck with a tissue.

'Sorry?'

'My wife's Spanish,' said the Prime Minister.

Wait a minute: you're talking to the Prime Minister, the man who—

I know. The man who takes us to war every other year and, in between, opens chemical plants, armament factories, airports and motorways. He's talking about his children but does he ever stop to think what their life will be like in a few years or sooner, when we run out of resources, as well as the time and means to make changes? Even if the Sticky Rock Café is a good cause, he shouldn't

be here at a party, looking for cakes and votes. He should
be at his desk, working on the real issue, the real danger:
the life or death of this planet.

What does he care? And what can you do, Ruby Q?

I can do this.

Ruby Q took the pen the Prime Minister was holding
out to her.

'I'll sign,' she said, with a smile. 'If you give me an
interview.'

The Prime Minister roared with laughter. 'Miss Cooper, I
know nothing about music. Even less about sheds.'

'No matter,' said Ruby Q, smiling sweetly. 'I want to
interview you about the state of this planet. I want you
to tell me and other teenagers what *you* intend doing to
save it from corruption and ecological meltdown.'

Ruby Q!

The Prime Minister's smile turned sour. His eyes narrowed.
'Ring my office on Monday morning,' he said, curtly.

'Thank you, Prime Minister,' said Ruby Q. 'But before
you inform your office to give me the brush-off, you might
like to know that I am interviewing the Face, the leader
of the GeeZers.'

No, you're— Aha, I detect a flicker of interest.

'Perhaps I could interview you together,' Ruby Q mused.
'You could discuss things. It'd give you both some good
publicity, for a change.'

Ooo, if looks could kill.

'And I could give you my autograph at the interview,'

said Ruby Q.

At that moment, MacCavity banged his caber on the ground.

'Ladies and gentlemen,' said Candelskin, skipping centre stage.

'And ferrets?' cried a voice.

The crowd laughed.

'Especially ferrets,' said Candelskin. 'Before you meet the Dipstick Five, I have a difficult request to make.'

An anxious murmur went through the crowd.

'The young men you are about to meet are former GeeZers.'

The crowd were abuzz.

That's not true.

I know. No way is Stanley Halls a GeeZer. And Mulch and the others were sales reps in Essex.

'It's a great story, for us all,' Candelskin continued. 'But today, limit yourselves to general questions, about clothes, food, hobbies, etc. Ask nothing about families and background. Remember, these vulnerable youngsters are undergoing treatment and are in need of our support.'

The crowd groaned, as one. Candelskin scanned the arena, sternly.

What is he talking about? Stanley, vulnerable? The others might be, Mulch, especially. But not our Stanley.

'I share your frustration,' Candelskin said. 'But those in charge of these youngsters insist. When I get the all-clear, you'll be the first to hear.'

There were grumbles.

'But as well as the information in your press packs,' Candelskin continued, 'I can offer you photographs by Lars Sparks, all for free, courtesy of the Company of Dekaydence.'

What? It was Lars who offered them.

The crowd's interest was re-ignited. Photos from the great Sparks. For free. Candelskin waved to someone in the audience and Lars Sparks rose reluctantly from his seat. Candelskin led the applause.

'And now,' said Candelskin. 'Will you welcome, please ...'

His words were lost in a tidal wave of cheers and applause. There was a fanfare and hundreds of black, silver, white and red pigeonoids and balloons flew into the sky, as down the arena steps came the Dipstick Five – Arnold Mulch, Nevis, Butt, Lizard and Stanley Halls.

The crowd went berserk: applauding, whistling, cheering and stomping. Candelskin guided the Dipsticks to five stools. The four young men in the odd suits smiled shyly but Stanley Halls, in his pyjamas, dressing gown and baseball cap, grinned and waved.

'What's it feel like to be a Dipstick?' someone shouted.

Stanley Halls dramatised resting his chin on his hand, as if thinking.

'I was round Nevis's place having a cuppa when ...' Mulch announced in his plodding monotone.

Oh no!

The audience stared at Mulch, puzzled or disbelieving. Ruby Q saw Candelskin look skyward before Mulch stopped abruptly, mid-sentence.

Stanley Halls did not need a second prompt.

'Stanley Halls says it's dipstickin' marvellous to be a Dipstick!' he hollered, punching the air. ''Cos it means I ain't never gonna get dressed!'

The crowd relaxed, roared with laughter and scribbled their notes.

'Where are you living now you're superstars?' someone called out.

'In the depths of Dekaydence!' Stanley retorted, rolling his eyes.

There were cheers and jeers.

'What star sign are you, Stanley?'

Some journalists groaned.

'Leo!' roared Stanley. 'So I'm a natural showman, man, and I needs a whole lot of lurve!' He wiggled his hips provocatively and winked.

There were appreciative whistles and yells of approval.

'What do you like to eat?'

'Anything so long as it's hot and fast, baby!'

There were wild hoots and whistles.

'What's the band's favourite colour?'

'Gold! Preferably solid!' Stanley shouted.

The crowd cheered.

'What do you do to relax, Stanley?'

'Sleep!'

'If you were an animal, what kind would you want to be?'

'I *am* an animal!' Stanley roared, running towards the front row.

He was so close Ruby Q could have touched him. She stared at him. He looked so familiar but ... He moved away, answering questions in his own cheeky manner. Occasionally, he encouraged the other Dipsticks to join in but the crowd had eyes and ears only for him.

Ruby Q decided it was time for her question.

'Who writes the words and music?' she called out.

The audience waited expectantly.

The Dipsticks said nothing.

How personal a question is that?

'Well, it's kinda like this—' said Stanley, hesitantly.

'That information will be released with the next CD,' said Candelskin, briskly. 'Ladies and gentlemen, please put your hands together for the Dipstick Five!'

The crowd obeyed, roaring Stanley's name.

The Prime Minister stood up to applaud and turned to Ruby Q. 'My secretary will contact you to make an appointment, one that's convenient for you and the Face,' he said, tersely.

'Jolly good,' said Ruby Q, and returned her attention to Stanley.

Great, now all you have to do is get an interview with the Face. Remind me, how many times have the GeeZers turned you down?

38 DOWN AND OUT

Piccolo hadn't escaped: MacCavity hadn't sent for him, and Piccolo didn't know what to make of it. If they suspected him of stealing the spideroid's web, they'd have come for him, wouldn't they? So was Candelskin breathing down MacCavity's neck? Or was his playing too fancy for MacCavity's taste?

Catgut was pushing him to work on the songs for the third CD, but Piccolo's enthusiasm had all but evaporated. Catgut was in despair.

'You'll be the death of us all!' he shrieked at Piccolo in front of the musicians, one or two of whom began to sob.

It made no difference. Piccolo resented every note, every word he composed. He despised himself for what he'd done, allowing his longing to become a musician to blind him to the dreadful reality of the situation he and many others were in. He hoped Will understood his predicament; he also hoped Will had escaped. If only he, too, could escape and get Will's message to the Face. Perhaps then he'd feel better about himself.

'Your face looks as if it'd stretch into Thursday week,' said Rallan, taking flagons out of the delivery hatch. 'Want to talk?'

Piccolo shrugged.

'Here,' said Rallan, dispensing coffee into mugs and handing him one. 'Don't take any notice of Catgut. He's a bully and a madman.'

'There are a lot of them around,' said Piccolo.

'Ah, there speaks the voice of experience,' said Rallan, lightly.

Piccolo said nothing.

Rallan stirred sugar into his coffee. 'Will you go home when this is over, to your mum and dad?'

'My dad's dead.' said Piccolo, tersely.

'I'm sorry.'

'Me too.'

'How –?'

'He was murdered.'

'My God, how – who—?'

'A Big Bloke,' said Piccolo, and walked off before the drummer had a chance to ask more questions.

He'd never told anyone about what had happened years before, when he'd woken up in the middle of the night and seen the Big Bloke's cosh turn his father's head to pulp.

39 MAN'S BEST FIEND

Suddenly, Will found his mind filling with memories of hunting trips his brother had taken him on as a child. He'd detested the experience, and everything surrounding them. A bunch of men and women in party mood fuelled by a tot or three of brandy, setting off with their hi-tech guns to stalk a wild animal. Chasing it, bringing it down. Not always with a clean shot, not always a quick death. A once graceful noble beast, whose young would not be far away as its carcase was hauled off.

It had made him sick beyond the confines of his stomach.

'You should be proud of our heritage,' his brother had said, fiercely.

It was the only time they'd argued.

As he looked into the haggoid's blazing red eyes and wondered what the hell to do, he saw an irony in the situation, a kind of rough justice. Even though he'd never fired a shot in his life, even though this thing was, after all, a piece of metal.

He dared not move. If he could distract its attention ... The only thing he had to hand, literally, was the torch. It was invaluable to him but –

The haggoid was edging slowly towards him.

He had no choice. He was about to hurl the torch at the creature when it made an odd whining, yattering noise.

What did that mean?

It did it again.

He stared at it: it was looking unsteady and its metal eyelids were drooping. What had the kennel boy told him? Could it be that its gut was full? Or that its software was about to crash? Either way, he felt sure that if it ceased functioning an alarm would go off at HQ, which would bring the Tartans running. There was only one thing to do.

He moved cautiously towards the haggoid, holding out the torch.

'Ross? Cromarty?' he spoke, softly. 'Good boy, I'm just—'

He was less than a metre away when the haggoid flew at him, pinioning him to the ground, its metal teeth millimetres from his face, its overheated metal body scalding his skin.

He made a grab at its stomach, desperately searching for the switch that would shut it down.

40 RICH TEXT FORMAT

After a spell underground in what, for him, was surprisingly rude health, Sir Harrison Catgut rose from his bed one morning only to collapse back into it. Complaining of migraine, he begged that someone fetch him cold teabags to cover his eyelids.

Rallan obliged and, on Catgut's instructions, told the Black Tartans that work on the third CD would have to be suspended temporarily. After sitting with Catgut for some time, he went to find Piccolo.

'Maybe if you sat and talked to him, he'd feel better,' said Rallan.

Piccolo shrugged, disinterestedly. 'Catgut doesn't do listening. And I'm tired of hearing his voice droning on. I need a break from all his shouting, nagging and moaning.'

'You might find this hard to believe,' said Rallan, 'but he's got it into his head that he's responsible for us all, you included.'

Piccolo gave a hollow laugh. 'What's in those teabags?'

Rallan smiled. 'He's fond of you, you know.'

'Is that why he treats me like an alien?'

'I think he's gruff because he hasn't a clue how to show

you his genuine affection.'

Piccolo glared at Rallan. 'Really? Like if someone beat up a kid, stubbed out cigarettes on their body, and shit like that? You'd be saying, "Hey, kid. Remember, these punks really love you."'

He stood up, abruptly, the chair crashing to the floor.

'You know nothing, drummer!' he said, bitterly, turning on his heel.

After lunch, Piccolo was sitting alone at a trestle table, over a mug of cold coffee, when he became aware of someone standing beside him.

'Mind if I join you?' said Rallan.

Piccolo shrugged.

Rallan sat down beside him.

'I'm sorry, Piccolo. I—'

'Forget it,' snapped Piccolo. 'Just don't nag about Catgut.'

'OK, but there is one thing,' Rallan said, quickly.

'I told you—' Piccolo went to get up.

'Some years ago, Catgut lost his only child.'

Piccolo froze.

'Right as rain on Saturday, dead on Sunday. They say it's what turned his mind. He was a brilliant classical musician before ...'

Piccolo sank back into his seat.

Of course, he knew he wasn't the only one to have suffered. But now here was Catgut. And, for all he knew,

Rallan. There was so much pain in the world. So many burdens people had to carry around with them, not just a backpack of short-term troubles but weighty loads to be borne for the rest of a life. Why? Piccolo couldn't get his head around why God, who'd created a world with beautiful music, could allow such disharmony to spoil it.

Catgut tossed and turned, sweated and shivered, rambled, and shouted orders to someone unseen. He flailed out, wildly.

Piccolo jumped up from his seat at Catgut's bedside to steady the water jug on the cabinet, which was when he saw something on a lower shelf. He looked around, waiting for a break in the Eye-Spies, and reached for Catgut's adservarum.

He slipped his hand into his pocket for the paper Will had given him, waited again, and then punched the number and the code into the adservarum. He waited. Then he texted Will's message. He waited some more, before erasing the evidence and returning the adservarum to its place. No one, or nothing, appeared to have noticed.

He wasn't convinced that it mattered if the Prime Minister was killed. But Will thought it mattered and that's what was important to Piccolo.

He sat back. Whatever happened, at least he'd sent Will's message. His heart was racing but somehow, he breathed more easily.

Someone grabbed hold of his wrist.

He started.

It was Catgut.

Wild-eyed and dishevelled, the composer was sitting up in bed, staring at him, clinging to him like a young child.

'Thank you, Young Person,' said Catgut, passionately. 'Thank you, for everything you've done. Without you —' Catgut fell back on the bed, his eyes glazed and unseeing.

For some reason, Piccolo thought of his father. He took a cloth from the cabinet and dabbed Catgut's sweating forehead.

 41 STANLEY HALLS UNCOVERED

'You did what?' said Jack, aghast.

My sentiments exactly.

Ruby Q was sitting with Jack and Taylor in the Martins' garden in the late afternoon sunshine, telling them about that day's Royal Gala launch, and she'd mentioned her interview with the Prime Minister.

'Ruby Q, you haven't got an interview with the Face, nor are you likely to get one, if you remember,' said Jack.

He's right.

'I know,' said Ruby Q. 'I'll have to try harder to get one.'

'I think it's an ex idea,' said Taylor. 'Every newspaper and TV station in the country will want to buy your interview. The only problem is, Ruby Q, you'll be rich and famous before I am.'

Ruby Q grinned.

Jack shook his head.

'Anyway, tell us about Stanley Halls,' said Taylor. 'He's far more interesting than the PM. And you've obviously taken a fancy to him.'

'No, I haven't,' said Ruby Q, blushing and indignant.

Yes, you have.

'Take a look at these. Does he seem familiar?' said Ruby Q, handing them Lars Sparks's photographs.

Jack laughed. 'He's the spitting image of my brother, Kane.'

Taylor stared at the pictures.

'I thought he looked familiar,' said Ruby Q. 'But I've only ever seen Kane fast asleep, sunbathing in your garden.'

'Amazing,' said Jack. 'If Kane stayed awake long enough, he could be Stanley's stand-in.'

Ruby Q and Jack laughed.

'This *is* Kane,' said Taylor, emphatically.

'It looks like him,' said Jack, ''cos the clothes are similar. That's all.'

'They're *his* clothes 'cos this *is* our brother,' said Taylor, firmly.

'Don't be silly, Taylor,' said Jack.

'I'm not. This is a picture of Kane,' said Taylor, raising her voice.

Jack was about to say something but Ruby Q got in first. 'Why don't we ask him?'

'We can't,' said Jack. 'He's staying with a friend 'til Saturday. And before you ask, his mobile's off. And we haven't got a clue which friend.'

Taylor looked thoughtful. 'We've always joked about him sleeping too much, thinking he'd been out clubbing the night before, but perhaps he was rehearsing.'

Jack humphed, impatiently.

Ruby Q frowned. 'OK, if Kane is Stanley,' she said. 'Why

didn't he tell you?'

Taylor shook her head. 'I dunno. He's very secretive. He hates me going into his room.'

'So do I,' said Jack. 'Does that make me a pop star?'

Ruby Q stared at the photographs. 'He said he flew in from the USA,' she said.

Jack frowned.

'Kane does a wicked American accent,' said Taylor.

'And he does have a great singing voice,' said Jack.

'So you know Stanley is Kane, don't you, Jack?' cried Taylor.

'No, I don't,' said Jack. 'But we can ask him on Saturday.'

'I can't wait that long,' said Taylor, petulantly. 'I want to know now. I'm going to call Dekaydence HQ.' She stood up.

'Good idea,' said Jack. 'You'll say, "Hi, Stanley Halls is my brother. Please put me through to him." Every girl in the land will be using that one.'

'I don't care. I'm still—' said Taylor, turning to go.

'Hang on,' said Ruby Q. 'I could try to get an interview with him.'

Will this be before or after you interview the PM and the Face?

Jack and Taylor stared at her.

'I could say it would help my article, which it would,' said Ruby Q.

'What an ex idea,' said Taylor.

Jack said nothing.

'It's worth a try,' said Ruby Q.

She reached for her mobile, which had started to ring. 'Hello ... Yes ...'

Jack and Taylor waited for her to finish her call.

'... OK, I'll do it!' said Ruby Q, finally.

Blimey O'Riley!

She closed the phone and sat staring into space.

'What's the matter, Ruby Q?' said Taylor.

'Was it the PM? The King? Or Stanley Halls?' said Jack.

'No,' said Ruby Q. 'But it was your brother.'

'Kane!' Taylor sat bolt upright.

'No,' said Ruby Q, keying numbers into her phone. 'It was your GeeZer brother, Cage.'

'What?' said Jack and Taylor simultaneously.

Ruby Q put a finger to her lips.

'Hello, Mr Candelskin's office? It's Ruby Q Cooper from *Shed Monthly*. I'd like to interview the Shed Music composer. I've heard his name is Piccolo ... You'll call me back? OK, thank you.'

'What's going on?' Jack demanded. 'What does Cage want?'

'Cage rang to say a boy, a GeeZer, is missing in Dekaydence,' said Ruby Q. 'The GeeZers want me to interview this Piccolo, the Shed Music composer, because they think he may know something.'

'What?' said Jack.

'That means you'll get to see Kane,' said Taylor.

'Maybe,' said Ruby Q.

'Ex,' says Taylor.

'Hang on, what's a GeeZer doing inside Dekaydence?' said Jack. 'They must have something on the company.'

'I don't know,' said Ruby Q, and blushed.

Ooo! You do!

'And why are they asking you to go in under cover?' Jack persisted.

Ruby Q shrugged, her blush deepened.

'Ruby Q, we're talking danger here. Cage has no right to ask you to do his dirty work. Especially after turning down your interview request.'

'Dekaydence are good guys, remember?' said Ruby Q. 'They're launching Sticky Rocks to help save the planet.'

'Maybe the GeeZers know something we don't,' said Jack.

'Look, I'll be OK,' said Ruby Q. 'I'm in Dekaydence's good books, aren't I? Who helped them choose Kane or Stanley?'

'Ruby Q, you know what happens to GeeZers when they're caught. We've seen the pictures on the internet,' said Jack, vehemently.

'You never showed me,' Taylor protested.

'I'm not working for the GeeZers, Jack,' said Ruby Q. 'At least not directly. I'm working for *Shed Monthly*.'

'You're determined, aren't you? Determined to go against your own common sense. So I reckon there's something else.' Jack glared at her. 'What is it, Ruby Q?

Why are you hell-bent on doing this?'

Ruby Q hesitated.

Sharing is what friendship is about, Ruby Q.

'OK, but don't breathe a word,' said Ruby Q. 'Cage told me that if I get the information they need, I'll get an interview with the Face.'

'Fab-ex!' says Taylor.

Jack shook his head. 'So even GeeZers aren't above bribery,' he said, angrily.

Ruby Q's phone rang again.

'Hello, yes,' she said. 'This evening? OK. Thanks for your help and please thank Signor di'Abalo for agreeing to it.'

'Ruby Q, this is madness,' said Jack. 'Getting an interview with Kane was one thing but this undercover stuff – Besides, what about your search for your family?'

'That has to go on hold,' said Ruby Q. She hesitated. 'There is something else. Cage rang off before I could say anything but the boy missing in Dekaydence HQ is Will. The one who wanted me to get an urgent message to the GeeZers. I let him down once. I can't let him down again.'

42 A WINDOW OF OPPORTUNITY

The musicians were having breakfast when two Black Tartans arrived and took away Rallan. Piccolo went to intervene but a look from Rallan warned him off. The musicians became edgier than usual.

Piccolo thought of the fate of the previous drummer and worried. What did they want with Rallan? He fretted for another opportunity to play for MacCavity, in order to escape. Once free, he'd find someone, anyone, to free Rallan, Catgut and the others. And he'd look for Will. As Will, he hoped, would look for him.

Not long afterwards, the Black Tartans returned for him.

They took him to MacCavity's office where, in the corner, the spideroid was spinning.

Without looking up from his paperwork, MacCavity signalled for him to play. Piccolo felt sick with fear and excitement, his palms cold and sweaty. Either way, he thought, this was it.

He lifted the piccolo to his lips. As he played, he wandered round the room, edging nearer to the open window. He saw the river sparkling in the sunshine, like a diamond necklace. Freedom was on the other side of the ledge. He could breathe it. He could taste it. Whatever lay below the first-floor window, it wasn't far to jump or fall. No higher than the cemetery wall. Then he'd run. And he'd find Will, wherever he was.

The window was less than a few steps away. In the middle of the piece, a crescendo, he made a run at it.

MacCavity stuck out his foot.

Piccolo crashed to the floor.

'Before you pop off, laddie, best you know that your friend, the drummer, is in serious trouble,' said MacCavity, his voice soft and dark. 'He's been using Catgut's adservarum. Texting messages.'

'What's it got to do with me?' said Piccolo, sulkily, trying to sound unconcerned. What made them think it was Rallan who'd been texting?

'Because you know what happens to people who break the rules,' said MacCavity, with a knowing smile. He picked up a tiny bottle from a shelf above the desk and gently stroked it.

Piccolo frowned. What was MacCavity talking about? He glanced at the tiny ornaments on the shelf, and realised. Everything, including the bottle, was a miniature. A tiny replica. Was that it? Was MacCavity telling him that Rallan was next in line for miniaturisation?

Piccolo retched the contents of his stomach on to the floor.

'I could do a deal, if you want to save him,' MacCavity said, at last.

'What do you mean?' said Piccolo, shivering and wiping

vomit from his mouth.

'There's a bucket in yon corner. First, clean up the mess.'

Piccolo rose unsteadily to his feet and did as he was told.

'Mr Candelskin's got a little job for you, laddie. Do it well, with no trouble, or ...' MacCavity downed the contents of the bottle, which he then threw into the bin.

Piccolo struggled to keep down what little remained in his gut.

Somehow, Will found the switch and the haggoid slumped on top of him. It took immense effort to heave it off. Ignoring the scalds and open wounds he'd incurred in the struggle, he searched the mechanoid's body and found a catch, threw it open, and stared at a bloated vacuum sac. He pulled it out, emptied the crushed debris of tins, papers, bricks, wood and a tartan handkerchief on to the ground, and replaced it in the body.

Tearing a sleeve from Piccolo's shirt, he secured it to the haggoid's collar and, gritting his teeth, threw the switch.

The haggoid staggered to its feet, its bright infra-red eyes scanning its surroundings. Catching sight of the crisp packet in Will's hand, it jumped at him.

But Will was ready: holding tightly to the makeshift lead round the mechanoid's neck, he let go of the packet. Scarcely had it left his hand when the mechanoid caught it in its jaws and devoured it. The creature stared at him, its eyes and long thin leather tongue greedy with expectation. Will reached into his shirt-sack: one round of sandwiches and a can remained. He dropped them on the floor and watched as they went in a flash of metal teeth.

The mechanoid sat back on its haunches, watching

him intently, dribbling oily saliva, its jaws seemingly grinning.

He remembered the boy in the kennels and shuddered.

'Right,' he said, as much to steady his nerves as distract the haggoid. 'We'll go this way. See if we can get you more stuff to eat.'

The haggoid's metal tail tapped the ground. It was uncanny how it appeared to understand, Will thought.

Holding the lead tight, he crawled out of the narrow pipe and jumped down into the main tunnel. He was sure it wouldn't be long before more guards, and more Eye-Spies, came after him.

He had to move quickly and trust his gut feeling that he was travelling north, and well away from Dekaydence.

Some tunnels were so small that he had to crawl along on his stomach, dragging the haggoid behind. Sometimes he thought he heard something and stopped. But the sounds appeared to be echoes only in his head.

Despite the creature's odd varied yattering, much to his surprise it gave him no trouble. Did its software register this activity as a game? Or him as a new leader? He'd no idea, and after a while he gave up worrying.

He was more conscious of the fact that he was wet through, chilled to the bone, and that the stench of sewage and mouldy dampness was reacting badly with his empty stomach. His eyes ached from the strain of squinting into the eerie gloom. He tried humming, but had to stop, as it seemed to encourage the haggoid to yowl.

The worst of it was the rats: utterly fearless, they ran across his feet, along his arms and body, over his head, brushing past his face. There'd been no problem persuading the haggoid to eat one; the problem was trying to tempt it to eat another.

But he urged himself on, reminding himself of the urgency to get to the Face.

The narrow tunnel came to an abrupt end. He slithered out of it and on to the ground a few feet below, the haggoid clattering down beside him.

The torchlight revealed that he was in a high-ceilinged cavern with several tunnels leading off it. He held up a finger to test for a flow of air in each, but, beyond the pervading damp chill, there was no movement. Which to take? The haggoid pulled him towards one. Will hesitated but then went with it. Really, he had no choice.

It was then he heard a distant explosion.

The haggoid yowled.

Will stood rooted to the spot, listening, watching for a sign that would tell him what was going on. Was it a gun? Had a tunnel wall collapsed? Would he be drowned any moment in a flood of river water or sewage? But nothing happened, except that the haggoid stopped yowling.

He hurried on.

At least he could stand up in this tunnel. But he was getting tired, losing concentration. The light from the torch was growing weaker and, from time to time, the haggoid slithered on the narrow, wet ledge, nearly landing him in the sewer.

It was when he turned a corner that he saw a spot of bright light. He stopped and listened for a sound. Nothing. He walked forwards slowly and, as he drew closer, realised it wasn't a light bulb as he'd thought but—

Daylight!

A shaft of dust-filled sunlight!

He hurried towards it and, looking up, saw that the light was coming from a manhole, immediately above his head. He glanced around. Joy of joys, there was a ladder attached to the brickwork. He felt he had wings as he flew up the rungs, the yattering haggoid scaling the wall alongside him.

All he had to do was ease the manhole cover upwards ...

Tentatively, he lifted his head into the open air. The bright summer sunshine made his eyes water and the sudden assault of noise deafened him. No matter. He was free! Within a few minutes, he'd find a phone box.

He clambered out on to the street, relishing the light and warmth on his body, and then realised something was wrong.

People were running about in every direction, screaming and shouting. Police were everywhere. Abandoned vehicles, too. After a few seconds he heard the distant sound of sirens.

He'd escaped the nightmare of Dekaydence but what new nightmare had he walked into?

44 MIXED MESSAGES

What's with this guilt, Ruby Q? You promised to go under cover for the GeeZers. It's what you always said you'd do. So get on with it.

It's OK for you. You didn't have to tell the editor of *Shed Monthly* the real reason why you're interviewing Piccolo. Now I'm lying to Candelskin and, therefore, Signor di'Abalo, who've shown such faith in me.

The Treasures work under cover. They don't tell Elsa when they bring you trays of food if you miss a meal. That's OK, isn't it?

Moral philosophy isn't my strong point, so I can't explain the difference. Nor do I know why the GeeZers are investigating Dekaydence. Nor how easy it will be for Piccolo to tell me anything, even if he does know anything. I only know that Sticky Rocks are a Good Idea and I owe Will. And for Jack and Taylor's sake, I must find out whether Kane Martin is Stanley Halls.

And the best of British, Sherlock.

At the entrance to Dekaydence HQ, a Red Tartan handed Ruby Q a security stud, which she clipped to her ear, and she went through the entrance gate. Before her, in a courtyard, stood a massive stone fountain erupting huge red and orange flames into the darkening sky.

Despite the summer heat, she shivered.

'Miss Cooper, good to see you,' cried Candelskin, his aftershave reaching her before the man himself. 'A thousand apologies, but we have the decorators in so we have to use the fire exit.'

He guided her over ladders towards a door wedged open with a paint pot, and led the way up a staircase to the third floor. Cables protruded from half-painted walls.

'I'm afraid you might find our young composer a tad sulky,' said Candelskin, as they proceeded along a corridor.

'Oh dear. Nothing I wrote?' said Ruby Q, only half in jest.

'No,' said Candelskin. 'When we rescued Piccolo from the streets, we found traces in his system of unusual fungoids. They've left a mark on his fragile and especially creative mind.'

So he's out to lunch.

'Are you saying Piccolo is incapable of speech?'

'No,' said Candelskin, with a little laugh. 'But the poor boy isn't at all himself. He stays here, under constant medical observation. Oh, and best not to inquire about his family. But not to worry, I'll be sitting in on the interview, in case you encounter any difficulties.'

Great! You're interviewing a highly strung artist in rehab, your questions are restricted and the boss will be breathing down your neck. I'd call the GeeZers and quit while you're ahead.

They reached a door, where two Black Tartans stood guard.

Ah. So it looks as if he's potentially dangerous, too.

One of the guards opened the door and Candelskin led the way inside.

Ruby Q was surprised to find herself in a bright atrium, filled with scented shrubs, songbirds and a fountain.

She saw him in a corner, a tall, thin youth, watching them warily, as his fingers tapped a restless beat on his arm. As she got closer, she noticed the rainbow-coloured stud in his ear, before she saw the look in his eyes. Was it nerves or anger? She offered him her hand, which he avoided, and the three sat down.

'I can't ask you questions about your background but—' she began, extracting her voice recorder and notebook from her bag.

'Don't see why not.' Piccolo shrugged. 'There's not much to say.'

'We like to protect people, and their families, from intrusion, don't we, Piccolo?' said Candelskin.

'I got no family,' said Piccolo. 'I'm an only. My dad's dead and my mother's a drunk. With luck, she's dead by now.'

Well, that's dealt with the tricky personal details.

'Was your dad a musician?' Ruby Q ventured.

'He was a postman but he played guitar in a band, semi-pro. He loved his music. Albinoni to Zappa. Anything. He wanted to ...'

He fell silent.

Ruby Q hesitated. 'Was it your father who gave you a piccolo?'

'Yep, when I was six,' said Piccolo, and his fingers tapped restlessly on his leg. 'He was disappointed. Wanted me to be a guitarist, like him. But that wasn't for me, man. I like to fly with this little guy.'

He took the piccolo from his jacket, holding it like a baby.

'It makes a beautiful sound,' said Ruby Q. 'Like running water.'

Piccolo looked up and stared at her. 'Your voice sounds like a flute. You a musician?'

'No,' she said, blushing, and wishing she could explain that money, or lack of it, had prevented her continuing with violin lessons, but the interview wasn't about her. She saw he'd lost his interest.

'Who are the musicians you admire?' she continued.

Piccolo regarded her intently. 'Sir Harrison Catgut,' he said.

'Gosh!' Ruby Q was taken aback. 'He's an acquired taste. What do you like about him?'

'He is one skidoodlin' balmy beer mat, for sure, but his music, like, it speaks to you, if you let it. D'you understand what I'm saying?'

Ruby Q glanced up from her notes. A look she couldn't translate passed between Piccolo and Candelskin.

During the course of the interview Ruby Q learnt more of Piccolo's varied musical taste but all the time sensed his discomfort. Was it his nerves or her interviewing techniques?

'It must be great to know your music is part of a new and exciting environmental campaign and will be heard by millions of youngsters,' she said, and saw his eyes cloud over.

'Yes, it's a great idea,' he said, flatly.

How odd. You'd think he'd be over the moon about it all.

Ruby Q waited but nothing more came.

This question could be tricky.

'So you support the GeeZers?'

She noticed Candelskin's inscrutable expression.

'Their hearts are in the right place.' Piccolo sounded nervy.

She waited but nothing more was forthcoming.

Mmm. Try a bit later. Don't forget Kane.

'What's it like working with Stanley Halls?' said Ruby Q.

Piccolo looked at Candelskin.

'They don't actually work together, Miss Cooper,' said Candelskin.

'Oh,' she said, surprised. 'In the press pack it says they're working together at Dekaydence's HQ until the fourth CD is—'

'Fourth CD!' Piccolo leapt to his feet and, for one moment, Ruby Q thought he was going to hit Candelskin.

'Sit down, dear boy. No definite decision has been taken as yet.' Candelskin smiled as he adjusted his shirt cuffs.

'But how can they *not* work together?' Ruby Q persisted.

'Time is not on our side, alas,' said Candelskin. 'Stanley is busy recording all day along the corridor in the Blue Zone while Piccolo—'

Well done, you've got one piece of info!

'While I'm locked up all day, composing,' said Piccolo.

'Piccolo! You'll give Miss Cooper the impression we're slave drivers!' Candelskin tittered, and Ruby Q noticed one of his eyelids twitching involuntarily.

'Oh, I know all about deadlines,' she said. 'But, as my father is fond of saying: "Where there's a will."'

She stared at Piccolo, but he was watching Candelskin, whose attention had been diverted by a call on his adservarum.

'Actually,' Ruby Q said, deliberately, 'what my father says is, "Where there's a will, there's a way out."' She held Piccolo's gaze. 'It's a grey area because you have to know where your will is.'

I think he understands you. Which is more than I do. Pesky riddles.

'You're right, Miss Cooper,' said Piccolo, slowly. 'I think you must search in the very sewers of your mind. Look at my song, "IoU".'

That's where Will is! In the sewers! Well done again, Ruby Q.

'For someone who isn't a musician, you know a lot about music,' said Piccolo.

'My father—' Ruby Q began, but Candelskin had finished his call.

'I'm afraid we must end this interview,' he said, with a quick smile. 'Something urgent has cropped up. A Tartan Guard will escort you to the main entrance, Miss Cooper, where a limousine awaits to take you home.'

'Oh.' Ruby Q stood up.

Pestilence.

'Good luck with your research,' said Piccolo, standing up.

'Thanks,' said Ruby Q, shaking the hand he offered. 'It's been good to meet you. And good luck with all the CDs – not that you need it.'

'I'll need all the luck in the world,' he said, looking deep into her eyes as Candelskin put an arm on his shoulder and led him out of the room.

45 BOMBSHELL NEWS

Will emerged on the Embankment, on the north side of the river, into a city in turmoil. He soon realised why.

Word was that the Prime Minister had been killed. A bomb had exploded at his official residence, No. 10 Downing Street. Others had been killed, too, including the PM's wife.

Already, Will heard people in the crowd blaming the GeeZers or a faction he hadn't heard of before, the Real GeeZers. He railed against himself for failing to get to the Face, imagining the fierce reprisals that would follow. For all GeeZers.

He had to think what to do. Beside him, the haggoid was gorging on several refuse sacks. He would've abandoned it, there and then, but for the havoc and destruction he knew it would cause. But what could he do with it? He couldn't take it back to the Royal Palace.

Before he did anything else, he must offload this mechanoid. He'd think about where and how along the way.

'Come on, Cromarty,' he said, and set off along Whitehall, towards Charing Cross, with the haggoid trailing cardboard and black plastic from its metal jaws.

Let me get this right. When we get to the Blue Zone, you tell the Black Tartan you need the loo. Then you sneak out of the loo, find Kane—

We're here! See the Blue Zone notice on the wall.

The guard is taking a call on his adservarum. What's he saying? Signor di'Abalo wants to see you.

What?

Great! Just what you wanted: an interview with the boss.

Yes, but not now. I must find Kane and I must tell Cage about Will. Besides, what can Signor di'Abalo want with me?

How do I know?

Ruby Q didn't have long to wait before she found out.

The Black Tartan led her outside, across the courtyard, to the top floor of a building fronting the river. A guard opened a door.

She walked into a bright, stylish, sparely furnished room, decorated in ivory, with a picture window overlooking the river and the City. A scent of lilies hung heavily in the room. In the corner, a stone fountain, a small replica of the one in the courtyard, gushed flames into the air, while on the back of an ivory sofa, two cats, one black, one white, were stretched out, fast asleep.

She heard music, and started. It was one of her mother's favourites: the Largo from Vivaldi's Fourth Piccolo Concerto in C major. The haunting melody reminded her of a day long before. A day at the seaside with her parents.

The day that photograph was taken?

Yes.

Chin up, old thing.

Someone behind her spoke.

'Miss Cooper.'

She heard the man's voice rather than his words. Liltingly musical, with a flavour of Irish and a dash of Italian, it was as warm and soothing as the room. And yet she shuddered.

She turned. Sunlight was pouring through the window, so when the man rose from behind the desk, she saw only a great shadow within a halo of golden light. He came towards her, seeming to step out of the sunlit cloak, and she found herself looking into the strangely handsome face of a tall man, simply but elegantly dressed, with eyes a luminous mixture of blue and green. He smiled.

'I am Lorenzo di'Abalo,' he said. 'Please ...'

He gestured to Ruby Q to sit on the ivory sofa, before taking a seat beside her. The white cat stretched out a paw.

'I hope your interview with Piccolo went well,' said di'Abalo.

'Yes, it did. Thank you,' Ruby Q replied.

'He's a talented young man, as I'm sure you, Miss Cooper, with your perceptive gifts, appreciate. Alas, he has a way to go before he recovers.'

'Yes, Mr Candelskin said.'

'It's not only drugs, Miss Cooper. It's more perverse than that.'

'What is it? What's wrong with him?' said Ruby Q.

Di'Abalo looked at her, keenly. 'He's been brainwashed, Miss Cooper.'

'Brainwashed?' Ruby Q repeated. 'He seemed perfectly fine.'

'Did you not encounter a trace of hidden anger?'

'No.' And then she recalled the moment she thought Piccolo was going to hit Candelskin.

'Miss Cooper, we can expunge drugs from his system but we didn't get to him in time to save him entirely.'

'Save him from what?'

'The GeeZers.'

What?

Ruby Q couldn't help herself, and burst out laughing.

'I'm sorry. But the GeeZers are like you: they're committed to saving the planet.'

'Which is why I want adults to listen to them, and their younger siblings. Why else would I spend my fortune funding Sticky Rock Cafés?'

'I don't understand,' said Ruby Q.

'Miss Cooper, are you aware of the Real GeeZers?'

She nodded.

'The Real GeeZers have broken away from their peaceful brethren but, within the original organisation of GeeZers, they have planted a number of indoctrinated, volatile young thugs, intent on undermining the entire movement.'

Ruby Q stared at him.

'Piccolo met one of these thugs,' said di'Abalo. 'His name is Will.'

Ruby Q tried to steady her features.

'We know that Will's plan was to enter and destroy this building.' Di'Abalo paused, and shook his head.

I don't believe it.

'It's unbelievable,' said Ruby Q.

'Nothing is ever as it seems, Miss Cooper,' said di'Abalo, with a rueful smile. 'Look at this white cat. Beautiful, even as it sleeps. Awake, it can kill. Nine lives, and two faces at least for each life.'

'I can't get my head round what you're saying.'

'I understand. But perhaps when I tell you the news ...'

'What news?'

'Thirty minutes ago, the Prime Minister's London home, No.10 Downing Street, was blown up.'

'Oh no,' said Ruby Q. If only she'd got Will's message to the Face. If only –

'Luckily, the Prime Minister had been called away suddenly on urgent business but his wife, his young son, members of his staff—'

'Wait a minute! You're not telling me the GeeZers or the

Real GeeZers ...?' Ruby Q felt her body go cold.

'Look at this, Miss Cooper.' Di'Abalo pressed a button on his adservarum and pictures flashed up on the opposite wall.

Ruby Q stared at the shots of a young man entering No. 10.

'Do you know him?' di'Abalo asked.

'No, I've never seen him before,' said Ruby Q, and inwardly breathed a sigh of relief: the young man wasn't Will.

'He's a Real GeeZer but he continues to work as a GeeZer and is close to the Face. A few days ago, using a recognised code, he called for an urgent meeting with the Prime Minister, which was granted. He entered the building a few hours ago and left an hour later. He is the one who planted the bomb.'

'How can you be sure?'

'Fingerprints.'

'That's not conclusive.'

'And laser footage of him planting the bomb in a lavatory cistern.'

'But why?'

'As I said, nothing is ever as it seems, Miss Cooper. Nothing is all black. Nothing is all white. But we know that the GeeZers are no longer as pure, green and environmentally friendly as we once believed.'

Ruby Q's head was reeling.

You must warn Cage, if he doesn't already know! And

what is all this about Will?

'I don't understand. And why are you telling me all this?'

'I think you're going to go far in your career, Miss Cooper, and I wanted you to understand this before you went any further.'

'But why?'

Di'Abalo sighed. 'Many years ago, I lost a close friend. He died because of his own innocence or foolishness, call it what you like. I want the Sticky Rock Cafés to be a living memorial to him because I want to prevent youngsters, such as you, following in his footsteps. I don't want true GeeZers to become terrorists whose only interest is power through destruction.'

He paused.

'When I heard about the bomb, I remembered you were here in my headquarters, safe. Somehow, it seemed appropriate to tell you.'

Ruby Q stared at di'Abalo, her mind in turmoil.

And in all this, what of the planet?

'It's hard to take it in, isn't it?' said di'Abalo.

Ruby Q stood up. She needed to go home. She needed to be alone.

'There is one more thing you ought to know, Miss Cooper.'

Ruby Q couldn't imagine what more there was to tell.

'The name of the young man in those pictures,' said di'Abalo. 'It's Cage Martin.'

47 SPECIAL DELIVERY

There were police blocks everywhere, so Will decided to lie low for a bit, choosing the colonnaded entrance of an evacuated building.

Given the filthy state he was in, he didn't look or smell very different from a street beggar. And in the mayhem, he didn't think the haggoid looked much different from a dog. As long as no one looked too carefully, especially at its eyes. But scarcely anyone gave them a second glance. People appeared to have turned inwards, reflecting on the day's atrocity.

The hot sun warmed his face and he closed his eyes.

The next he knew it was dark. A man's voice was shouting abuse at him. He was kicked in the ribs and felt agonising pain. Someone shrieked and he heard footsteps hurrying away. He felt his arm almost torn from its socket as the yowling haggoid strained to chase after a figure running down the street. There was blood everywhere, much of it dripping from the mechanoid's jaws.

A few late-night revellers glanced at them but hurried on. Beggars, blood, trash. Nothing unusual there.

But he had to be careful not to draw attention to himself. Not now. Not after coming through so much.

The haggoid made a yattering noise. Will cursed. The

damn bag was full again. He'd have to move fast.

He staggered to his feet and moved on, as quickly as he could, keeping close to buildings, merging into the shadows as police cars came close, until he came to Trafalgar Square.

Even at three in the morning, with a curfew, there were people about, tourists mainly who could show their special permits. He crossed behind Nelson's Column, into Whitcomb Street and along until he reached the junction with Shaftesbury Avenue.

He glanced at the haggoid: its usual high-octane energy was fading. He hadn't much time. In fact, he might have to empty the bag there and then. He slipped into a doorway opposite an all-night store, where a well-dressed drunk was having difficulty finding the exit.

'Here, Cromarty,' said Will, reaching for the switch.

The haggoid opened its yattering jaws and slowly sank to the pavement. A shrill ear-piercing whine hit the air.

'Christ!' said Will, looking up.

The drunk was standing on the pavement, grinning at him. Will saw the adservarum he had in his hand. He was lifting it to take a picture when—

A Dekaydence newspaper van pulled up between them. The driver ran into the shop, carrying a pile of early editions. Will didn't hesitate. Using all the strength he could muster, he picked up the haggoid, lurched across the road and dropped it into the van, making off as fast as he could along Wardour Street and slowing down only when he could mingle inconspicuously with the early morning stallholders in the market in Great Peter Street.

48 CURIOUSER AND CURIOUSER

Ruby Q was desperate to get home and sit alone in her room to think about what di'Abalo had told her. She also had to decide what to tell Jack and Taylor. She was sure they knew nothing about Cage planting the bomb, but if they did? The limousine drew up at Elsa's house.

Oh, no. Jack and Taylor are on the pavement.

'Did you find Kane?' Taylor demanded through the window.

'No, sorry,' said Ruby Q, getting out of the car, unable to look either of them in the eye.

'Oh,' said Taylor, disappointed. 'Didn't Piccolo talk about him?'

'No,' said Ruby Q. 'Apparently, they never get to see one another. I was hoping to snoop around but I got called in to see Signor di'Abalo.'

'What did he want?' said Jack.

'To tell me about the bomb at No. 10.'

'Isn't it awful?' said Taylor. 'One of the PM's sons was killed and the PM's wife is in hospital, hanging on by a thread.'

'And once again, the GeeZers are blamed,' said Jack, angrily.

Ruby Q said nothing.

'Did you find out *anything* about Kane?' Taylor persisted.

'No. Sorry, Taylor,' said Ruby Q.

'Oh, I can't wait 'til Saturday,' Taylor wailed.

'It can't have been easy playing detective and journalist,' said Jack.

'It wasn't, not with Candelskin breathing down my neck,' said Ruby Q, deciding to say nothing about Will, in case it led to talk of Cage.

'Did you find out anything about Will?' said Jack.

Now what? You can't lie to friends.

'Not exactly, Piccolo kept talking about his favourite musician.'

'Oh,' said Jack, disappointed.

'Yes,' Ruby Q hurried on. 'It's a chap who was knighted for his loud modern music. My dad says he's not sure if it's worse to play or listen to his stuff but Piccolo—'

'Who cares? I want to know about Kane,' said Taylor.

'Taylor!' said Jack.

'Ruby Q's too busy now with her career,' Taylor cried. 'Everything else can go hang. And that includes her whole family and now ours.'

She turned on her heel and stormed off home.

'God, sorry, Ruby Q,' said Jack. 'I don't know what brought that on. Time of the month, maybe?'

'Oh, for heaven's sake,' Ruby Q snapped. 'If that's what they're teaching you on your courses, Jack, I'd give up on them now.'

She turned on her heel and stormed off into Elsa's house.

I say, Ruby Q. That's a bit unfair.

Ruby Q ran up the stairs. Through the landing window, she saw Jack standing alone on the pavement, staring at the sky.

You want to rush back outside and tell him everything, don't you? You want him to take you in his arms and tell you it's OK. But I know you, Ruby Q Cooper: you're too darned stubborn, aren't you? And you still find it difficult to trust anyone, even yourself.

Come on, you've got two articles to write for Shed Monthly *– one about the Sticky Rock Café launch and the other on the Piccolo interview – and a tight deadline.*

But what do I tell Cage when he calls? And Jack and Taylor?

Worry about that later. For now, grit your imperfect British teeth and do one of the few things you're able to that you have in common with your dad and Elsa – work through your troubles.

Ruby Q was tired and her mind kept returning to what di'Abalo had told her. But she struggled on and, eventually, completed the first article on the Sticky Rock Café launch, and sent it to the Editor's new email address.

She sat back in her chair and re-examined the list from Cataract, Cyclops and Mote. It recorded staff loaned to other institutions and included the names of nine women but not her mother's. She had a thought: what if her mother, possibly like Kane, was calling herself by another name? Suddenly, she saw her mother in every one of the listed names.

She stood up to close the curtains and saw on the floor one of the business cards Jack had designed. She hadn't noticed it before but he'd created a website for her. It was late but she decided to take a look. Not surprisingly, it was fun and smart, and had her own email address – which gave her an idea. She checked her bank account, looked for and found an Italian arts magazine in a web search, and went to bed.

I can't sleep with you tossing and turning. Didn't your dad tell you never to go to bed on a full stomach or an argument? Agh! It's those pesky clowns again!

Ruby Q woke up in a cold sweat, and lay in bed, thinking, until it was time to get up for breakfast.

Instead of working on the second article, Ruby Q sat on the bed, listening to Piccolo's song, 'IoU'. Of course, she knew already where Will was: in the sewers. Piccolo had told her himself. But was he trying to tell her something else, through this song? And might it throw any light on what di'Abalo had said?

As she read the words on the CD sleeve, she puzzled at Piccolo's obsession with the composer, Sir Harrison Catgut. She decided to do a web-search on Catgut but first try out the letters IOU.

Gordon Bennett! Zillions of entries! Mostly companies offering loans. Steer well clear, Ruby Q. But what's this?

An entry for the Imperial Orchestra of the Union. Grief, there's a bell ringing in your head.

I remember now: Dad said he'd never work with the IOU because they were such an arrogant bunch. Hang on, what's this on the 'Stop Press' news page – Sir Harrison Catgut!

What a coincidence!

Listen.

'Unconfirmed reports received today are claiming that twenty IOU musicians, together with the acclaimed composer Sir Harrison Catgut, are missing presumed dead in a plane crash somewhere over remote mountains in South America ...'

South America! For a split second, Ruby Q panicked. That's where her father was. But then she relaxed: his text message had arrived long after the date of the plane crash.

She read on. No wreckage or bodies had been found despite extensive searches but locals said the weather on the day of the flight was atrocious and that such tragedies in the region were not uncommon. She wondered how Piccolo would take the news of his hero's untimely death, and looked again at the words of the song.

> *Help! Save our society,*
> *Where criminals go free,*
> *Overflowing with refugees*
> *And so few are fed.*
> *Help! Save our society,*

Full of hyperbole
Riddled with allergies
Yet empty of bread.

Though life is no picnic
Call me a lunatic
Let's do our arithmetic
Before the world ends.
Help! Save our society.

I or U'll pick up the pieces
Before they all fleece us
Kill or disease us.
It's time to leave our sheds

Of ignorance before
I or U are skewered
By evildoers
Who appear to be super,
Duper, good, honest troopers.
Come, let us go free,
Help! Save our society!

Ruby Q frowned: Piccolo's song and the orchestra shared
the initials IOU. And there were other initials, in every
verse, every chorus, of the song. Save our society.

   Or, to put it another way, SOS. Is that word play?
   Or could it be a cry for help?

Ruby Q stared at the news story on the web page. Missing, presumed dead. Missing, no bodies found. Missing ...

She'd gone into Dekaydence HQ to find out about two missing people, Kane and Will. What if Piccolo was trying to tell her about missing people? Not Will, not Kane, but someone else. Someone whose name he couldn't mention. But who? And why?

You're imagining things. And I'm only encouraging you. Let's stop and get on with your work.

No, not yet.

Ruby Q went back to the words of the song.

'Who appear to be super, Duper, good, honest troopers.'

She mulled over the words.

What did di'Abalo say? 'Nothing is ever as it seems.' Well, suppose, just suppose di'Abalo and Candelskin are not as they seem. What then?

This isn't getting us anywhere. All I know is that if what di'Abalo said about Cage is true, the Martins are in for a terrible shock.

49 UNDERGROUND DEPRESSIONS

News of the attack on the Prime Minister had filtered underground. It gave the musicians something to gossip about other than their own predicament. Catgut, who'd met the PM at some function, said he wasn't the least bit surprised that someone wanted to murder the bastard. It then occurred to Catgut that, given his own predicament, someone was planning to do the same thing to him. He'd thought that he and the IOU musicians had been booked to go on tour abroad but ...

For Piccolo, hearing the news about the PM was the worst news. It meant he'd failed. He already felt he'd failed the thousands of innocent teenagers who'd soon be drawn into Sticky Rock Cafés through his music, and then would be brainwashed and lost. Now he also felt he'd failed Will.

Candelskin had told him that they'd all be freed when the fourth CD was finished. Piccolo didn't believe for one minute that Candelskin would keep his word but he knew he had to play for time, literally, until the girl from *Shed Monthly*, who seemed bright enough, deciphered what he'd told her and raised the alarm. It was a long shot, but what other option was there?

★ ★ ★

'How can you be sure we won't tell?' Piccolo had asked after Candelskin had made his promise.

Candelskin had smiled smugly. 'An antidote,' he'd said. 'Guaranteed, you won't recall a thing.'

'Like the head pad? Like the Professor's miniaturisation?'

'Best not to dig too deep, dear boy. Ignorance can be bliss, believe me.' Candelskin had adjusted his shirt cuffs, and sighed.

When the Black Tartans returned Rallan, apparently unharmed, Piccolo's mood lifted.

The big bearded man had tears in his eyes when he hugged him.

Piccolo didn't know how to react: it had been years since anyone had touched, let alone held, him with anything approaching tenderness or affection.

'Thank God, you're OK,' said Rallan.

'You too,' Piccolo mumbled, gruffly.

'They told me to keep your nose to the grindstone so as to finish the fourth CD within seventy-two hours.' Lowering his voice, Rallan continued, 'By the way, they know it was you who used Catgut's adservarum.'

50 ACTING CAGEY

After supper Ruby Q checked her emails. There were two messages: one from the Italian art magazine, confirming that her advertisement searching for the artist (and her aunt) Lily Nera would appear in the next – the Christmas – issue. The other message was from the Editor of *Shed Monthly* advising her that her article on the Sticky Rock Café launch needed 'more thought'.

Ruby Q's heart sank. Her career was over before it had begun.

Don't be silly.

The front doorbell rang and, moments later, Jack burst into her room, his face red with fury.

Ruby Q's heart sank further.

'You won't believe this,' said Jack. 'The police have raided our house. They think Cage is behind the bombing at No. 10.'

'Do you think he is?' she said, trying to sound casual.

Jack's shocked look was enough to persuade her. Almost.

'Cage couldn't harm a fly. He joined the GeeZers to save the planet for animals. He doesn't go a bundle on humans.'

'Including the Prime Minister?'

'What do you mean?'

Ruby Q's heart thudded hard against her chest. 'How do you know Cage hasn't changed? How do you know he wouldn't kill to save the planet?'

Jack stared at her. 'You don't understand, Ruby Q. When you grow up with someone, you get to know them inside out. And I tell you, Cage couldn't do it.'

Ruby Q nodded. Jack was right. What did she know about brothers or sisters?

'You're not convinced, are you? Why not?' Jack demanded.

She shrugged.

'Listen, Ruby Q, my brother's face will be plastered over tomorrow's papers. If you know something, I want to know it, too.'

Ruby Q hesitated.

Come on, Ruby Q, he's a good friend.

'Jack,' she said, falteringly. 'When I was in Dekaydence, Signor di'Abalo showed me a picture of Cage going into No.10.'

'Really? What does that prove?'

Ruby Q swallowed hard. 'Nothing, but they've also got Cage on laser, planting the bomb.'

Jack shook his head.

'I am sorry, Jack,' she said, quietly.

'Don't be!' said Jack, sharply. 'Cage is as likely to have joined the Real GeeZers and bombed No. 10 as – as our cat! This is a set-up, Ruby Q. But if they've managed to persuade you, so that you don't believe me, what chance does Cage—?'

Ruby Q sat bolt upright. 'Is Kane home yet?'

'No,' said Jack, distracted. 'But what's that—?'

'Jack!' she said. 'If Taylor is right and Kane is Stanley, it won't be long before someone makes the connection between Cage and Kane!'

Jack stared at her, stunned.

'We've got no choice, Jack. They might use Kane as a bargaining tool to get Cage to surrender. And you've seen the stuff on the web. They torture people to get information.'

'God, Ruby Q!'

'That's why we must get into Dekaydence and find Kane!'

'This is madness,' said Jack. 'Apart from anything else, we don't know for sure that Kane and Stanley are one and the same person.'

'Jack,' said a voice behind them. 'You want Ruby Q to believe you and yet you won't believe me or her.'

Ruby Q and Jack turned to see Taylor, standing in the doorway.

'The Treasures let me in,' she explained. 'I came to tell you that Cage rang. He wanted to reassure Mum that he isn't the bomber. He's safe but he won't be able to contact us for a while.'

'Thank God he's safe,' said Jack, and he slumped on the bed.

'Ruby Q's right, Jack,' said Taylor. 'We must get to Kane.'

'I don't believe this,' said Jack. 'Neither of you seem to realise we could be dealing with seriously dangerous people here. You can't casually stroll into their building. Think of the security, let alone—'

'I've got a security stud. I'm sure it'll get me in,' said Ruby Q, remembering the Dekaydence stud which she'd put away in a drawer. 'I'll go first thing tomorrow. It's Sunday. There'll be fewer people on duty.'

'This is ludicrous, but, if you're determined, I'm coming with you,' said Jack.

'Me too,' said Taylor.

They stood, in silence, each lost in their own thoughts.

'Actually, Ruby Q,' said Taylor, 'in the film of your life, which'll star me, of course, there has to be a scene where you enter the enemy camp.'

'I s'pose that makes it OK, then,' said Ruby Q.

She saw Jack look away. Right now, she realised, he was the one in need of support.

51 BACK AT THE YEW TREE

When Will returned to the Royal Palace, only one person inquired about his holiday; only one person asked why he'd returned home early and what had caused his injuries. Everyone else appeared as shocked and self-absorbed about the No. 10 bombing as the King, who was busy organising extra security in and around the Royal Palace and for the Royal Family.

Will's young cousin followed him everywhere, quizzing him about the islands, the weather and his companion. In fact, he found she'd moved into his room while he'd been away, cluttering the place with cuddly toys and trunkloads of clothes. He turfed her out and checked the monitoring equipment, ensuring it hadn't been tampered with, let alone discovered.

He tried contacting the Face, and Cage, but the lines were dead. And there were no messages. The illegal websites had been shut down and news reports, on Dekaydence channels, told of GeeZers, Real and original, being rounded up and held by the police. He felt like a compressed spring. Who to contact? What to do?

Two days after his return, he determined to visit the cemetery, a place he knew was known to the Face and Cage, as well as Piccolo.

He slipped out of the Royal Palace at dawn on Sunday morning when the family was preparing for church and few staff were on duty.

The light was as sharp as lemons and the air felt heavy, as though stunned by the heat. He kept close to anything that offered shelter. The streets were mostly deserted, but he heard noises and saw figures running or hiding between the few shadows. He had no way of telling whether they were friend or foe. But then, he reasoned, they'd think the same of him.

At one point, a limousine came roaring down the road. He dived in among a pile of stinking refuse sacks, abandoned on the pavement. The car screeched to a halt and then kerb-crawled, as if searching for something. Or someone. When it was driven off at top speed, he leapt out up to snatch mouthfuls of fresher, if baked, air.

The trees round the cemetery drooped, as lifeless as shrouds. He saw that the allotment gate had been forced open. Judging from the footprints and weeds growing up, he reckoned it had happened a few weeks before. The place seemed deserted. Nevertheless, he entered it cautiously.

The shelter had been destroyed, its contents strewn all over the dry, bleached grass. He was examining the trunk of the yew tree, finding its hiding places still intact, when he felt something brush past him.

He grabbed at it, and got hold of its throat. Whatever it was, it was wild. It fought like a tiger, kicking out and trying to bite his hand, which was trying to stopper its mouth. He dragged it to the ground and leant on its ribs. Beneath a filthy balaclava, he glimpsed its face, thick with grime. It was a child.

He might have been kinder, but only the night before, he'd seen the King's state papers: the authorities were recruiting youngsters, paying them good money to inform on siblings, friends and anyone who might be linked in any way to GeeZers.

'Who are you and why are you following me?' he demanded, angrily.

52 AN INSIDE JOB

'Why do we have to stand in for the boggin' guards with their boggin' allergies to paint?' Grout grumbled, as he and Bodkin entered Dekaydence HQ through a fire exit door, held open by a large pot of paint.

'Cost cuttings,' said Bodkin.

'But it's Sunday. Nothing happens on a Sunday, even in security.'

'It's only for an hour or so,' said Bodkin. 'Then we're off to the Test and Repair Centre. Professor's orders. We gotta replace the American accent in the Dekaydence Guides' software, and make it more Union-friendly. What do you think, Grout – Latin or Serbo-Croat?'

'I don't like being cooped up in this glass box. It's like I'm an exhibit,' said MacNoodle, looking round the Dekaydence HQ entrance lodge.

'Och, I like it,' said MacMinor, his head buried in a puzzle book.

'You would. It's about your size,' snorted MacNoodle. 'Och, I must get out. I'll take Cromarty for a walk, to stretch his wee rusty legs.'

'They're not rusty. You're just trying to make me feel guilty,' cried MacMinor, as MacNoodle set off with the haggoid. 'At least you got it back, you ingrate.'

'Good morning,' said Ruby Q, bright and breezy.

A book flew out of the Red Tartan's hand and, as he bent to pick it up, she signalled to Jack and Taylor, who slipped under the barrier.

'Och, Miss Cooper. It's you,' said MacMinor, sitting up.

'Hi,' she said. 'Could you give this letter to Piccolo? I know it's Sunday but there's an important question I forgot to ask him.'

'Nay problem,' said MacMinor, taking the envelope.

'Thanks. Have a Nice Dekaydence Day,' she said, walking off as the guard turned to answer his phone.

She ducked down, slipped under the barrier and ran to the fire exit door, where Jack and Taylor were waiting. Jack pocketed his phone and they raced up to the third floor.

A map on the newly decorated wall lit up, showing a flashing red cross.

'Good morning,' said a woman's voice, oozing a sincerity carved from syrup. 'I'm a Voice Map. How can I help you?'

'We're looking for the Blue Zone,' said Ruby Q.

'Actually we're looking for Ka— Stanley Halls,' Taylor interrupted.

Ruby Q and Jack looked at her, horrified.

'Might as well go for broke.' She shrugged.

'First right, second left, third door right,' said the Voice Map.

'And today's password?' said Taylor, casually.

'Oscar.'

'Thanks,' said Taylor.

'You're welcome,' said the Voice Map. 'Have a Nice Dekaydence Day!' The map went dark.

'Easy peasy,' said Taylor, smiling as they set off along the corridor. Ruby Q wasn't so sure.

'Intruders. Level Three,' the Voice Map announced, sharply.

'Somehow, I don't think they're on their way to church,' said Bodkin, as the monitors revealed three figures running along a corridor.

'Schedule S for Security advises contacting Mr MacCavity's office,' said Grout, reading the security manual.

'No way. McCarbon's on duty,' said Bodkin. 'That means paperwork in triplicate.'

'Schedule A for Alert says when all else fails contact Mr Candelskin,' said Grout, scrolling through data.

Bodkin grimaced. 'They're moving too fast to be decorators,' he muttered. 'So who are they and what do they want? Wait a minute – isn't that girl with the weird hair, the troublemaker, who was Blooza Jousa-ed?'

'Are they GeeZers, Mr Bodkin?' said Grout.

'I think they must be,' said Bodkin, his eyes glinting. 'Crazed GeeZers. In which case we must deal with them, mustn't we?'

A clock on the computer struck eleven. Grout stood up.

'It's time to go to the Test and Repair Centre, Mr Bodkin.'

'Someone has to wait here for a boggin' guard to show. It'd better be you.'

'Oh,' said Grout, disappointed.

'Alternatively, we could both stay and do a bit of cost-cutting of our own,' said Bodkin, feeding a disk into the computer. 'Do you know what fun is, Grout?'

Grout frowned.

'Candelskin don't know either. Which is why we tell him nothing about this. Understand?'

Grout nodded and began picking his nose.

Ruby Q heard voices at either end of the corridor.

'Quick, we're being followed,' she said.

'Oscar!' said Jack, trying a nearby door handle.

'Oscar!' said Taylor, trying another door.

The voices were coming closer.

'Oscar!' said Ruby Q, and the door nearest to her opened.

'And W is for War,' said Bodkin, sitting back in his chair.

Ruby Q, Jack and Taylor piled into a dimly lit room and shut the door. They heard voices, speaking softly, on the other side of the wall.

'What are they waiting for?' Jack whispered.

'I don't know. Reinforcements?' said Ruby Q.

'While they're making up their minds what to do, I'm going to find somewhere to hide,' said Taylor, and she walked off.

It seemed a good idea, so Ruby Q and Jack followed her.

Bodkin pressed a button. The voices outside the Test and Repair Centre fell silent.

A light flashed on the control panel. Grout went to answer the telephone call but Bodkin stopped him: it would be over soon and he didn't want Candelskin interrupting his fun.

Taylor stifled a scream.

Ruby Q did likewise when she saw the skiing automatons hanging on coat hangers on a tall rail.

And then she heard something.

'And X is for Excitement!' said Bodkin, gleefully.

The trap doors of the cages opened slowly. Something told Ruby Q that they had to quit this place. Fast. But it was too late. She saw three metal dog-like creatures moving stealthily towards them, their jaws snapping and grinding like hungry pliers. Jack put an arm round Taylor's shoulder. Ruby Q wondered how, at such a time, she could feel jealous.

'If they attack, use your rucksack as a shield and edge

to the door,' Jack commanded in a low voice, taking his rucksack from his back.

A few empty crisp packets fell out of the rucksack and drifted to the floor. One of the mechanoids leapt into the air and gulped them down. The other two yowled angrily. In desperation, Jack threw them a handful of pencils, triggering a nasty spat between all three. Ruby Q expected whoever was outside the door to rush in, but they didn't.

'Give them anything!' cried Jack, throwing down his course notes.

Ruby Q ripped pages from her notebook, which the mechanoids instantly devoured, and then spotted a half-open cupboard alongside her, full of magazines. She grabbed a handful. A mechanoid leapt up, snatching the lot from her hand.

Taylor screamed.

Ruby Q turned and saw her on the floor, struggling with a mechanoid, which was holding her rucksack in its metal teeth. Ruby Q seized more magazines, and hurled them into the air.

The three mechanoids flew at the rubbish, yowling horribly.

'Let's get out of here!' cried Jack, hauling Taylor to her feet.

'I said all along those haggoids were a waste of metal,' snarled Bodkin, adjusting a dial. 'Let's see how the kiddiewinkles cope with my new hologram.'

Ruby Q, Jack and Taylor were a metre from the door when there was a flash of light and the room vanished. They stared round in disbelief.

They were in a wide savannah. It was hot. Overhead, a flock of birds drifted lazily on an air current. One swooped towards them and, as it came closer, Ruby Q saw its huge beak open. She realised it was flying directly at Taylor. She shrieked a warning. Jack pushed Taylor out of the way and hurled his rucksack into the air. The bird squawked, flapped its wings and flew off.

More birds flew towards them, like great dark arrows.

They looked round, searching desperately for somewhere to hide, but there was nowhere.

'Get down on the ground! Hold your rucksack high!' Jack shouted, snatching a penknife from his pocket.

Taylor winced. Her hand was bleeding from the mechanoid's bite.

They heard the wind in the birds' wings, a rattle in their throats. They were that close and then ...

Nothing. Silence.

They peered out from behind their rucksacks. The birds had gone. So had the savannah. They were back in the storeroom. And the mechanoids appeared to be fast asleep.

'What's happening?' said Taylor.

'No idea, but let's not wait to find out,' said Jack, and

he led the way to the door.

Ruby Q was wrapping Taylor's hand in a handkerchief as they stepped out into the corridor.

'What's happening?' said Bodkin, as he watched the hologram disappear and felt the weight of a heavy arm on his shoulder.

He caught a glimpse of black tartan.

'We must get out of here! And quickly!' said Jack, as he closed the door. He turned round and his face fell.

Two Black Tartans holding thin dark pens, which he took to be a lot deadlier than a simple writing implement, towered above Ruby Q and Taylor, while an elegantly dressed man wearing a pungent aftershave stood near by.

'Please, don't go just yet,' said Randall Candelskin, adjusting his shirtcuffs.

As the Black Tartan hauled him out of his seat, Grout panicked and kicked some switches on the control panel.

53 WHERE THERE'S A WILL ...

Will had to find out who the child was and why it'd been following him. It was kicking at him as he held his hand over its mouth to stifle its screams. It started to gag. He rolled it over, and it gasped for breath. He was losing patience. He grabbed it by the scruff of the neck and pulled its head back so that it couldn't shout out.

'Who are you? What do you want?' He lifted his fist, and then wondered what the hell he was doing, thinking of striking a child. What had he come to? The child raised a feeble arm to protect itself.

'It's me, dumbo,' it gasped before passing out.

For a moment, he stared at the small limp figure dressed in rags. He ripped off the balaclava and saw the halo of dark curls surrounding its face. He felt his soul freeze. He saw it now. Somehow, this bedraggled filthy creature, lying unconscious at his feet, was his studious little cousin, who'd filled his room with her teddies, who was so polite and respectful. He saw it now. Why not before?

'What in God's name are you doing?' he cried, as he tried frantically to revive her.

54 THE WHITE ROOM

In his panic, Grout had inadvertently set off a cacophony of fire alarms, water sprinklers and Voice Maps, which startled everyone, except Jack. He hurled his rucksack at one Black Tartan and lunged at Candelskin, shoving him into the other guard. Candelskin fell to the floor, screaming. Jack was horrified to see in his own hand a penknife covered in blood.

'Quick!' he cried, dropping the knife, and he took off down the corridor.

Taylor followed.

Ruby Q was too stunned to move, until Candelskin shouted at the guards, 'Don't let them get away!'

Ruby Q sprinted after Taylor and they both raced after Jack, who was way ahead of them. They ran along the corridor, down steps and into another corridor, the guards not far behind. They saw Jack turn a corner, followed and found themselves alone in a passageway littered with paint pots and dustsheets.

'Down here!' Jack's head popped up out of the floor.

They clambered into the hole and Jack threw a dustsheet over the trapdoor before snapping it shut. They crouched in the narrow space between floor and roof, scarcely daring to breathe. Seconds later, they heard boots marching to and fro overhead. The guards were searching the rooms. Ruby Q reckoned it wouldn't be long before the dustsheets were removed.

The light from Jack's torch revealed a staircase leading down into darkness. The footsteps were directly above them. Jack nodded and they hurried down the steps. They hadn't gone far when they heard the trapdoor being lifted. They quickened their step until they found themselves at a dead end, on a narrow ledge, alongside a train, its carriages packed with children.

'It must've stopped between platforms,' said Jack. 'Quick!'

They scrambled along the ledge and climbed into the empty caboose on the end carriage, crouching down below the balustrade. The train set off as the two Black Tartans arrived on the spot where they'd been standing seconds before.

'I wonder where we're going?' Jack whispered.

Neither Ruby Q nor Taylor said a word.

The train drew into a station. They saw a sign: 'The Globe: alight here only for the Palace of Dekaydence'.

'Stay down,' hissed Jack.

On one platform, crowds of youngsters were disembarking. On the platform opposite, more youngsters waited to board the train; among them were two Red Tartans.

'This way,' said Jack, and they joined the crowd of arrivals.

They headed for the escalators with the Adventurers but, at the top of the staircase, they saw more Red Tartans. Jack veered off, leading them through an open slatted door into a small store cupboard. Ruby Q and Taylor squatted among the brooms and buckets, as Jack took a bunch of keys from the wall and began trying each key in the lock.

'Do you think you killed him?' said Taylor.

'I don't know,' said Jack, busy with his task.

'Maybe you just wounded him,' said Taylor.

'Look,' said Jack, sharply, 'I forgot I had the penknife in my hand. Anyway, they were trying to kill us.'

Ruby Q said nothing. She didn't think it was quite the moment to tell Jack he'd attacked Randall Candelskin, di'Abalo's right-hand man. But it was odd, she thought: she'd have sworn Jack could never do such a thing.

Isn't that exactly what Jack said about his own brother?

Yes. Worrying isn't it? Makes me wonder what might provoke me to attack.

Elsa?

Be serious.

Jack was staring at something through the slats. Ruby Q followed his gaze. It was one of the mad, dog-like creatures, with blazing red eyes. Suddenly, its metal teeth tore a chunk out of the door.

Taylor gasped.

Jack shot her a furious look.

'They're nay here, Mr McCarbon, sir. We've checked everywhere.'

Ruby Q recognised MacMinor's voice, and jumped as a long thin leathery tongue reached through the slats to within millimetres of her face.

'Are you sure, MacMinor?' snapped McCarbon. 'And what is wrong with that infernal mess of wiring, MacNoodle?'

'Sorry, sir. It's the haggoid's software, sir,' said MacNoodle, hauling the mechanoid back from the door. 'This one had the sporran off Mac—'

'That's enough,' McCarbon shouted, rattling the door handle.

Jack quietly slid his foot against the bottom slat.

'I want everywhere checked again. So find those lazy Sassenach cleaners and get the keys for this cupboard,' snarled McCarbon, kicking the door before marching off with all but two Red Tartans.

'Surely we'll get overtime for this?' said MacMinor.

'Och, there's no telling you, is there, MacMinor man?' MacNoodle sighed, and they walked off, dragging the yowling haggoid behind them.

Tartan voices echoed all around.

'And we still haven't found Kane,' said Taylor, unhappily.

'I'm sure he'll be fine,' said Ruby Q.

She didn't delude herself that Taylor believed her. After all, she didn't believe herself.

In fact, Ruby Q didn't know what to believe any more. Not many weeks before, she'd felt lonely, friendless and down in the dumps. Then she'd found friends who'd got her a job in journalism. She'd discovered the place where her mother had worked once and learnt of an unknown aunt. She'd helped choose Stanley Halls for the Dipstick Five and her first article for *Shed Monthly* had been a hit. She'd heard from her dad, and had an interview lined up with the Prime Minister and an exclusive with the Face. She'd been on her way.

Now where was she? She'd messed up her first-ever mission for the GeeZers. It appeared she was in league with the would-be assassin of the Prime Minister. She'd put a friend in an intolerable position and he'd committed a murder.

Don't forget, your writing has gone to pot.

Thanks.

Ruby Q sank back, depressed, into the overalls hanging on the cupboard wall. They had a delicious scent of marzipan.

'Jack!' whispered Taylor. 'Ruby Q's disappeared!'

'Don't be silly,' said Jack.

'Jack!' Taylor insisted.

Jack looked round. He couldn't deny it: Ruby Q had disappeared.

Grief, what happened?

We're in another store cupboard. The floor went spinning. I must've leant against something.

Ruby Q tried to find a lever, anything, to make the floor rotate and take her back. But in vain. She called out to Jack and Taylor. But in vain.

How about panicking?

No.

There was nothing else for it, Ruby Q told herself after a moment's thought: she'd have to return by another route. It mightn't be the best of disguises but—

She slipped on an overall, picked up a mop and bucket, and walked out of the cupboard on to a spiral stone staircase.

I'd go up.

She hadn't gone down more than a few steps when she heard music. It was one of her favourites: Dido's lament. The music enveloped her as an embrace, drawing her to it. She reached the bottom of the staircase and stood in a small, poorly lit hallway. The music was coming from behind a heavy wooden door. She was holding the handle when she noticed a metal grille in the wall, high above her head. If she upturned the bucket and stood on it, on tiptoe, to check things out ...

The room was bright, everything in it dazzlingly white, except a tetrahedron-shaped glass container, about two metres high, which stood on a white plinth. Two men in white coats sat at a control panel.

Someone screamed.

It was a girl, about her own age. She was being dragged across the room by two Black Tartan Guards. She was sobbing and struggling as the Black Tartans took her into the glass tetrahedron and strapped her to a glass cross.

The guards left, the doors slid shut and as a metal crown, packed with wires, descended on to the girl's head, Ruby Q saw that the Dekaydence stud in the girl's ear was flashing, as Will's had done. The music grew louder, drowning her cries. Ruby Q wanted to bang on the wall, to rage through the grille, but she knew it would be of no use.

The light in the tetrahedron grew brighter. So intense that Ruby Q had to look away. When she looked again, the light had dimmed. She covered her mouth to hold back her own scream: the girl was hanging limply on the cross, a childlike smile on her face. The stud had stopped flashing.

The two men at the control panel were shaking their heads as they studied some data when a man in a dark suit she hadn't noticed before stood up and uttered a piteous cry that sliced through her ribs and pierced her heart. He turned and Ruby Q saw his face: it belonged to Lorenzo di'Abalo.

She almost fell off the bucket. What was going on? Had they killed the girl? And if so, why? Was this what they'd done to Will? Would this be Jack and Taylor's fate, if they were caught? She must get back to the cupboard; she had to find them. Whatever was going on, she had to get them out of this place.

She ran as fast as she could up the staircase, flight after flight, beyond where she'd been, until she came to a door. It was locked. A key was hanging near by on the wall. She listened. Nothing. No noise from the other side of the door. And no one was following her. Yet. She took the key, turned the lock, and slowly opened the door ...

Oh no! We're in the Great Hall of the Palace of Dekaydence, surrounded by hundreds and hundreds of Adventurers. The noise is excrutiating.

OK, so we'll mingle. And merge into a group leaving the building.

'Lookie, lookie, we got a rookie!' said a familiar voice. 'The carrot brain's got a cleanin' job. Or has she come back for more trouble?'

Innit stood there, the dark-eyed girl on his arm, a sneer on his lips.

'No, but I s'pose that's why you're here,' Ruby Q retorted.

'What else would I be doin' 'ere? Stamp collectin'?'

The girl sniggered.

Ruby Q bridled: once, she'd been a keen collector.

Look, you've got better things to do than argue with this creep. Like getting us out of here.

''Ere, where you goin'? It's crunch time!' said Innit,

cracking his knuckles.

Ruby Q tried to lose herself in the crowd. She heard Innit behind her, jostling others out of the way. He was a big lad in a big bad mood and no one wanted to argue with him.

She was two strides from the Fanged Doors, Innit and his girlfriend not many steps behind, when the doors snapped shut.

What now?

I don't know.

There was a drum roll, the lights dimmed, and the huge TV monitors focused on the great elemental sculpture in the centre of the hall, which was dissolving into a mist of gold and silver stars.

'It's a new game!' Innit shouted excitedly to his girlfriend.

At least he's distracted. But what about us? How do we get out?

Through the door. It'll open again when this finishes.

A stage rose into the air, out of the glittering mist.

This looks familiar.

A spotlight fell on a figure, striking a dramatic pose, and everyone in the room but one went wild.

'Stanley! Stanley! Stanley Halls!' they screamed at the handsome young man in pyjamas, dressing gown, boots and baseball cap skewed sideways, who was grinning from ear to studded ear, punching the air and blowing air kisses.

Get ready to run for the door. Ruby Q, are you listening?

Despite her plight, Ruby Q couldn't help but smile at Stanley.

'Stan's the Man who will Shed his stuff!' shouted the Adventurers.

'Hiya, people! How y'all doin'?' Stanley drawled into a microphone.

'Fine!' responded the hall of Adventurers.

'I'm here on my ownsome,' Stanley sighed, dramatically.

Adventurers aaghed, sympathetically.

'So there ain't no live music,' said Stanley.

Adventurers booed good-humouredly.

'But, hey, any moment, you'll be watching our new DVD! And buying our new CD which goes on sale today, right here!'

There were cheers and whistles of approval.

'But guess what? We got a lucky winner here today!' said Stanley.

'Ooo!' cooed the crowd, excitedly.

'Bet you didn't even know there was a competition!'

'No, we didn't!' yelled several Adventurers, while the rest laughed.

'Well, there wasn't a competition!' Stanley chortled. 'The winner was chosen for their shoe size or something!

No one tells me nuffin'!'

The Adventurers roared with laughter.

He is good, isn't he? But get us closer to the door. Now!

'And our lucky winner has no idea who they are until – *now*!' cried Stanley, punching the air.

Ruby Q!

Adventurers applauded and looked around expectantly, which was when Ruby Q realised two Red Tartans were standing behind her.

Oh no!

'Oh yes! This lucky Miss Adventurer has won free membership of the Palace of Dekaydence until her eighteenth birthday!' said Stanley, cheerily. 'And she gets to meet the Dipstick Five, including *me*!'

'Listen,' Ruby Q cried out. 'There's a girl. She's hanging on a glass cross. She's ...'

But the Adventurers were too busy cheering to hear her words.

The Red Tartans escorted her into a hovering black Orbobubble.

'Bye bye and buy buy! And next time it could be you, you, you!' Stanley shouted, as the stage descended into the ground and the giant elemental sculpture re-formed.

In the Black Orbobubble, Ruby Q heard the Adventurers cheer as the Dipstick Five appeared on screen, performing their new CD. She was in a daze.

A few weeks ago, everything had seemed relatively straightforward. Now she didn't know who or what to believe – who really was fighting to save the planet and who was not.

Dekaydence had launched the Sticky Rocks as an initiative to help save the planet, which was great, but what was going on underground in the dazzlingly bright white room? Whatever it was it looked anything but great. Signor di'Abalo was certainly right about one thing: nothing was ever as it seemed.

The Orbobubble sped through the Palace and out of the Globe, landing in the Palace's country park, alongside a Red Tartan Bus.

There, between three Black Tartans, she saw Jack and Taylor.

They look relieved to see you.

Believe me, the feeling's mutual.

'No talking,' said a Red Tartan, as Ruby Q opened her mouth. 'Or sign language,' as Taylor made a gesture.

They were led on to the bus, to the upper level, where a man sat at the front, his back to them.

'It's the competition winner, sir, and the other two,' said a Red Tartan, saluting.

Ruby Q sniffed the air as the man turned and smiled.

Ruby Q, Jack and Taylor gawped.

'Hello there,' said Randall Candelskin.

55 FIGHTER

Will cursed the fact that he had only basic first-aid skills. But his young cousin was a fighter in more ways than one and it wasn't long before they were able to make their way back to the Royal Palace.

The journey was uneventful: it was Sunday morning and, as usual, the capital was bustling with crowds intent on soothing their sorrows at car boot sales, supermarkets, DIY stores and, rarely, places of worship.

His young cousin spoke little and he asked nothing. It was only when they were standing in the corridor outside her room that she put a finger to her lips and beckoned him in. As he closed the door quietly behind him, she kicked him hard in the groin.

'Jesus!' He crumpled up with pain.

'Pay-back for what you did to me in the cemetery!' she spat at him, eyes ablaze. 'But don't worry, it's a one-off. I don't hold grudges.'

'What the—?' Will gasped, struggling to stand up.

'You don't get it, do you?' She had the look of a wild cat.

He collapsed into a chair.

She was right beside him. 'For all your A-grade exams, you can't suss it out, can you?'

He looked at her through narrowed eyes: what did

she know?

'Look,' he snapped. 'Whatever you want to say, spit it out, because I'm tired, in bloody pain no thanks to you, and I want to go to bed.'

'Don't treat me like a moron. I've saved your skin,' she retorted.

'What are you talking about?'

'God, for a clever clogs you're dumb! Do you think I enjoyed living out of suitcases, surrounded by stupid bloody toys, in your squalid little room while you were away?'

Will looked confused.

She hit her forehead in disbelief. 'I moved in with boxes of my stuff to protect your equipment — that is your spying equipment — from prying eyes. I made a huge mess so that no one would want to come into the room, let alone get in to snoop around.'

Will stared at her.

'Look, dumbo,' she said, impatiently, 'I know you're a GeeZer. I've known for ages. And when you said you were off on a Highland fling, I knew you must be off on some secret mission. I thought I'd cover for you. Get it? God, I don't know why I bothered.'

Will was trying to absorb what she'd said. After all, this was his little cousin who'd always looked the picture of innocence, and acted so.

As if reading his thoughts, she tossed her head. 'I am twelve, you know,' she said, haughtily. 'Years that is, not months.'

56 EVERYTHING'S FINE AND CANDY

'I-I thought J-Jack had—' Ruby Q stammered.

'Killed me?' Candelskin suggested, fingering his torn jacket. 'He did the next best thing. He ruined my Maccaroni.'

'Maccaroni!' Taylor gasped. 'He designs only six suits a year, one for someone in each of the six continents. How absolutely ghastly for you.'

'Quite,' said Candelskin. 'Nevertheless, I felt I had to come and offer you my sincere thanks.'

What?

'Sorry?' said Ruby Q. 'Thanks for what?'

'For alerting us to the enemy within,' said Candelskin.

Jack and Taylor looked blankly at Ruby Q, who shook her head.

'And I have to offer you our most sincere apologies,' Candelskin continued. 'Overall, it must have been a truly terrifying experience.'

I think I've missed something somewhere.

'As you know, Dekaydence is committed to helping youngsters get back into the community. Unfortunately, you encountered a young criminal unable to change his ways.' Candelskin gave a sad little smile. 'But for you,' he said, 'we might never have discovered that Bodkin was a viper in our midst.'

'You mean we ran away for nothing?' Taylor demanded.

'Alas, yes,' sighed Candelskin, glancing out of the window as the Tartan Bus travelled from the Palace of Dekaydence towards the City.

'The Voice Map automatically alerted Security that we had intruders, but a computer blip meant it took a while to pinpoint your whereabouts. By then, you'd taken to your heels. Understandable in the circumstances but quite unnecessary.'

'So, why the celebrity show back there?' Ruby Q nodded at the Palace of Dekaydence.

''Fraid it's a bit of a trademark of mine,' said Candelskin, adjusting his shirt cuffs. 'Making a crisis out of a drama. Adrenalin rush, and all that. The opportunity to put more Wagner into life, if you take my meaning.'

Ruby Q cringed.

Yuck! Wagner reminds me of those waxy overblown plants Elsa keeps imprisoned in the greenhouse.

'But, while you've kindly alerted us to certain security lapses,' said Candelskin, 'there is the little question of what you were doing inside Dekaydence without authorisation.' He regarded Ruby Q, quizzically.

'It's my fault,' she said, blushing. 'I forgot to ask Piccolo an important question. When I dropped off a letter at reception, it suddenly seemed too good an opportunity to miss. I thought I could just pop in and ask him for myself. And I asked my friends to come with me.'

'You need only have asked me,' Candelskin sniffed.

'I didn't think you'd work on a Sunday,' mumbled Ruby Q.

Candelskin nodded. 'Best we draw a line under the entire episode and get you home,' he said. 'I'm sure you're keen to have a wash and a bit of a brush-up. I'll order the limousine, but not to worry, we'll put dustsheets on the seats.'

Taylor's eyes lit up at the mention of the word limousine.

Ruby Q said nothing. She couldn't erase the vision of the girl hanging on a glass cross in a white room, not many metres below a playground where thousands of children came to have fun. And she still wondered about Cage and Will.

'Randall, don't sulk, dear boy. It doesn't become you. The girl reporter is not my confidante: you are,' said di'Abalo, stroking the black cat and flicking languidly through a magazine. 'At some time, look at your horoscope. It promises you fabulous riches and clothes.'

Candelskin nodded.

'Tell me how the Prime Minister is coping,' said di'Abalo.

'Very badly,' said Candelskin.

'Excellent. The sympathy vote will be a bonus.'

'No, you haven't heard the latest,' said Candelskin. 'The Prime Minister's wife is out of the coma. She's seriously injured but she's alive.'

'Ah!'

'The Prime Minister is furious,' said Candelskin, lowering his voice.

Di'Abalo shrugged. 'She may yet die.'

Candelskin adjusted his shirt cuffs. 'That remains his preference, Signor.'

57 HEIR TODAY

'Why should you want to cover for me?' Will asked his cousin.

'How can you ask me that question?' she snapped, sitting down on the bed. 'I support the GeeZers. How could I not?'

'I see.' He nodded.

'The thing is, Will,' she said, 'you don't see.' She got up and went to sit on the arm of his chair. 'You think it was your decision to come and live with us. Yours, and maybe your mother's. But it wasn't. Grandpa, the King, decided.'

'Even if that were true, which—' Will began.

'Look at yourself,' she ordered, fetching a mirror from a table.

For the first time that evening, Will laughed. So did she.

'OK,' she said. 'You're not exactly camera ready. Especially with that gaping hole in your ear. But you are a good-looking man, Will. And you're bright and nice. For the most part.'

'What are you driving at?'

'You're a threat, Will.'

'A threat?'

'You still don't see it, do you?'

He shrugged.

She gave him a pitying look.

'Will, you're a threat to my father and my brother succeeding to the throne. That's why Grandpa brought you down from the Highlands. He wants to keep an eye on you. He wants to keep you away from the wild tartan men plotting in the north. You know the story: if my great-grandfather hadn't killed his older brother, your great-grandfather—'

'That's an old wives' tale,' said Will, dismissively.

'Like the tales spread about Tommo? That he was a stupid, wild drunk. Don't say it's never crossed your mind that your brother was murdered by my grandfather?'

Will shut his eyes and looked into a dark empty space.

'Will,' she whispered. 'You know there are those who believe you're now the rightful heir to the throne.'

She knelt before him. 'And I'm one of them.'

Will sat motionless, his eyes closed, in silence.

'That's why you've got to get out of here, Will,' she urged. 'It's not safe for you. If they ever found out about you and the GeeZers, the King wouldn't hesitate. I think he's itching for an excuse to have you murdered.'

Will opened his eyes and, for the first time, saw fear in her eyes. He took hold of her shoulders.

'Would you run away, if you were me?'

She went to speak but found she couldn't.

He smiled. 'That's your answer. I have to stay here. The GeeZers, or whatever's left of them, will need me. If we don't carry on fighting for the planet, my brave fiend, the day won't be far off when there won't be a crown to inherit, there won't even be a kingdom.'

58 ESCAPE HATCH

If they knew he'd used Catgut's adservarum, they'd probably intercepted his message to the Face, thought Piccolo. He was safe only because they needed him. For as long as they needed Shed Music.

Given the episode with the octopoid, he'd grown nervous about using a tunnel as a possible escape route. And he'd given up on the girl reporter. Even if she'd cracked his coded message, who could she go to for help? Chances were, Piccolo decided, the authorities knew what was going on inside Dekaydence. There was no one who could save them, except perhaps the GeeZers. And that would happen only if Will had escaped.

Piccolo didn't want to admit it, even to himself, but he doubted Will had made it out.

His mind went round in circles.

He was working less than half-heartedly, as if in a dream, or rather a nightmare, longing for the day's end when the wire attachment released him into a paradise. Was this what Bianco had meant by the Promised Land? The trouble was, Bodkin no longer performed the task. Grout came alone. Or accompanied by another equally incompetent white-coated assistant.

Which was why, one night, when he was screaming at the Big Bloke standing over his father's dying body, Piccolo thought he heard his father calling to him.

'Piccolo!'

He tried to reach out to his dad but something held him back.

'Piccolo!'

Piccolo opened his eyes and the Big Bloke and his dad disappeared. He found he was drenched in sweat, the head plug loose on the pillow. Rallan was standing over him, his hand on Piccolo's shoulder, as an Eye-Spy hovered close by.

'You're OK, son. You're OK,' said Rallan, soothingly. 'It must have been one hell of a nightmare.'

Piccolo sank back, exhausted.

If only it had been a nightmare, he thought.

It was the next morning, when he and Rallan were on breakfast duty, unpacking the delivery hatch, that Piccolo had the idea. It shot through him like a bolt of lightning. Why hadn't he thought of it before?

'What's up?' said Rallan. 'You look like a dog with two tails.'

There were several musicians around and the Eye-Spies hovered close by. Piccolo said nothing but nodded at the delivery hatch.

Rallan followed his gaze. He looked puzzled.

Piccolo moved his eyes slowly up and down.

It took a few seconds for Rallan's frown to change to a grin.

'Go for it,' he said, under his breath.

'You could come with me,' Piccolo whispered.

Rallan shook his head. 'I don't think so,' he said softly, tapping his belly. 'But do me a favour – when you get out?'

''Course,' said Piccolo. 'After I call the cops.'

Rallan gave a melancholic smile. And Piccolo knew then that Rallan shared his doubts: that in all likelihood there was no one out there who could help, save the GeeZers.

'I'll give you a phone number,' said Rallan. 'I need to tell someone I'm sorry.'

59 AT HOME WITH A HAGGOID

The moment the limousine drove off, Ruby Q told Jack and Taylor everything. About the White Room. About the IOU website, Sir Harrison Catgut and the plane crash. And everything di'Abalo had told her about Cage and Will being Real GeeZers.

'I don't believe this,' Jack exploded.

'There's more,' said Ruby Q. 'The girl in the White Room was wearing a Dekaydence stud, identical to everyone else's, except hers was flashing. Like Will's.'

'Maybe they flash when the cell life is low,' said Jack.

'I don't know,' said Ruby Q. 'But at the end of it all, the girl had the same loopy smile as the Dekaydence Guides.'

Jack frowned. 'Are you saying that this glass box makes people loopy?'

'I don't know. I can't figure it out.' Ruby Q shrugged.

'But why, Ruby Q?' Jack persisted. 'And how?'

'I've no idea but—'

'You think they've used it on Kane?' said Jack, suspiciously.

'No!' cried Taylor.

'I don't know,' said Ruby Q. 'But we should warn

him – get a message to him, or go back in and tell him face to face. Whoever he is.'

'I don't want to go in there ever again.' Taylor shuddered.

'None of us does,' said Jack. 'Is there anything else, Ruby Q?'

'Yes,' said Ruby Q. 'Piccolo asked me to look at his song, "IoU". It keeps repeating words with the initials SOS. I couldn't work out what it might mean. Then I remembered Candelskin said that Piccolo was staying at Dekaydence so that they could keep an eye on him during his detox programme. But I think they're holding him prisoner.'

Jack whistled through his teeth.

'I think we all need a cup of Mum's herbal,' sighed Taylor.

Ruby Q, Jack and Baghilde, the Martins' cat, followed Taylor into the Martins' house. As she reached the kitchen door, Taylor muffled a scream and took a step back. Ruby Q and Jack looked over her shoulder.

A Red Tartan Guard stood at the kitchen window with his back to them, a haggoid lying at his feet. The cat, its tail standing up like a stiff brush, rushed into the kitchen, yowling.

The Red Tartan spun round to face them.

It's Stanley Halls! Or is it ...?

'Kane!' cried Taylor, and ran to give her brother a hug.

'What on earth are you doing here?' Jack spluttered.

'I live here, remember.' Kane grinned, speaking in his regular south London accent. 'Mind the haggoid, Taylor. And lay off, Baghilde.'

'Did you escape?' asked Ruby Q.

'What?' Kane chuckled, a dimple appearing in his cheek.

'How did you get out?' said Jack.

Kane yawned through a laugh.

'They had a works outing to the Palace of Dekaydence and I didn't fancy it. Thought I'd pop home and see Mum. And when a guard said he'd give anything to be in my shoes – well, he's about my height, so we swapped clothes and wallop.'

'You hit a Tartan Guard, too?' said Taylor.

'No,' said Kane. 'MacNoodle's me mate. Why should I hit him? He even leant me his pride and joy to show Mum. Didn't he, Cromarty?' He gently nudged the prostrate haggoid.

'Mum'll be pleased,' said Jack, sarcastically.

'But they're vicious machines. Look at my hand!' cried Taylor.

'You must've teased it,' said Kane, ''cos they're pussycats.'

'That aside,' said Ruby Q, 'how did you leave the building?'

'I grew wings and flew over the ruddy walls,' said

Kane. 'What d'you think I did? I walked out through the gates like us normal persons tend to do.'

'So no one stopped you?' Ruby Q persisted.

'Why should they?' said Kane.

'Because, Kane Martin, wicked things are going on in Dekaydence,' said Taylor. 'And talking of wicked things, why didn't you tell us what you were up to? Why did you tell Dad you were staying with a friend?'

'I didn't,' Kane protested. 'I told him that a Red Tartan had invited me in for a cup of tea and a singsong. Things kinda progressed from there. Candelskin will tell you. He lent me his adservarum.'

'So the adservarum might've been fixed,' said Jack, knowingly.

'Did they put you in a glass container?' demanded Taylor.

'Well,' said Kane, slowly, 'I did sneak a go in Candy's flotation tank.'

'Kane, I must tell you what's going on in Dekaydence,' said Jack.

'Later, bro,' said Kane, picking up the haggoid. 'I need a few days off. I can't cope with being happy 24/7. It's too draining at my age.'

He was at the door when Ruby Q thought of something.

'Kane, has your security stud ever flashed?'

Kane roared with laughter. 'I recognise you now. You're the one who wrote the article, aren't you? Well cheeky that was. I loved it.' And he was out of the door.

'At least he's home, safe and sound. And we don't have to go back to that horrible place ever again,' sighed Taylor, sitting down at the table.

'Yes,' sighed Jack, slumping down beside her.

'Didn't you hear what he said?' Ruby Q demanded.

They stared at her, uncomprehending.

'He said he wants a few days' rest.'

They looked blank. 'Which means he's planning to go back.'

They stared at her, horrified.

'He won't go back when he hears what I have to say,' said Jack.

'Want a bet?' said Ruby Q. 'I doubt he'll believe a word you say.'

'Why ever not?' said Taylor.

'Because he won't want to,' said Ruby Q. 'He's a natural performer. I don't believe he could give it up. Whatever we said. After a few days, he'll miss it and go back. Or worse, they'll come looking for him.'

'God!' Jack exhaled.

'So what do we do?' said Taylor.

Ruby Q shrugged.

'We watch him,' Jack announced, firmly.

'Good. Include me in any rota.' Ruby Q stood up. 'But not tonight. I must get my articles done to give to your dad first thing tomorrow.'

'Best push off then,' said Jack, not unkindly. 'And good luck.'

'Yes,' said Taylor. 'I hope you don't have to work too late.'

Ruby Q hoped so, too.

When she got home she realised that she never did discover anything about Kane's stud. Or if he'd experienced the White Room.

Even if he had, would he remember?

60 BURNING ISSUES

It's been a day and three halves, but you must do the Piccolo interview and rewrite the article on the Sticky Rock Café launch.

I'm not in the mood. The screen's a blank and so am I. And why am I doing this when there are hugely more important issues to tackle?

As in the White Room? Your mum, dad, Auntie Lily, Kane, Cage, Will, Catgut? Not to mention the planet?

In a nutshell, yes.

It's harder now you know something's wrong at Dekaydence and suspect more, but deadlines cannot be missed.

OK.

Ruby Q began the rewrite of the Sticky Rock Café launch article. In words, she painted pictures of the day, the scenes, the people. It wasn't easy, but she persevered, until she reached the end. She set to work on the Piccolo interview, building the article, bit by bit, with quotes from the composer and descriptions of how he looked and behaved. Eventually, after checking and revising both, she printed off a hard copy for Mr Martin to take to the office and emailed a copy to the Editor.

She stood up, stretched and went to the window. It was dark outside. The only sound in the house came from the old clock ticking in the hallway. She realised she'd missed supper and any chance of getting something from the locked larder. But what ate into her deeper than hunger was loneliness.

She hadn't heard from her father for days. She hadn't seen Elsa, let alone talked to her. The Treasures were kind but they were always busy. And while it was great to have Jack and Taylor as friends, at the end of the day they had their own family. Ruby Q riffled through the fading memories of her mother, wondering, not for the first time, if she'd done something to send her mother away.

Was that someone at the door? No, but there's a tray of food and today's Daily Unigraph. *Good old Treasures.*

As Ruby Q devoured peanut-butter sandwiches, milk and a slice of fruitcake, she flicked through the newspaper. There were endless stories on rationing, shortages, cuts, increased taxes and the new anti-GeeZer police squad. Something caught her eye and she turned to the business section.

It was the lead story: the Company of Dekaydence had won the King's Award for Industry for its continuing research work into wayward teenagers, and di'Abalo was rumoured to be in line for a peerage.

Ruby Q dialled Jack's number. The line was busy.

She waited and tried again. It was still busy. She couldn't wait. She slipped out of the house and, on the pavement, bumped into Jack and Taylor.

'I was trying to ring you,' said Jack.

'I was trying to ring you,' said Ruby Q.

'Jack, for heaven's sake, tell her what's happened,' said Taylor.

'Is it Kane?' said Ruby Q, seeing the shock on their faces.

'No,' said Jack. 'Have you heard the news about Dekaydence?'

'I've just read it. That's what I was coming to tell you. Di'Abalo's set to become a peer of the realm.'

'No, that's not it!' cried Taylor. 'Dekaydence HQ is on fire!'

'What?'

Images of Piccolo, Will, the Dipsticks, the Red Tartans, Candelskin and di'Abalo flashed through Ruby Q's head.

'They've no idea how many are trapped inside,' said Taylor.

'Di'Abalo and Candelskin are safe. Apparently, they weren't on site,' said Jack. 'But guess what? It's all over the news, on TV, radio, and in the early editions of the papers: GeeZers are to blame.'

So was di'Abalo right? Is this the work of the Real GeeZers, and Will?

'I must get over there,' said Ruby Q.

'What for? And what about the curfew?' said Jack.

'Jack, I've got to go.'

Jack and Taylor exchanged looks.

'I must look for Piccolo.'

'If it means that much to you,' said Jack. 'We'll go, but—'

'If Kane drives, it means we could keep an eye on him,' Taylor suggested.

'With his driving, we'll need to,' Jack muttered. 'First, we'll have to persuade Dad to lend us the car.'

'Leave that to me,' said Ruby Q. 'Come on.'

Mr Martin was slumped in front of the TV, with beer and an Arsenal football match, and needed little persuasion that Ruby Q's copy had to be delivered that night to the Editor's home. He'd quite forgotten the curfew.

Kane proved more difficult. He wasn't happy to be woken up. And he wouldn't budge unless the haggoid came with him.

'Where are we going?' he yawned, starting the engine, as the haggoid set to work gnawing on an old spanner Jack had found for it.

'Near London Bridge,' said Jack, vaguely, switching on the radio. 'Lost and Found' floated out and Kane cheered up sufficiently to sing.

There were roadblocks everywhere but, with an old map, Jack directed Kane to a street about a mile from Dekaydence HQ. They parked. Even at that distance, they felt the heat and saw the flames leaping high above the tall buildings. Clouds of bitter black smoke billowed towards them and the crowds, which included hundreds of near-hysterical teenagers, pressed against the heavily manned barriers.

Rumours were as rife as the police cars, fire engines and ambulances filling the surrounding streets. Someone shouted, and the throng was moved further back for fear of collapsing buildings and gas explosions.

Jack looked at the map. 'This way,' he said, and he led them into a side street.

'I know where we are,' said Kane. 'At least, I thought I did.'

Oh my word!

The Company of Dekaydence HQ was engulfed in flames, and firefighters, struggling to contain the fire, were being beaten back by the heat.

'God!' said Kane, holding the haggoid, which strained at its leash.

'What now?' said Taylor.

Jack shook his head.

'Listen,' said Ruby Q.

'I can't hear—' said Jack.

'Shhh!' hissed Ruby Q.

Above the haggoid's yowls, she heard a familiar sound.

'What is it?' whispered Taylor.

But Ruby Q had darted off down the road. They followed but she reached him first. He was leaning, unsteadily, against the wall. He was covered in soot, and his face was bleeding.

'Piccolo,' she said. 'It's Ruby Q Cooper. We met ...'

Taking the instrument from his mouth. Piccolo nodded slowly.

'Are you OK?' she said.

Yes, it is an idiotic question but someone has to ask it.

Piccolo nodded again.

'Is anyone else with you?'

'No,' he said, his head lowered. 'Not one of them.'

Oh, no.

'You mean Catgut and the IOU were in there?' said Ruby Q.

The look in his eyes was answer enough.

My God, Ruby Q! That is what SOS meant!

And I missed it. I was too busy listening for what I wanted to hear.

'How did you get out?' said Ruby Q.

'The delivery hatch, but it got stuck. I waited and – and then, I don't remember. There was an explosion but – oh, I dunno.' Piccolo stumbled over his words.

'Hey, Pix,' said Kane, in his Stanley Halls American accent.

'Stanley?' Piccolo peered at him.

'Yeah, how ya doin', man?'

'How d'you escape?'

'I was kinda out already, taking the haggoid for a walk,' said Kane.

Piccolo nodded.

'Hey, man, I hadda thought,' said Kane. 'If you've got no plans, you could come home with us. Chill out for a bit.'

Piccolo stared at him. 'Your mum a good cook?'

'The best,' said Kane, proudly.

'Your dad a good man?'

'He has his moments.'

'Then you're a lucky man, Stanley Halls. And don't forget it,' said Piccolo. 'But I got to get moving.'

'Man, are you sure?' said Kane.

'Yeah,' said Piccolo.

'But it's cold and it's wet and you're hurt,' Taylor blurted out.

Piccolo's glare silenced her.

'Is there anything we can do for you?' said Ruby Q. 'Perhaps give you a lift somewhere?'

'No, someone's coming for me,' he said.

'OK, if you're sure,' said Ruby Q, doubtfully.

'Would you like this little ol' haggoid for company, Pix?' said Kane.

'Piss off,' said Piccolo, with a quick smile.

'OK, man. But you take care, Pix, d'you hear me?'

'If you need anything, call me,' said Ruby Q, handing Piccolo a business card.

'Sure,' said Piccolo. He hesitated and then spoke quietly so that only she heard his words. 'There is one thing you can do. The Sticky Rock Cafés – they're a con. Investigate them, Ruby Q Cooper. They ain't as green and friendly as they seem. They's deadly, they is ...' His voice trailed off. Something in the distance had caught his eye and he moved off.

'Piccolo,' Ruby Q called out. 'Piccolo.'

'No more, man,' he said angrily, rounding on her. 'You do your job and just leave me alone.'

Somewhat taken aback, she watched him go and then, with the others, headed back to the car.

'It's daft to leave him there,' said Taylor, as Kane drove off.

'What could we do?' said Jack. 'Drag him home against his will?'

'But he's hurt,' cried Taylor. 'It's not right, we should—'

'Shut it,' said Kane, sharp and south London again. 'Give it a rest. Think about the poor sods who've been killed. When I wake up some more, it'll scare me witless, 'cos one of them could have been me.'

The rest of the journey was spent in silence.

When they got home, Elsa's house was locked and bolted and in darkness.

'Stay with us, Ruby Q. Mum won't mind,' said Taylor.

Too tired to argue, Ruby Q accepted, gratefully.

Before she turned off the bedside light in the Martins'
spare room, she checked her phone. Instantly, she
was wide awake. She had a text message from her dad.
Another of his golden oldies. A track from *The Crazy
World of Arthur Brown* – 'Fire!'

That's what I call spooky.

61 PICCOLO'S PACT

Piccolo could've sworn he'd seen someone in the distance but no one there was there. Not that he was expecting anyone to come for him. Neither was he expecting anyone else, friend or foe, to come out alive from the rubble. And he did want to be left alone. He wanted to think about what he should do. Where he should go. He wanted to stay in the shadows, waiting, until it hurt less to breathe.

He thought of the old days, when his mother and the Big Bloke used him as a punch bag. It was a wonder he had any bones intact. It was a wonder he'd survived.

But he was determined to survive some more. He wasn't cut out to be a GeeZer. All he wanted to do was to play and compose. Surely there must be some place he could do that?

When he thought of Will, his mind reacted like fire on dry grass, and he had to keep stamping on the ideas that came – that his friend had died in the inferno or been killed, or worse, by the guards.

He decided to return to the cemetery. It was the only place he knew. And the only place where he knew Will would come for him, if he could.

He made his way, agonisingly slowly, along the

roads by the river, halting when anything stirred. The streetlights were out but he had to be careful. If it came to it, he couldn't run, let alone climb a high wall.

At one low point, he almost wished he'd accepted the girl reporter's offer of help. He decided to call her the next day or the day after. Whenever his mind was clearer. She'd obviously understood his message about Catgut and the IOU, but too late. He tried not to think about how and why he'd survived while the rest, including Rallan, had perished. One day, he decided, he'd tell their story, as well as his own.

Eventually, he walked through the allotments and arrived at the cemetery gate. A lemon segment of moon revealed the place to be deserted, and as untidy and overgrown as ever. He sank to his knees and propped himself up against a gravestone. This was home to him. Here, he'd found friendship; here, he'd grown up.

And here, he made a pact. With whomsoever might be hanging out in any old heaven. He vowed that he'd never see Will again, on condition that Will was kept safe.

He closed his eyes.

He dreamt he was cocooned in dark, soft warmth. That he was lifted up and carried across London, swooped down and into the ground, and laid gently on the floor. He heard distant voices.

'What's this? It looks half-dead, apart from that damn

flashing stud.'

'It's the musician I told yous about. The friend of your beloved Will.'

'Cut it, Bianco.'

'OK, man, OK.'

'What am I supposed to do with it? Casserole it?'

'Thought he might come in useful.'

'How?'

'"If music be the food of love, pl—" Christ!' Bianco wiped the cold soup from his hair. 'For a peacenik, you've got a nasty streak, Face!'

'I got plenty of nasty streaks, Bianco, especially for dealing with people like you who have a foot in both camps and a conscience in neither.'

They were sitting on the floor, opposite Piccolo, the Face busy on an adservarum.

'I've been thinking,' said Cage, quietly.

The Face switched off the adservarum, and began chewing on a twig.

'Yeah?'

'The time's come to fight fire with fire.'

'Explain.'

'We need marketing, Face.'

'Have you gone raving mad?'

'Listen, we're getting nowhere. We need a higher, better profile and journalists sympathetic to our cause.'

'Bullshit!'

'And we need a symbol. Something simple that'll go on everything we do, on every surface in the land. So that no one is in any doubt who we are, where we are and what we're doing. We need to drop leaflets by the ton, we need T-shirts that we can sell and—'

'And music?'

'Yes,' said Cage. 'And music.'

The Face spat out a piece of bark in Piccolo's direction. 'Hence the special delivery?'

Cage shrugged.

62 WALKING BACK TO HAPPINESS

Ruby Q woke early, and wondered where she was. Then she remembered the events of the previous evening. Could it really be true that four Dipsticks were dead? Along with Catgut, the IOU and countless others? If only she'd realised what Piccolo was trying to tell her. Perhaps if she'd told di'Abalo about Will's message. But then who to believe? If the Sticky Rocks were a deadly con, were they linked to the White Room?

If, if, if! That's a great way to beat yourself up. Get back to reality: Mr Martin needs your articles in five minutes.

But if the Dipsticks are dead ... And the Sticky Rocks are—

Look, you can't do anything at the moment except focus on your priority which, as a professional journalist, is to deliver your copy on time.

Ruby Q dressed hastily and rushed next door. Handing over the envelope, she realised Mr Martin knew nothing of the Dekaydence fire and had quite forgotten that she was supposed to have delivered her copy to the Editor the previous evening. Mr Martin was in his own heaven: Arsenal had beaten Manchester United by an unprecedented three penalty goals.

When she returned home, Ruby Q found that the Treasures had laid out her breakfast, but she was hungry only for news of the Dekaydence disaster. It was the lead story in *The Daily Unigraph*: at least a hundred people were thought to have died in the fire, including all the Dipstick Five.

So no one, except us, knows that Kane went missing.

There were pictures of the blazing buildings and of Candelskin, looking sombre, while an outraged editorial condemned all GeeZers. There was a pull-out supplement on the Dipstick Five, with news that profits from Shed CDs would be donated to the Sticky Rock Café project.

The hall clock struck eight and the telephone rang. It was Young Miss Burgess at *Shed Monthly*.

'Hello, Miss Cooper. The Editor wants you to write a tribute to those poor young men, for next month's edition. She's in a crisis meeting but will be in touch with you after lunch.' She blew her nose.

Crisis meeting? Of course, the death of the Dipsticks means the end of Shed Monthly *and Mr Martin's job. And yours, Ruby Q.*

'But there is some good news, dear,' said Young Miss Burgess, briskly. 'The Features Editor on *The Daily Unigraph* was on the phone yesterday. She'd like you to write for them— Hello, dear? Are you there?'

Ruby Q, did you hear that?

'Yes. Goodness. I can't take it in,' said Ruby Q.

'Understandable,' said Young Miss Burgess. 'The Editor says if you want to discuss it with her, she'd be more than happy to advise.'

'That'd be great,' said Ruby Q.

'Oh, and she said your copy for this month was excellent, though quite what we're going to do with it ...'

Will you still get paid?

What a question at such a time!

You've got to eat, Ruby Q.

Mmm.

Ruby Q poured herself a coffee.

A job with The Daily Unigraph*! Well done, old thing!*

The doorbell rang and Jack and Taylor walked in.

'Hi,' said Ruby Q. 'Want a coffee or something?'

'No thanks,' said Taylor, sitting down.

'We've got something to tell you,' said Jack, standing stiffly.

'Me too,' said Ruby Q, excitedly.

'We'll go first,' said Taylor quickly, nudging Jack.

'Yes.' Jack coughed. 'I've been surfing this morning. Looking at the website of the Imperial Orchestra of the Union. They've added a name to the list of missing musicians. Ruby Q – it's your dad's name.'

'What?' said Ruby Q.

What's he saying?

'I think your dad was in Dekaydence with the other

IOU musicians.'

Ruby Q shook her head. 'Not possible. I had a text from him last night when we got back.'

'Ruby Q,' said Jack, 'check the time the message was sent. The website was updated this morning. It says one of musicians on the trip with Sir Harrison Catgut fell sick and had to be replaced – at the same time your dad went away.'

Ruby Q couldn't speak.

'I checked the Musicians' Union rules on their website,' said Jack. 'They can register only one drummer called Rallan Cooper on their books at any one time until—'

'Until he dies,' said Ruby Q, impassively.

She sat in a trance. She saw her father reading to her, mending her bike, laughing uproariously and waving goodbye.

'Are you OK?' said Taylor, nervously. 'I mean ...'

Her words bounced off the bubble Ruby Q felt she was in.

'Ruby Q?' said Jack.

Ruby Q looked vacantly at Jack and Taylor.

'The text message he sent, it makes sense if—'

'What did it say?' said Taylor.

'"Fire"!' said Ruby Q, and she stood up.

'I've got to go to Dekaydence HQ,' she said.

'I don't think that's a good idea, Ruby Q,' said Jack.

'Jack, my dad isn't dead!' she cried. 'I know it. But

I must check out Dekaydence. I have to take a look around!'

'OK, OK,' said Jack. 'But I'm coming with you.'

'Me too,' said Taylor.

I know you're right, Ruby Q. But what if we're both wrong?

Jack spoke to the Treasures before he set off with Ruby Q and Taylor to catch a bus to London Bridge. They travelled in silence, Ruby Q staring out of the window.

It seemed the long hot summer was coming to an end. Great dark clouds scudded across the sky and a wind rippled the river. A large black bird was cruising high above on a current of warm air. A lucky sign, she thought, and she wished herself to be the bird, seeing and feeling the world from a different perspective.

They arrived to find the site looked markedly different from the previous night. The barriers had gone and the Company of Dekaydence HQ lay in smouldering ruins, cordoned off by yellow ribbons. A lone policeman stood on duty under what was left of the entrance archway, with one word remaining of the company's title – 'Dekaydence'.

'This way,' said Jack, and Ruby Q and Taylor followed him down a side road, deserted but for an old white van.

The   boundary   walls   remained   intact   and

impenetrable, but behind a dense mass of ivy, they discovered an old door. Jack hacked at the thick tendrils round the frame and all three leant against it until the door budged sufficiently for them to squeeze through.

They stepped into a grey landscape of smoke, brick and dust, once the company's courtyard, where, remarkably, the Fountain of Fire still stood, gushing not proud red talons of fire but a thin spiral of black smoke.

A flash of lightning streaked across the darkening sky.

'Whatever we do, we can't be seen doing it,' said Jack, nodding at the policeman. 'So, keep close to the boundary wall.'

Jack led the way. It wasn't easy trying to clamber quietly over rubble. And neither he nor Taylor realised that Ruby Q had headed off in another direction.

She went to sit on the base of the Fountain of Fire.

Perhaps your dad didn't like to admit to you that he was playing with an orchestra he'd told you he despised.

All I can think of are his messages: 'Help!', 'We Gotta Get Out of This Place' and 'Fire!' If Dad was a prisoner here, like Piccolo, he was trying to get me to help him, wasn't he? I could've saved him!

It was raining heavily but Ruby Q's face was already wet with tears. She stared out across the courtyard and saw a figure in a dark hooded cloak standing on the opposite side of the road, beyond the building, the cordon and the policeman. She knew who it was. It was the one person who could tell her for sure that her father had not been underground with Catgut and the IOU. It was Piccolo.

He was beckoning to her. She scrambled over the rubble, heading for the entrance, slipping and slithering on the debris. But she didn't care. The sun was coming out from behind the clouds and, on the other side of the road, Piccolo was waving to her. Laughing and crying with joy, she waved back.

'I'm coming,' she cried. 'Wait for me. I'm coming!'

Jack, Taylor and the policeman were scrabbling over the rubble towards her, shouting, but Ruby Q had eyes and ears only for Piccolo.

She was soaked by the time she reached the entrance. She slipped under the cordon and stepped on to the pavement. He was there, on the opposite side of the road, his hood drawn up against the driving rain, waiting for her. His arms were outstretched, as if ready to embrace her.

A rainbow appeared above his head like a halo, the seven glorious colours shimmering in the sunlight. Red, orange, yellow, green, blue, indigo, violet. Such a beautiful sight. Ruby Q felt her very spirit laugh, sing and soar like a bird. She stepped off the pavement and ran towards him.

She heard a yowl. She heard a horn. She smelt burning rubber and heard a screech of brakes. She heard a scream.

Ruby Q!

The sun was warm on her face when she opened her eyes, and she was dimly aware that it had stopped raining. A young woman in a paramedic's dark green uniform was kneeling at her side, smiling and saying something she couldn't decipher. Jack, Taylor, Kane and the policeman were staring down at her. She heard something else.

'Cromarty.' She mouthed the haggoid's name.

But someone was missing.

'Get this device out of the way,' said the paramedic, sharply.

Ruby Q heard the haggoid yowl as it was dragged away.

'I must—' she said, trying to sit up and failing.

'You must not, young lady,' said the paramedic, firm but kind. 'You lie quite still until we make sure you're OK.'

'I'm fine,' said Ruby Q, although her brain felt like meringue. She closed her eyes. She was back in her bubble, with voices floating by.

'She thought her father was in there,' she heard Jack say.

'Ah, terrible business, sir. Terrible.'

That's the policeman.

'Amazing – the driver didn't stop.'

That was Kane.

'Shame none of us got his number.'

Someone sighed.

That was you, Ruby Q.

'Jack,' said Ruby Q, opening her eyes.

'I'm here, Ruby Q,' said Jack.

'Where's Piccolo?'

'I don't know. Why?'

'He was here, Jack,' she said, struggling to get up.

'Please keep still, young lady,' said the paramedic.

'Jack, he was here, on the other side of the road. He was waving to me. I was running— Ouch!' Ruby Q clutched her head.

'I'll take a look, Ruby Q,' Jack said, soothingly.

Ruby Q closed her eyes. Voices drifted in and out of her head.

'Has she got concussion or something?' said Taylor.

'I don't know,' said Jack. 'Something's wrong. She said Piccolo was here. But you saw: the road was deserted. There was no one else about. No one, until Kane and the haggoid appeared.'

'Yes,' said Taylor. 'Thank goodness the Treasures sent him to come and find us. I never thought I'd be so pleased to see a haggoid.'

Taylor paused for a moment. 'Jack,' she said. 'I know this sounds stupid but that white van was heading right for Ruby Q until Cromarty ran across the road towards her. I think the van swerved only to avoid hitting the haggoid.'

Jack said nothing.

He's looking up at the sky, Ruby Q. The sun is shining but dark clouds are rolling eastwards up the river towards us. It'll rain again. Or maybe it won't. Jack is realising that nothing in life is certain. And that there are things in the world he doesn't understand and maybe never will.

'OK,' said the paramedic. 'We're taking her to hospital. One of you can come with us in the ambulance and the others can follow in the car.'

'Oh, Ruby Quby!' sobbed Taylor. 'Will she be all right?'

'We'll have to wait and see,' said the paramedic, gently.

Ruby Q sighed. Her eyes were shut but she saw the dark clouds overhead. She knew it was raining again as Jack climbed into the ambulance and sat alongside her. And she knew that Kane was following on in the Treasures' car, with Taylor and the haggoid.

The ambulance is setting off. The blue lights are flashing and the siren is silenced so that you're not disturbed, Ruby Q.

Yes, I know. As I know that the policeman standing under the Dekaydence archway is pulling up his collar to keep dry.

As I know that, on the opposite side of the road, a

figure in a dark hooded cloak is watching me as the ambulance turns the corner. I know it isn't Piccolo. A gust of wind lifts the hood and, for a moment, I see a mop of thick curly yellow hair, a white face with heavily painted black features and an improbably wide, bright red grin.

Ruby Q!

Don't worry: they can't hurt us now.

63 TWELFTH NIGHT

Flurries of snowflakes drifted through the night over London and past the windows of the Globe. But in the penthouse's dining room overlooking the river, the seven people attired in evening dress were warmed by a magnificent fountain of fire in the corner of the room, as well as by the delicious food and wines served by the attentive waiters.

Seated at a table decorated exquisitely in the traditional red, green and white of the Christmas season, they were bathed in the light of myriad candles and enveloped in chamber music played, discreetly, through hidden speakers.

'More champagne, Prime Minister?' said Lorenzo di'Abalo, raising his golden goblet and lowering his voice. 'Or should I say Mr President?'

'Not official yet, Signor di'Abalo,' the Prime Minister replied, with a nervous smile, as the waiter replenished his goblet with vintage Dekaydence champagne.

'But a foregone conclusion, Prime Minister. Why, tomorrow my own papers and TV channels will tell me so,' said di'Abalo.

'Really?' The Prime Minister's eyes glistered.

'Oh yes. Your name will be known throughout the

Union, and indeed, way beyond.'

The Prime Minister gurgled with pleasure and downed another goblet of champagne. He was holding out his glass for more when the guest sitting to his left poked him in the ribs.

'You want to watch him, that Signor Diabolical, or should I say, Lord di'Abalo of Croy Polloi, that hell-hole in souf London,' said Petty Masters, chewing loudly on a cream cracker. The fashion designer was in party mood; her voluminous white tulle ball gown was embroidered with road signs and on her head was a small red-and-white traffic cone, which matched her flashing earrings.

On her other side, Candelskin grimaced and adjusted his shirt cuffs.

The Prime Minister smiled and gazed across at the auburn-haired woman in the dark green dress, seated between His Mediumness, the Crown Prince, and the Scandinavian photographer chappie. Not that it mattered, thought the Prime Minister, but he was a single man, almost. It was only a matter of time.

'Explain yourself, Miss Masters,' di'Abalo laughed, rekindling everyone's good humour.

'Oh, I shall, Signor Diabolical,' retorted Petty Masters, tossing her head. 'It's all well and good, sittin' here celebratin' the Sticky Rocks' success in the sluggin' Union, but look what you give me for Christmas – you with your alleged gift for presents.'

She emptied the contents of an old plastic bag on to the table, and out tumbled a pair of exquisite red shoes, with tall, spindly ebony heels.

'If anyone here enjoys mountaineerin', they can have 'em. I like to keep my feet on the ground,' she said and, hitching up her skirts, she waved in the air a thick-stockinged leg, at the end of which was a hobnailed boot.

Candelskin and the Prime Minister stared, aghast. The Crown Prince guffawed. Lars Sparks and the dark-haired woman sat impassively.

Di'Abalo applauded and laughed. The guests relaxed.

'Ah, Miss Masters,' said di'Abalo, gesturing to a waiter. 'Allow an old man to indulge his fantasies, once in a while. In any event, I hope you'll accept this, a gift for Twelfth Night from your Malvolio.'

A large parcel was placed on the table in front of her. Stuffing several crackers into her mouth, she began ripping away the exquisite yellow silk with yellow and green silk flowers. She tore open the box and looked inside. Her eyes widened. Carefully, she extracted a pair of antique deep-sea diving boots.

'They've been distressed especially for you,' said di'Abalo.

There was a ripple of applause. Petty Masters gazed at the boots, her eyes shining in happy wonderment. Candelskin breathed a sigh of relief, and the Prime

Minister eased his neck in his collar and downed more champagne.

A waiter placed a gift before each of the other four guests. Each present was wrapped exquisitely in silk, with silk flowers and ribbons, in colours from the rainbow.

The auburn-haired woman held up a necklace on which hung a heart-shaped diamond that sparkled in the candlelight.

'Allow me,' said di'Abalo, rising as Phlegm moved his chair.

'Thank you. It is very beautiful,' she said, in a deep, slightly accented voice, as di'Abalo fastened the clasp. She lifted her head and swept a renegade lock of hair back from her face.

The Prime Minister watched her, entranced. For a moment, he forgot the card in his hand promising his gift, a delivery the next day of a hundred bottles of vintage Dekaydence champagne.

Di'Abalo went to the window and watched as the other guests unwrapped their presents. Candelskin hastened to his side.

'Neat,' cried the Crown Prince, pressing a silver inaudirum into his ear. 'Hey, it's playing the Shed Music songs from the summer.'

'I prefer the latest sound from the GeeZers' group, Rome's Burning,' said Lars Sparks, taking from a box a black cashmere sweater even more exquisite than the one he usually wore.

The Prime Minister looked up, alarmed.

'They make a good sound, don't you think?' Lars looked at the auburn-haired woman. who met his stern gaze.

'Indeed, Herr Sparks, but perhaps ...' She lowered her voice. 'This is not the best time to talk of such matters.'

'And why should that be?' said Lars.

'We are trying to keep it quiet, at least until after the election,' said the woman, leaning towards him, 'but the Prime Minister's remaining son has had a breakdown, and they think he's involved with the GeeZers.'

'Ah.' Lars nodded.

Across the room, Candelskin was telling di'Abalo that intelligence sources suggested that the boy, Piccolo, was writing the songs for Rome's Burning, but he sensed di'Abalo's mind was elsewhere.

'I didn't realise you were going to invite her,' said Candelskin, nodding to the auburn-headed woman.

'Ah,' said di'Abalo.

'The Prime Minister seems to like her,' Candelskin persisted.

'So it seems,' said di'Abalo. His eyes flashed mischievously. 'Randall, you're not fretting because you think I've forgotten to buy you a present? As if I could, dear boy. After all you've done for me.'

Randall looked abashed.

'You're not to open it until you get home,' said di'Abalo, handing Candelskin a small package wrapped in all seven colours of the rainbow. 'And I won't have you worrying. Piccolo is no longer of any importance to us and alas, Randall, accidents happen. It is a tragedy but also a housekeeping measure. We console ourselves with the fact that the Dipstick Five are more valuable to us dead than alive. And we move on, dear boy, we move on.'

It was after midnight when the party broke up and the limousines returned guests to their homes.

Humming an obscure piece of Wagner, Candelskin unlocked the front door of his fashionable London townhouse. It had been a successful evening. Di'Abalo was even more a man at the centre of things, courtesy of his – Candelskin's – good offices.

Now, with the Prime Minister elected President of the Union, they would be moving into a bigger league. It would be an adventure. A time to relish more power. Candelskin smiled. For his reward, he knew, he wouldn't have to wait until he got to heaven. He decided on a celebratory drink before retiring.

He wandered into the drawing room, switched on the lights and froze.

'Good evening, Mr Candelskin. We meet again,' said a man sitting on one of his delicate Louis XV chairs.

Candelskin knew him at once: Geach.

One of Geach's men watched over him as he packed a small suitcase before they took him to their offices, below ground, somewhere off Piccadilly. He was allowed one communication.

The voice at the other end of the telephone caught him unawares. It was the auburn-haired woman. But before he could say anything, di'Abalo came on the line. Candelskin could tell from his voice that he already knew the news.

'This time, Randall, it is not possible to get you off,' said di'Abalo.

'But it means prison. It means …' Candelskin felt his palms, the back of his neck and, worst of all, his armpits begin to sweat.

'Randall,' said di'Abalo. 'You know I am with you always.'

Candelskin didn't trust himself to speak.

'Randall,' commanded di'Abalo. 'I shall not forsake you. Ever. Do you understand?'

The line went dead.

Candelskin covered his head with his hands, and gave a strangled sob.

It was much later, after they'd ripped the security stud from his ear, after he'd journeyed through shock, despair and terror, and he was sitting alone in a prison cell in clothes made of a rough cheap fabric that chafed his skin, that Candelskin remembered di'Abalo's gift which, for some reason, he'd packed. They'd scanned and examined it, returning it to him with a knowing smirk. He took it from his suitcase.

It had been rewrapped carelessly but still the bright colours of the crumpled packaging contrasted starkly with his cheap, gloomy surroundings. He pulled at the flowers and ribbons to discover he was holding a small, leatherbound and obviously rare old book. He opened it and stared at the title page, uncomprehending. It was a bible.

As the dark-haired woman left the room, the cats reclaimed the ivory sofa.

Di'Abalo, his bowtie loosened and jacket discarded, stood by the window, watching the lightning flash across the sky.

Phlegm entered the room quietly, with a goblet on a silver tray, and crossed to the Fountain of Fire.

'It'll be hard for Mr Candelskin in prison,' he said, holding the goblet into the flames.

'Indeed,' said di'Abalo, staring into the dark sky. 'But it'll be good for his soul.'

Phlegm nodded, and held out the tray.

Di'Abalo smiled his singular smile as he took the fire-filled goblet.

'Not long now, Phlegm,' he said, kindly, and swallowed the raging flames to the last smouldering drop.

64 NEW YEAR RESOLUTIONS: PICCOLO

Piccolo has lost track of the number of safe houses they've stayed in and how often he's been woken in the night to get up and out, then and there. Everyone sleeps on piles of old newspapers and everyone's body is a permanent suitcase, for speed of movement and so as to leave no trace behind. Sometimes he imagines the scent of apple blossom but that's all it is, imagination, and he wonders if Bianco made it to the Promised Land.

Sometimes, like tonight, when faced with yet another mud-coloured vegetable broth and a bitter winter's night, Piccolo's taste buds insist on reminding him of the mouth-watering Dekaydence sweets and hot puddings. And that sets him thinking, mostly of Will.

'You're a miserable sod,' the Face snarls at him.

Piccolo says nothing. He's learnt to keep his mouth shut.

The Face gets up off the floor and begins pacing round the bare room, lit only by the icy light from the moon pouring through the window.

'Why don't you piss off?' the Face snaps. 'Now that you know who Will is and where he is. You could live together happily ever after.'

Piccolo carries on slowly eating his soup.

'Save your energy, Face, for the planet,' says Cage, wearily.

'God, I'm sick of the lot of you,' the Face shouts, storming out of the room.

Piccolo breathes a sigh of relief. He's never understood women. His mother had been a mystery and now the Face—

'Don't let her get to you,' says Cage, quietly.

'I try not to, but she won't let up. And I don't now why.'

'You don't see it, do you?' says Cage. 'She's jealous. She doesn't seem to know it, or else can't admit it, but she fancies Will something rotten. She's jealous of your friendship. And now that the music you've written has raised more funds for us than we could've dreamed of ...'

Piccolo nods, rubbing the aching wound on his ear, which they'd made removing the stud.

'Does she ever see him?' He tries to sound casual.

Cage sighs. 'Not any more. Maybe he found her too much of a control freak. As some of the rest of us do.'

They sit in silence, sipping their soup.

'You've no idea how jealous she is of you, have you?' says Cage.

Piccolo shakes his head.

'When we made contact again with Will, she ordered

us not to tell him that you were here.'

Piccolo looks stunned.

'That's love for you, Piccolo,' says Cage.

Piccolo says nothing.

'You could contact him yourself,' says Cage.

Piccolo shakes his head.

'Why not?'

Piccolo shrugs. What would a prince want with a pauper? Besides, Piccolo has made a deal with the Almighty, and he isn't about to risk breaking it. If it keeps Will safe.

'It's time I moved on,' he says.

'Home?'

'No!'

Cage hesitates for a moment. 'Will knows you're safe, Piccolo,' he says. 'I told him.'

Piccolo nods. 'Thanks.'

'Does that make a difference?' Cage asks.

'No.'

'So what will you do? Where will you go?'

'Somewhere I can get some peace and quiet,' says Piccolo.

'Sounds good,' says Cage, wistfully.

'Yes,' says Piccolo.

'OK, my turn to wash up,' says Cage, picking up the bowls. He smiles, a dimple forming in one cheek, and leaves the room.

Piccolo listens to the departing footsteps and swiftly

goes to his newspaper bed and takes out the Face's adservarum, which is hidden in the newssheets. He tries the number he knows by heart. Nothing. He's texted and emailed the address on the card the girl reporter gave him. If only he'd known that she was Rallan's daughter. He could've said something, offered her some comfort.

Something in the newspaper catches his eye. He smooths out the creases. According to the article, a Dekaydence TV crew, filming in a remote South American jungle, has come across Sir Harrison Catgut and the missing IOU musicians wandering about in a complete daze. After a medical, they are to be flown home.

Piccolo feels his pulse rate soar. They didn't die in Dekaydence! It might be a fantastical Candelskin-fabricated story, but they're out. They might be drugged, in an antidote-induced daze, but they're free. Candelskin has kept his promise. And Rallan will be reunited soon with his daughter.

Suddenly, Piccolo knows exactly where to go. The only place where he's able to play and compose. Where he'll be understood or, at least, accepted. He smiles: he might not get much peace. Despite Sir Harrison Catgut's boast of living in the remote depths of the countryside, Piccolo can't imagine for one moment that his ego would allow him to do so quietly.

65 NEW YEAR RESOLUTIONS: RUBY Q

Someone has forgotten to switch off the lights on the Christmas tree. Ruby Q knows that it's the same person who forgot to take down the tree on Twelfth Night. She knows that while patients sleep, soundly or otherwise, the nurses are in the staff room, gossiping and making hot chocolate in what are the early hours of the morning.

She's been in hospital since summer.

At least, part of her is there.

She smelt the flowers the Treasures brought her regularly. She heard Young Miss Burgess tell her that Dekaydence had bought *Shed Monthly* and everyone's job was secure. Elsa brought in a copy of her latest novel and Taylor told her that Kane had gone to America to seek greater fame and fortune. Jack told her that Piccolo was composing underground music for the GeeZers, who Cage admitted were in a bad way because of the rise in numbers and strength of the Real GeeZers.

But there's no news of Will.

Jack told her that Catgut and the IOU musicians

hadn't been killed in the Dekaydence disaster and were, allegedly, returning from South America. Which means she'll soon see her dad.

He also told her the breaking news of a volcanic explosion in Yellowstone Park in the USA, which has wiped out much of the West Coast and caused tidal waves and havoc throughout the Pacific. A million or so have been killed, millions more injured. A shocked American President has declared a state of emergency, while scientists on a newly re-established illegal website are predicting worse to come.

'I've also come to say goodbye,' says Jack. 'I can't wait any longer. I must join the GeeZers, before it's too late. Taylor will tell me how you're doing. Unless you want to tell me yourself, Ruby Q.'

He waits but, as usual, Ruby Q says nothing and, eventually, he leaves. Ruby Q remains inside a bubble in her head. She's there, but only in part.

But I'm still here, Ruby Q. Watching out for you. Like now. I can see a figure in a green velvet hooded cape slip into the ward. I can see a figure, but not the face. The figure brushes past the Christmas tree and something falls to the floor. It stoops to pick it up and hurries on light feet to the end of the bed where you're lying, attached to tubes and wires. A hand reaches out from under the cloak and puts something on the bedside cabinet; it goes to brush a lock of hair from your face but hesitates and then withdraws back into the cloak.

'Wake up, Ruby Q Cooper,' the figure whispers, softly.

Did you hear, Ruby Q?

'Wake up,' the figure repeats, more urgently. 'There's not much time left.'

The figure looks round the ward, like an animal scenting the wind for signs of trouble, hears something and is off, through the fire escape, into the night. Agh! There are two clowns, dressed as nurses, and one of them is heading straight for you!

'Wake up, dearie,' a voice pleads.

Ruby Q doesn't move. Her eyes and body are still.

'Anything new?' says a second voice.

'No,' sighs the first.

'I don't know why they don't pull the plug,' yawns the second. 'It's a waste of hospital resources.'

'Shame on you,' the first tuts. 'What if she were your child?'

The voices move off, arguing quietly.

Ruby Q stirs. She's had long enough in her bubble. She opens her eyes. It's hard to focus but she sees two nurses at the next bed.

I swear to you, Ruby Q, there were clowns here.

I believe you. I saw them too in my dream.

You weren't dream—

I also dreamt I had a visitor. I heard her voice, smelt her perfume. I couldn't see her face but I knew it was my mother.

But ...

Something on the bedside cabinet catches Ruby Q's eye. She thinks it must be a decoration from the Christmas tree: it sparkles so much. Unsteadily, she reaches out to touch it. It's extraordinarily pretty, a necklace, with a glass heart, which catches the light, reflecting all the colours of a rainbow. She frowns, trying to remember something.

She decides to get up. She has a lot to do. Her father will be home soon. And now she's convinced that she'll find her mother before too long. She must contact the Features Editor on *The Daily Unigraph*, to pursue the offer of work. She knows she has to find out what's going on in Dekaydence, in the White Room and the Sticky Rock Cafés. Something deep down tells her that the information will be vital to the GeeZers in their fight to save the planet.

66 NEW YEAR RESOLUTIONS: WILL

The sun is casting a honeyed light over the frost-covered grounds of the Royal Palace. There isn't a breath of wind to stir the few clusters of snowdrops or the ancient oak trees in their winter skeletons. Will is lying in a boat, becalmed in the middle of the lake, adjusting his new adservarum, a Christmas present from his mother in Scotland.

The Prime Minister, dressed in mourning black, watches him from the window of the Armageddon Conservatory.

'What is he doing?' he asks the King.

'Nature studies,' the King replies.

'You don't think—'

'He is monitored, Prime Minister, as you know, and he behaves impeccably, which makes me wonder about your spies.'

'Sir?'

'I am not having the Armageddon Conservatory torn to pieces, Prime Minister, on flimsy, so-called intelligence.'

Will, watching them on the adservarum, breathes a

sigh of relief. So does his contact at the other end of the line.

'Sir, you will recall, we found cameras hidden in the state room.'

The King snorts. 'Put there by your own Ministry of Internal Defence, I understand.'

The Prime Minister looks startled. He coughs nervously.

'Don't think I don't have my own sources of intelligence, Prime Minister, even far away in the Union,' says the King, with a knowing smile.

The Prime Minister blinks and returns a blank smile.

'But I shall miss our little *tête-à-têtes*,' sighs the King. 'Certainly, it'll feel mightily odd having the country run by a firm of accountants instead of a Prime Minister and Chancellor of the Exchequer.'

Will sits up.

'Cataract, Cyclops and Mote are the country's *top* accountancy firm,' says the Prime Minister, haughtily, 'with offices throughout the world. They'll be reporting daily and directly to my office in the Union. And the savings to the UK's economy of not having a Chancellor, an Exchequer, index-linked pensions and health care – Well, we'll be able to afford more guards to protect your majesty and your throne.'

The King nods.

'Cataract, Cyclops and Mote work for your friend, don't they? Lorenzo di'Abalo?'

'I believe so, sir.'

The King sighs. 'No doubt, you need a change of air,' he says, awkwardly.

The Prime Minister stands staring at the boat.

'Will your daughter go with you?' the King inquires.

'I'm not sure,' says the Prime Minister. 'If my poor wife had lived ...'

The King nods at his butler standing in the corner, who steps forward with a tray, on which sit two tumblers of whisky.

'Please ...' says the King.

The Prime Minister takes a tumbler and swallows deep.

'Bad business,' says the King, frowning. 'Damnable GeeZers!'

In his boat, Will grits his teeth.

'Which is why, sir ...' says the Prime Minister, indicating Will.

'Look to your own, sir,' growls the King.

The Prime Minister blushes a fierce beetroot colour.

It's Will's turn to smile, albeit grimly. The new IWs are full of it. The Prime Minister's elder son, Jesus, is reported to have gone mad after his mother and young brother were killed in the explosion at No. 10, and is on the loose, with an insatiable taste for the blood of those he believes guilty.

Will switches off the connection to the conservatory.

'Well, Mr Smith, what now?' says Cage, from the other end.

'Well, Mr Smith,' Will replies. 'What do you think?'

'Infiltrate the world's top accountancy firm?'

'Why not?'

'Understood,' says Cage. 'Mr Smith, do you think it wise to remain in your lodgings, given the inflammable objects surrounding you?'

'Aye,' says Will, softly. 'To fight fire with fire, Mr Smith, you must live within fire, the better to understand it.' He closes the connection.

As he rows back to shore, Will thinks of his brother, Tommo, rowing him across the loch last spring. Less than a year ago, yet it seems like an age. What has happened since? Who else has died? Scores of teenagers in the Dekaydence blaze, including the kennel boy, and millions in America and beyond, while millions more face a future limited by a dying planet, caused by the ignorance and arrogance of adults.

Like most other politicians in the world, Candelskin and the Prime Minister seem blinded by a voracious hunger for power. But the ordinary man and woman in the street, who take their information from newspapers and TV owned mostly by the Company of Dekaydence ... Will frowns. Beyond working hand-in-glove with the government, and now the Union, to control young people and eradicate the GeeZers, what other evils might Dekaydence be up to? And why?

As he clambers on to the moorings and ties up the boat, he thinks of Piccolo, in the countryside, living his dream, playing and composing. Will feels a rush of envy, which he hurriedly pushes away. He doubts he'll ever be able to return to his quiet life in his beloved Highlands. And now it's even more dangerous to rekindle a friendship.

There is much to do. His brother had known something about Dekaydence and had been prepared to put his life on the line to prove it. It was a brave act but Will realises bravery isn't enough. Not now. Maybe it never has been. It is cunning that is needed. And ruthlessness. And other qualities Tommo hadn't possessed. But which Will now realises he does.

What would his brother have said, he wonders, if he'd known that his kid brother, who loathed blood sports and lived with his head in books, had committed himself to the cause of the Real GeeZers? And had agreed to become their leader?

The sequel to this book

GREEN FIRE

is coming spring 2009

GARRET BOOKS

🎧
Hear the music

🔊
Listen to an extract
(read by Martin Jarvis)

Go behind the scenes of

DEKAYDENCE™

at
www.dekaydence.com